Xenagogue

By

Huckleberry Rahr

ISBN eBook: 978-1-959981-61-9
ISBN paperback: 978-1-959981-62-6

Editor: Weslee Imrisek
Developmental Editor: Angela Grimes
Cover Art: Getcovers.com
Formatting: Huckleberry Rahr

Books in the Pebble Stone Series

1: Xenagogue

2: Yugen

3: Zephyr

Books by Huckleberry Rahr

- Jade Stone Chronicles
  - Wolf Healer
  - Epsilon
  - Alphas
  - Traitor
  - Pack
  - Battlefield
  - Pack Present
- Pebble Stone Chronicles
  - Xenagogue
  - Yugen
  - Zephyr
- Ember Savita Chronicles
  - Veiled Phoenix
  - Moonstone Phoenix
  - Battle Phoenix
- Hidden Magic Series (working titles…)
  - The Aura of The Chameleon
  - The Chameleon's Duplicity
  - Truth Exposed
- The Search – Short Story, eBook only

Acknowledgements

After writing Epsilon, I took a break from writing. I actually debated only writing Wolf Healer and Epsilon. My son never liked this idea, he always pushed for more. My issue was, I wasn't sure what adventure to send Jade on.

As soon as I decided to continue writing, both he and a good friend began asking for Pebble's story. They wanted to know where she came from and what would happen to her. The problem was, I needed to finish Jade's adventures, and Bevin's and all the rest.

Well, once I got done there, I had other worlds and creatures that wanted to get their stories told, and who was I to deny them their day in the sun?

As it goes, one thing led to another, and several books later, I've finally come back to let Pebble shine. All three of her books are ready for you to enjoy.

I'd like to thank Elizabeth Daly, Kay Wyatt, Angela Grimes, and Wes Imrisek for beating the words of this book into submission. I'd also like to thank Nadine Kriska for answering all my questions about teaching a college biology class. If I've misrepresented, that is all my fault, not hers. She's an amazing instructor!

To The Readers

Xenagogue is the first book in the Pebble Stone Chronicles. This trilogy can be read as a separate series from the Jade Stone Chronicles. That said, there are spoilers in this series since it takes place after the end of Jade's books.

Chapter 1 – It's Not Cheating

'*As a breeze shuffles the grass, the needles tickle the feathers.*'

I huffed a laugh at my wolf's puzzling words and upped my speed, leaping to avoid a fallen tree. Playing hide and seek as a werewolf was a fun and useful training game and I knew if I wasn't careful, I could win too quickly.

Although there were teams of werewolves running in the woods, I wanted to search alone. I wasn't part of this pack, and though I knew some of the members, the ones I knew best were either not running, or were the ones we searched for.

'You know that doesn't help me, right? Your wise words of wisdom—' In a pine tree ahead of me I saw Jade, my sister, in her black swan form, trying to sit frozen. She was one of the targets, and she didn't want to be noticed.

There was an impression of my wolf's amusement as I continued to run. It wasn't that I could directly talk with my other soul, I just got a feeling of emotions from the pesky beast ... and obscure premonitions. *'Your backwards talking still helps me not,'* I mocked, speaking as a certain backwards character would.

This was my second day in California. Well, second day this trip. High school finals had been a couple of weeks ago, then I walked the stage and earned my diploma. It had taken me until middle school to transition from homeschooling to public school, and I loved to learn, but finally making it to college was an exciting rite of passage for me. Half the California pack came out to cheer me on as I graduated. It made sense, considering so many of them originated in Wisconsin. They were my family.

Once I received my diploma, I spent time with my friend, Hollis, before she went to visit relatives in Spain for the remainder of the summer. Since she didn't know about werewolves, it was a nice escape from some of the stress I felt from new responsibilities. We wouldn't see each other again until it was time to move into the dorms.

I was so excited that we were going to be starting at the University of Wisconsin this fall.

While she spent the whole summer away from Wisconsin, my time in California would last for only a couple of weeks. My sister was getting married. I didn't know who this surprised more—me and my parents, or Bevin and José, her lifelong friends, and wolf alphas.

My sister had a menagerie of animals she shifted into. A swan, a wolf, and a panther. The ability to shift to more than one animal was rare, super rare, but Jade was unique in a lot of ways.

Jade asked me to stand up with her at her wedding, and how could I not?

An itching in my left shoulder told me to veer in that direction. My wolf loved to help me with this extra sense, usually in wolf form. It was hard to explain to others my relationship with my beast. Sometimes it came in riddles, other times images, but more often a feeling. Usually the sensation wasn't so blatant. Three trees later, the irritation grew worse. Up in the tree lay Owen, my brother, in his light brown panther form.

That's two. Once I found all three, I'd head back to the house. As long as our marks noted us, they'd let their alphas know the order they were found by the searchers.

A few months ago, my parents had asked me if I wanted to start training to take over as alpha of the Wisconsin pack when they stepped down. Though the request made me nervous, it also excited me. I arrived for the wedding a bit early to speak with the boys, this pack's alphas, about what it was like to lead, especially as young alphas of a werewolf pack. The California pack formed when they were both still in college.

Backing up, I closed my eyes and turned until the niggling itch gave me a direction. It was light so I ran, leaping bushes, and avoiding the other werewolves in the woods. I loved the feeling of moving on four paws. The wind combing my fur and the extra smells and sounds I picked up.

California smelled and felt different than Wisconsin, thrilling me and my wolf. Eucalyptus filled my nose and the ground was rougher. The songs of the birds threatened to distract me, but this was a race, a challenge, and I only had Sarah left to find.

A black panther, larger than life, and the hardest of the three to locate, she was amazing at disappearing. As I searched, I smelled the other wolves and didn't want them following me. This was a competition. Using everything I'd learned from Dad over the years, I tried to disappear from the others' senses.

I smelled rabbits and small rodents. Despite this being the land of a werewolf pack, they protected the ecosystem, not depleting or running off any of the other wildlife.

As I ran, I hoped the action would release more of the tension my body held. The pull of my goal got stronger— Sarah was close. I stopped and searched until I found the deepest shadow. *There! Gotcha!* The black panther blinked once, acknowledging me. No shifting and making noise for this beautiful beast.

A thrill surged through me as I ran back to Were House, the California pack den. Bevin and José waited for the wolves to return once they'd found the three hiding players. I hoped I was first. I couldn't imagine anyone finding the three as quickly as me—well, maybe José, but he wasn't playing.

When I entered the backyard, I spotted the boys sitting with enough baby car seats to run a garage sale or an upscale boutique. Bevin and Jade had been best friends probably since Jade had been born. In high school, José joined their group. Bevin had always had a crush on him. Years later, Bevin and José became the first openly gay alphas, starting a new pack in California. When they asked Jade if she'd help them have kids, she agreed. Now the three of them had three kids to raise. The other two were Owen and Sarah's.

Bevin held Calista, a miniature of Jade, with dark hair, almost black, and the same jewel green eyes. She passed as a miniature of me, too. Though I was adopted, Jade and I resembled each other. José held Binium, or Bini, the smallest of the triplets. Just as Calista resembled Jade, Bini resembled José with matching dark hair, which was currently a mess, and dark brown eyes. Both babies looked ready to run.

I trotted over, my claws clicking on the patio.

"Pebble!" Bevin called out in a soft, excited whisper. "You're the first one back. Will you go out again, or hang out with us?"

José snorted. "We could use the help, and I know we're on your 'to-do' list while in California. But running is always fun."

I sat, laughing at them with my tongue lolling out. Not only did they have their own trio of terrors—the six-month-olds crawled everywhere if given a chance—Owen and Sarah's twins slept in the car seats. Soren and Lilly were only a month old, but watching five kids couldn't have been easy, even for these two.

Bevin leaned closer, smirking. "Of course, if you want to continue to prove your superior ability to hunt those three down by cheating with your wolf's mojo, go right ahead." His eyes twinkled like blue sapphires with his smile.

A low growl bubbled up from my gut. I knew he was teasing me, but I hadn't cheated. The reason the two of them sat watching the kiddos was because they could cheat at this drill. They were connected to their pack and drawn to their people—all except Sarah who wasn't technically a member of their pack. They couldn't help but find Jade and Owen. That said, they both knew I had a weird sensitivity with my wolf. I always seemed to know things.

José chuckled. "He's joking, Pebble. No one thinks you cheated. You did find the troublesome trio very quickly, but you're also very clever."

With a yip, I turned and trotted over to my clothes. I liked being in wolf form, but I was also worried that my nieces and nephews may end up in the pool.

I closed my eyes and spoke to my wolf, *'human.'* She sighed, not wanting to give up her time to run, but we'd have another chance later. The shift rolled over me like a wave, as if emerging from a cocoon. There was pain as bones elongated and body parts transformed, but this had been part of my life for as long as I could remember, and the pain wasn't an issue, at least not anymore.

Once my paws changed to hands and feet, I pulled on my shorts and tank top. Coming around from the semi-private half-wall, I went to collect Calista, who wiggled and cooed.

Bevin smiled up from where he sat. "Thanks, she has more energy than ... I don't know. If we could bottle it, I'm sure we'd make millions, though."

"Like you lack for energy," José scoffed. "You work, you work at a second job, you run after a sports league of babies, and you still do more things. I don't really get it. I, on the other hand, just want to sleep in. Do you remember sleeping in? Wait, no, you've always woken up early. Insane."

A laugh bubbled out of me. This fight had been going on forever.

Until recently, I was always too young to really hang out as an equal. They were all in high school when the Stones found and adopted me at five-years old. Even though Jade and Owen were my two adopted siblings, everyone here felt like immediate kin. They all helped in raising me.

I laughed, making faces at my niece. She giggled, reaching for my hair. It was too short for her to do any damage. Unlike Jade, who wore her black curls long, I'd cut mine short. Small waves and curls framed my face. No fuss and easy to manage. But the young ones loved grabbing the ringlets.

As I played, wolves started filing into the back yard. They came in groups of twos and threes. Bevin took six-month old Esperanza from her car seat, all three babies ready to play. Her bright blue eyes watched the wolves as if she understood what was happening.

It amused me to watch the kiddos interact with the wolves.

I went to sit in the yard, placing Calista down near some of the pack. She crawled to a wolf, Alex, white as a new snowfall. Calista crawled up, pulling at Alex's fur and ears.

Alex gave me a pained look. Smiling wide, I got up to rescue them from the clutches of the deadly baby.

A few minutes later, two panthers and a swan came into the backyard. Bevin stood. "Since Soren and Lilly are still fast asleep, I say one more round."

'Heya, sis, why didn't you stay wolf? Don't you want to play another round?' Jade's concern flowed into me. As a swan her scent was always weird, and it didn't give anything away about her emotions. From what I'd learned from the others, this was a good thing. Scenting prey animals meant wanting to hunt. Despite not being able to

use my nose to figure her out, I sensed her emotion from her words.

'Yes and no. Bevin and José with five babies is a lot. I'm helping them.'

'Fair. We can take a run later, maybe tomorrow. You should get more paw time than you got. There are enough people who can watch the kiddos.'

I smiled, trying to send a feeling of love and happiness to Jade. *'Thanks, I'd like that.'*

"Got it, everyone?" Bevin finished up.

Nope. I thought to myself. *I didn't get a single word. Oh, well. Since I'm staying here, I guess it doesn't matter.*

The swan launched and the two panthers ran. I watched them, glad that Sarah and Owen had more time to play. Even though there was a pack, a month into parenthood, I doubted they were doing much but being with their babies. This was really good for them.

José wrapped his arm around my shoulders. "You okay? You seem somber. I'm not used to having a wolf I can't sense without working for it."

I shoved into him lightly. "What, you have to do it the old-fashioned way? What will you ever do?"

"I know! It's awful." José slapped the back of his free hand to his forehead.

Laughing, I picked up Calista, and we headed back to the car seats.

Bevin grunted. "Pull up a seat, let's talk."

"Does that sound ominous? I mean it does, but should it?" I narrowed my eyes before I relaxed in the lounge chair, bouncing the baby on my knee.

"No, I just know that there's probably a lot on your mind. You just finished high school, you're about to start college. Right there you have enough. But then, in a few years, you'll be taking over the Wisconsin pack."

I deflated. "Oh, yeah, that."

José reached over to rub my arm. "Are you okay with that? You don't seem excited."

For a moment I looked up into the infinitely blue sky with a few fluffy clouds. Then I gazed first into the sapphire blue eyes of Bevin, my sister's closest life-long friend—she'd always told me to trust him with anything— then José's warm gaze. They pulled me in with their need for me to confide in him.

I smirked. "You're better at that than my parents. Did you know that? I don't know if it's because you're younger, or because I've always idolized you two, but you're good."

José turned to Bevin. "Can I get a plaque that says I'm idolized by a teenager?"

"No." Bevin didn't even break into a smile.

I giggled. "Okay, but really. I *am* happy that Mom and Dad trust me with the Wisconsin pack. And the pack seems excited, too. It's just ... you have each other, Mom and Dad have each other. I don't ... I don't know. I do see what they do running the pack, and I've been helping. They call me in to help with decisions. I just ... I can't imagine doing it all alone."

Bevin pulled out a phone and tapped on it. A few minutes later, Oscar's two younger teens came out and collected the triplets. Then they headed back in without even a 'hi.'

The California pack's chef was a terror to those not allowed in the kitchen, but a delight everywhere else. His kids would probably grow up to be just as sweet. For now, they were moody teens, something I knew all about. That said, they weren't wolves yet, too young. It usually didn't happen until someone was my age or older. They probably had a few years yet.

I wonder if they'll become wolves.

I watched them go. "Talkative."

José shrugged. "They can be, but they saw who was out here and guessed we needed to focus. They're good kids."

I pulled my gaze from the two—who managed to get the house door shut without dropping a baby—and turned back to find Bevin squatting down in front of me. "Pebble, you know that your parents will wait for you to be ready, right? You have time. And though it's nice having a second who is alpha level, you can have a partner who helps with running the pack who isn't an alpha. Someone like Jade who can help with the pack without holding anyone up here." He tapped his head.

A tension I'd been holding seeped out. "I hadn't thought about that. I was just fixated on the fact that I had to run the pack and had to find the perfect other alpha. I know that when you travel to the other packs it's about meeting and learning, Am I also expected to ... I don't know, search?"

José reached out for my hand. "Oh, Pebble. Have you talked to anyone else about this?" I shook my head. "No wonder you're so stressed. No. You don't need to find a partner until you're ready. If you're anything like your sister, that will be in about twelve to fifteen years."

I barked out a laugh, and Bevin smiled, leaning over to give me a hug. "Much better."

The hug centered me and muscles that hadn't relaxed in months finally settled. "Gods, I may actually rest tonight."

José's smile was warm but sad. "You may or may not know this, but I originally didn't want to be a wolf. Add to that being alpha. It isn't easy, but in the end I'm happy this is my life."

He and Bevin were the best couple I knew. The way they worked together, supported each other, and always knew what the other needed almost had me reconsidering my disinterest in dating. If I knew it would end up like them, friends for life, maybe. It just didn't seem worth the effort.

A couple of wolves ran into the backyard.

Bevin watched them. "Well, our time is up for now, but we'll talk more before you head back to Wisconsin."

"Again with your ominous words. I don't know about you, Bev. Super scary."

Chapter 2 – Who Am I?

The shirt in front of me didn't feel like the right one for the day. I pushed it aside, looked at the next one hanging, and shivered. *No, that's not right.* The hanger squeaked on the pole as I pushed it over and checked out the next shirt, and the next.

A chill slivered down my spine, and I jumped back. *What am I doing?* I looked at the closet. It wasn't mine ... not the one in California, not the one in Wisconsin. *Is this a dorm closet? Is this a vision of the future? Are these even my clothes?*

With a shiver and jerk, I looked over my shoulder and a phantom of a person stood in the middle of the room. One arm lifted, reaching towards me.

Fear surged through me, and I woke up with a gasp. "What the hell was that?"

I sat up in bed in the guest room at Were House. My head swiveled left and right, but there was no one else in the room. My heart beat staccato as I breathed hard. A low amount of light streamed in through the window. I'd slept through the night, but it was still early.

Jade would be up, but she liked to do her mornings alone. *Maybe we can walk into town together. Talking with her would be nice.* I wrinkled my nose, I knew I was forgetting something. *It'll come to me once I've had coffee and really woken up.*

Slipping from bed, I padded to the closet to find an outfit. I paused, thinking about that phantom person. Before grabbing a shirt and jeans, I slowly rotated one more time to ensure I really was alone in the room.

"Don't be an idiot, Pebble. Use your nose. Of course you're alone," I mumbled, rolling my eyes.

I huffed out a breath, grabbed some clothes, and headed to the bathroom across the hall. After a quick shower, I put my dirty clothes in the hamper in my room and made my way to the dining room.

The scent of coffee and my sister welcomed me. "Morning, Jade."

"Hiya, sis. You're up early." Her wide smile warmed my heart.

I sat next to her and leaned over for a hug. From the corner of my eye, I saw Oscar come from the kitchen with a large mug of coffee and a plate of bacon and eggs. *Gods above, he's magical.*

"Thank you, Oscar!" He was already back in his domain.

"Child." There was laughter in his voice.

The coffee was rich and a bit sweet. Heaven! "You and Brooke are picking up Mom and Dad from the airport today?"

I knew their schedule. Sarah had created calendars for everyone.

"How did you know?" Jade actually sounded skeptical.

"You do know everyone has roles, right? Sarah has given us our very own where and when for the next week." I started eating my breakfast.

My sister sighed. "Oh, yeah, that. She tried to give me one. It's on the table over there." She waved vaguely towards the living room.

I laughed. "Man, I've missed you."

"Back atcha!" she said. She sipped her coffee with a sigh. "So, what's on your 'to do' list?"

"Nothing this morning. I think I'm going to walk into town. This place will become busy over the next few days with everyone coming for your wedding and then the big day. I'd like to get some downtime before the crazy that is your ceremony."

Jade's eyes narrowed. "I don't know if I should be offended or jealous. You know you could come to the airport with us."

"True, and I do love spending time with you. But there's also the ice cream shop, which is a huge argument for town."

Jade growled low in her chest. "Now that's just rude. You'd go there without me? What kind of sister are you?"

"Only the best, and you know it. I'll walk into town a second time when you get home. You know that ... because I am, in all ways, *your* sister."

A laugh bubbled out of Jade and the room filled with the citrusy scent of her joy.

Owen plodded in, came over to hug each of us, and sat. "Hey, the Stone siblings, alone. What trouble can we get into?"

"No." Bevin's voice came from the other direction. Amusement bubbled in me at how serious he sounded. As alpha, he had to deal with Jade and Owen all the time. As their best friend, I knew he was mostly kidding ... probably. "I knew I sensed something wrong in the Force," he continued. "The three of you together can never be trusted. Any two of you is bad enough, but all three? Gods, save me!" He dropped into a seat looking mostly asleep.

I smiled at him. "I have no idea what you're talking about. The pack house in Wisconsin was never in danger with the three of us." I leaned in. "Bevin, has anyone ever told you that you can be a bit dramatic?"

Jade nodded. "I know, right? All the time with him and his extravagance."

"Can you imagine living under this scrutiny?" Owen added.

Oscar placed a mug of coffee and plate of food out for Owen and Bevin, then joined us. "You know you asked for this, right, my boy?"

Bevin, who'd been sitting with a snarl on his face despite his citrusy scent of amusement, broke, and chuckled. "Yeah, I guess."

Owen leaned back. "You have work today, right, boss?"

"Yeah. José and I work all this week. I know Jade took two weeks off, but someone needs to be bringing money in." He smirked.

"Hey, I'm working, too." Owen ate a piece of bacon. "I have two swans I'm training. One's only been a swan for three weeks."

"How many does the government have now?" I asked.

"Six. The program has evolved. The director has created mini groups that go on site as nighttime surveillance. There are always two wolves and one swan. The people who get this elite team only know they're getting a highly trained top government group, nothing more. That means I don't have any other swans in-house to help." Owen sounded down, but I knew my brother, he was always excited to train people.

José ran out. "I'm going to be late." He continued out the door.

Others from the pack ran through as well, coming from their rooms, and heading to work. Oscar handed several bags of food as they passed by.

I stood. "I'm heading out for my walk to town. Enjoy your days, everyone."

Milo popped up from the basement. "I need to head to the Youth Outreach Center. Did I hear you were walking into town? Would you be okay with company?"

For a moment I hesitated, but then I nodded. "No, yeah, I mean, yes, walking with you would be fine. I'm heading in for ice cream." I smiled.

"So, Pebble, are you enjoying your time in California?" Milo's androgynous appearance and dark Asian features gave them a compelling look. It was probably one reason people who came to the Youth Outreach Center felt drawn to stay—they were charismatic.

I took a moment to answer Milo. We'd never spoken much. Years ago, when Jade had been a senior in college, the two had dated. They'd stopped dating because Milo thought Jade was 'too much.' They liked Jade but would like her more if there was less overhead maybe. It always annoyed me that someone would think anything but the best of someone I'd always admired.

That said, Milo and Violet were a good match, and I knew Milo was a good person. They'd helped a lot of people within the pack and community as a whole working at the Youth Outreach Center. In the end, they were worth speaking with, and I had to remember that.

"Yeah, I'm enjoying myself. It's a nice escape from spending all my time in Wisconsin and all the pressures there."

The scent of sandalwood filled the space between us. Great, they were concerned about me. That hadn't been the point.

Milo half-turned to look at me, studying my face. "Why do you feel like you need to escape Wisconsin? Aren't you happy there?"

I sighed. "I just misspoke. I am happy. Just finished high school, about to start college. It isn't ... it's ... I mean. I ..."

Milo stopped, forcing me to stop with them. They faced me. "You know, you don't have to tell me anything. I'm okay with that. We can talk about our favorite ice cream flavors and why your sister insists on only ordering one thing, unless it's Thanksgiving and then she wants some monstrosity of a 'special' flavor they offer. Or, if you'd rather, we can discuss nothing. But ... I'm a safe space, always and forever. I understand a lot. Werewolves, pack, there is something that connects all of them. Though I live there, I'm not a wolf, I'm separate. Use me as a sounding board if you want. A few of the others do." They shrugged. "Or don't."

It occurred to me that Jade and Milo must walk to town often. Jade loved both the ice cream shop and the café. After all these years, being a partner to a pack wolf, Milo was part of the pack, and my sister had moved on. Milo wouldn't be pack if they weren't trustworthy. Moreover, from the nudging of my wolf, Milo had a good heart.

After another moment of searching my face, they nodded, turned back towards town, and resumed walking.

I blew out a large breath, letting my cheeks puff out. The day before the boys had helped a little, but there were things I hadn't been comfortable bringing up. Maybe Milo was right. Or maybe they knew someone else I could speak with.

Jogging, I caught up with them. "Okay, I'm not really trying to escape Wisconsin. I love it there. And I am proud and mostly happy that Mom and Dad asked me to take over the pack."

When I didn't say anything for a few seconds, Milo looked at me again. "But?"

I nodded. "But. Right." Breathing to calm my nerves, I stared into the clear blue sky. "Eventually I'll need to find a partner, someone to run the pack with me."

"And that's a problem?"

"Yes? No?" My muscles were starting to tense. This was where I usually lost most of my friends when I tried to get the words out.

Before I could say more, Milo continued, "Have you ever dated or *wanted* to date?"

The tension traveled from my shoulders up my neck towards my head. "Yes ... well, no. I once thought I may want to date my friend Hollis, but then realized I just liked her as a friend. Beyond that, not really. I don't look at people and think, 'Hey, I want to date that person.' Like, ever."

Milo nodded. "Do you want to find a partner? Or do you prefer not being with someone else at all?"

A shiver ran down my spine. "You know, the idea of getting physical with someone I don't know ... I just don't understand that. I mean, maybe someday, but it's just not something I've ever felt towards anyone."

"What about people you do know? What if you found someone, became friends with them, and then it progressed. Like this Hollis person? What if she *had* turned out to be someone you connected with on a more intimate level?"

Milo didn't look at me. It didn't feel like they were pressuring me. They just presented questions as we walked. Slowly, I relaxed. *A friend like Hollis who wasn't Hollis.* "Yeah, that seems better. Get to know someone first. Become friends. Let the rest evolve naturally. I could see that being a possibility."

"Why don't we head to the Center? I want to give you some literature. Then we can go get that ice cream. Maybe you can figure yourself out and see that you're not alone."

My jaw dropped. "You think there are others out there who feel like this? Like me? Everyone I know just wants to date and, like, kiss everyone. I feel so ... alien. Couple that with my wolf, and I often feel isolated. It's one of the things I love about being here. I can just be free. No one expects anything from me."

Milo wrapped their arm around my shoulders. "Yeah. You're a weirdo, just like the rest of us, but that doesn't mean what you're feeling right now hasn't been felt by others." Something in me uncoiled. I wasn't sure if I wanted to sing or cry or laugh.

We walked for a few more steps. "So, why *does* Jade insist on always getting the same flavors of ice cream?"

Chapter 3 – A Family Affair

Sarah sat on a couch holding Lilly and I sat on the floor holding Soren. He gazed up at me with bright green eyes, so similar to Jade's, though his face was a match to Sarah's. His coos warmed me to my soul. Esperanza and Calista rolled from their backs to their bellies and back again, giggling as they bumped into each other. Bini slept off to the side, able to sleep through anything his sisters did.

The girls' heads banged together, and they both started to cry, sharp and loud. Soren tensed, but didn't join in, as if this were normal around here. For a moment, I froze, too, uncertain what to do. Then Brooke and Oscar came from the basement and kitchen, respectively, and each picked a baby up, bouncing them on their hips.

"Wow, these kids are never far from adult care, are they?" I watched in wonder as the girls quieted.

As much as I loved that my nieces and nephews had so much care in their life, part of me ached for the baby I'd been all those years ago. I didn't remember much of my life before Jade and Owen's family adopted me when I was five, but the memories I had weren't anything like this.

I remember my parents running in and out of a door telling me to be quiet or I'd scare the customers. If I had to guess, we had an apartment above the store they worked in? Owned? They left me alone during the day, either in the storeroom or in the upstairs apartment. Sometimes I watched TV, but usually I remember quiet times, wishing there were more. I wasn't sure what that more was ... I just knew there had to be ... more.

When I thought back on that time, I had some flashes of being scared of a wolf attacking me. I couldn't really remember if either of my biological parents were there when it happened. It was all shrouded in fear ... the intense fear of a child facing a monster. My first real memories were the social workers not believing me about the wolves attacking me after I was found on the highway next to the car with my dead parents in it. And then Jade and Owen telling me everything would be okay because they *did* believe me.

There was a wolf in Florida who had known my parents, but part of me was scared to talk to him. Both my adopted parents had offered to take me there, but so far I'd said 'no.' I was surrounded by love in the Wisconsin pack. Why open up old recollections when I was so much happier now? I knew I should go and learn more about my lost memories ... but not yet.

Oscar chuckled. "There's a whole pack that wants nothing more than to spoil these rugrats."

Pulled from my thoughts, I gazed up at him. "Who stays with them during the day?"

Sarah got up from the couch and handed me Lilly. It took me a moment to figure out how to manage two before I figured out how to hand her Soren. "I just fed her, let's swap so I can get Soren fed before your parents arrive."

She sat back down on the couch, situating Soren across her body. I looked down into the bright blue eyes of Lilly just as they began to close. Her content and peaceful demeanor told me she was ready for a nap.

Gazing down at her son, Sarah said, "I've been home. I took the summer off. Oscar is usually around, as are others, depending on day and time. Were House is rarely empty. It's really nice always having a helping hand, especially with five kids, mine and theirs." She nodded at Brooke.

As I held Lilly, Oscar placed Esperanza down next to her brother. The two curled close together as they slept.

Brooke watched him. "She's always the quickest to calm down, Esperanza. I'm guessing when she gets older, she'll have the best chance of being epsilon if any of them are. Bini sleeps well, like his dad ... like José." Calista still fussed, though the young girl seemed happy to have Brooke hold her.

Oscar grunted. "Why do you think I reached for her?" He smiled. "Now, the Wisconsin alphas will be here soon, and I'd like to have food ready for them. I think you have things under control."

Sarah gazed down. "Oh, good, Soren's asleep. How about Lilly?"

I searched her small face. "It looks like it."

"Why don't we put these two in my room until after the excitement of everyone arriving dies down? Your parents can meet the triplets first, then these two afterwards. Give the youngest time to sleep. Five grandbabies in one visit. They have a lot of baby time ahead of them."

I shrugged. "Technically they've met the first three."

Sarah shrugged. "That was at their birth. Though, I guess that counts. The three have much more personality now."

We stood and carried the twins to Sarah's room while Brooke stayed with the triplets. As we headed back out, I heard a car drive up. Looking out the window, I saw Mom's face in the approaching car's window.

A smile spread across my face. It had only been a few days, but I knew how happy my parents would be to see the kiddos, both their kids and the young ones.

As Sarah walked back to the living room and the babies, I waited by the door, cracking it open. When the crew got there, I swung it open, earning a big hug from Dad. "Hiya, Applesauce, how ya doing?"

"Hi, Dad. Good."

"Hopefully not too good. We've missed you and I don't want you thinking about staying out here. Don't pull a Jade and apply to college in California last minute." He raised an eyebrow.

I snorted, shaking my head at the joke.

"Now you've done it," Mom teased. "You've given her the idea. She has a place to stay with people she loves. You had to open your mouth."

Dad sighed dramatically.

I gave Mom a hug and directed them to the babies. She barely stopped herself from squealing. I heard a small squeak before she dropped her bags and went to scoop up Bini. He scarcely stirred as she cuddled him into her chest. "He's gotten to be so big ... and handsome."

Right behind her, Dad collected Esperanza from the floor. "Look at you my darlingest of darlings." He sat. "I have a big lap, bring me another!"

Amused, I brought him Calista.

Sarah smiled. "Welcome back."

Mom's face dropped as she searched the living room and dining room. "And where are the rest of my grandbabies?"

Jade came in and went over to Brooke, wrapping an arm around her fiancé.

"Asleep. I thought you'd like to re-meet these three first before seeing Lilly and Soren."

Mom grumbled and Dad smiled. "Well, that makes sense. I can't imagine how all of you are juggling five babies, though I hope it isn't actual juggling."

Oscar came out of the kitchen. "I have coffee, tea, and snacks, if you want to join me in the dining room."

"Oscar!" Dad said jovially. "It's great to see you, my old friend. I'd love to sit, especially if you're joining us."

"Soon, River. Very soon. Let me finish up the meal."

Jade helped Dad with Calista so he could more easily transition. Just as everyone started to walk to the dining room, I felt a pin prick in the side of my head, the tell-tale sign of a visual premonition. I tried to get to a couch before the thing took over ... everything. My hip hitting the floor told me I hadn't made it.

"Pebble!" Sarah's concern washed over me, but I was engulfed in fire.

Fire. A huge explosion of fire. A bird flying from its depths, wings ablaze. A cliff, tall and mighty. The bird flies up the side, with beauty and grace. Freedom, excitement, exhilaration. My heart beat fast with the emotions of the bird. *It freezes. It tumbles. It falls.*

Unlike most werewolves, I got premonitions. Dad believed this ability developed because I was attacked so young. There wasn't a time in my life I didn't remember not having a wolf. This more complete joining between me and my wolf probably gave me my visions.

Opening my eyes, I found Dad's gaze on mine. He knelt next to me, holding my hand. I knew he'd be there. He always was.

It was hard to talk after such intense images, so I said the only words that made sense. "Fire, bird, cliff, falling. He's going to get hurt if we don't stop him!"

Chapter 4 – Siblings

The phantom hand reaches for me. A shiver runs down my spine. I take a step back, but I run into the closet. Is it my closet? What room am I in? There is a feeling of desperation coming from the being.

Sitting up, a tremor ran down my body, sweat dampened my shirt, and I huffed out a breath. Seeing this in my dreams once was a nightmare. Having it repeat ... Gods above, was this something new from my wolf?

At breakfast, Owen and I sat together drinking coffee. Several people milled around the pack den, watching the kiddos, working from home, or tried to stay out of the way.

Everyone assumed my premonition meant Phoenix, one of the California pack members who loved to rock climb and ran an adventure tours company. I had no reason to disagree.

Bevin and Jade were getting ready to head out. I watched the two as Bevin carried a green go-bag full of food to the table by the front door. "Are you sure I can't go with you?"

Bevin came over to me and squeezed my shoulders, then slid his hands down my arms until he could clasp my hands. "Pebble, we know you want to come and help, but Jade and I have been doing this ... well, for half our lives, now. We have it down to a system. We'll go faster if it's just the two of us. If we need more help, you'll be the first person we call."

He meant José or Owen, but I appreciated his attempt to make me feel better. I knew as pack mates, they could find Phoenix faster, but I felt a growing need to help. It was the alpha power building in me. Being side-lined made sense but frustrated me.

As the two finished their preparations, Oscar sat in the living room playing with the five kids. Sarah sat on one of the couches and Brooke on the other.

I smirked at Oscar. "While you're playing with the kiddos, do you allow others into the kitchen?"

"Child," his low voice admonished me.

Sarah snorted. "You know it's only Jade who can't go *into* the kitchen. The rest of us can use the room ... we're just limited."

Jade rolled her eyes as she gave Calista a quick hug and kiss, making her way down the line of kiddos. "I've given up fighting the kitchen fight."

I narrowed my eyes at her, then turned to Sarah. "Does anyone actually believe that?"

"No, absolutely not. We keep waiting to see what happens when she goes in there." Sarah smiled wide at Jade, then watched as one of the cats ran over to curl into Bini's side, stretching before plopping down and purring. "I'm going to make popcorn when *that* fight goes down."

Jade scoffed. "You're just needling me because with all the babies here I have to stay calm. Just remember, Sarah, I know where you sleep."

"And I know your trainer."

Owen chuckled.

With a grunt, Jade put the last baby down. "You're awful. Why are we still friends?"

"Because you love me."

"Some days," she mumbled. "Bevin, we should go before I get violent with one of my alphas." The two headed out, Bevin chuckling. I followed their progress, really wanting to tag along.

Owen tilted his head. "Want to go for a run? It's been awhile. Just the two of us?"

A tsunami of emotions shot through me. I wanted to be with Jade and Bevin. The premonition had been mine, and for once, I could see how one of my premonitions translated to the real world. At the same time, I loved having time alone with Owen. He was a great person to talk to. Not everyone realized that behind his laid-back surfer personality, he had a good heart and a wicked smart brain. When he lived in Wisconsin, going to college in Whitewater, we'd go for runs a lot to help me work through my problems. In a lot of ways, he knew me better than Jade or my parents.

Finally, I smiled and nodded. "Yeah, I'd like that."

Owen drove us to a path on campus that wound along the woods. It was a quiet, mostly private, walking and biking path. The school used it when classes were in session, but it was summer, so it appeared empty.

We stretched. "Okay, sis, this isn't about speed. It's been a while and I wanna talk. I need to get into that crazy brilliant and wacky brain of yours."

I smirked. "Maybe." And I ran.

Any shifter ran fast. We had to modify our speed if there were regular humans around who didn't know about us. Owen and Jade, who both had more than one animal, could run even faster than most wolves. Despite that, and the fact that they'd both trained with professionals, I was their little sister, and I wanted to smoke them!

He caught up to me easily, chuckling low. "First of all, are you going to do any sports when you get to college?"

"Maybe," I said again with a grunt. "Coach Nelson is pushing me to do track and volleyball. They were my best my senior year. He even threatened to call the university coaches if I don't join."

That got Owen laughing. "I wouldn't put it past him. He likes his athletes being athletic. He stayed in touch with both Jade's and mine and Sarah's coaches while we were in school."

"Well, for you it made sense, you're now a trainer. You like all of that. Jade needed it for her early admittance, and Sarah, well, she loves all of the sports."

"And you don't?" His voice was soft.

We ran for a bit while I debated how to answer him. "I do like running, but I feel like I'm cheating when I win. I like volleyball, but that's more the team aspect, and meeting other people, than the sport itself. I figure I'll get that from living in the dorms. Maybe if Hollis joins something I'll join with her. Otherwise, sleeping in sounds good. Focusing on classes. I can get my exercise with whatever torture book Dad sets up for me."

"Okay, that's fair. As long as you've thought this through. Dad will make sure you stay in top form."

We continued to run for a bit, Owen pushing my speed. It felt good to be able to run without holding back.

He finally asked, "Have you come up with a major yet, or are you still undecided?"

"Um." I hadn't told anyone yet. In high school, I'd excelled in physics and biology. I had taken AP history and English. I wasn't quite as strong in academics as Jade, but I'd pushed myself. I enjoyed learning.

Over the last two summers I had interned at Dad's IT company. I'd learned how to program and even had a mentor for hacking into systems, thanks to some people Dad didn't know about.

Despite all that, I didn't think I wanted to take over Stone industries. That made three for three. None of Dad's kids would end up with an IT affinity, working for him with an eventual goal to take over. Dad would have to look towards someone else. Maybe José, who'd been working for him since he graduated, could take over the business? From him, it could go to one of the grandbabies?

I bit my lower lip, figuring Owen was a good sounding board. "I was thinking about psychology. I seem to have an instinct with people and a lot of my friends come to me with their problems ... you know, like—"

Owen smiled wide. "Like me and Jade. You really are our little sister in every way. That day we found you was the best day ever, you know that, right?"

I would not cry. He always made me feel like the best gift he'd ever received. Even when I was a bratty five-year-old and he was a teenager. Everyone in the family made me feel loved and wanted, but Owen? He made me feel special.

We got to the midpoint of our run and turned around.

"Yeah, like you two. And I think if I'm going to be alpha, I want to be able to help when people come to me. I know the pack has a few people who can do this, but ... I don't know, I want it to be me."

"I think that's fantastic. So many packs think it's only submissives who care for the well-being of their wolves. Bevin and José make sure they also care. Mom and Dad do as well. I think your studying psychology is wonderful." The jasmine scent of his pride blanketed the space between us and filled me with joy.

We ran for a bit more before I realized we were close to the end. "Catch me if you can!" I sprinted, putting in as much speed as I could.

Owen kept pace, no matter how much I pushed myself. I loved that there were two people in the world I couldn't outrun.

I put on more speed and Owen laughed as we reached the end of the path. "Not bad, Pebble. You're really getting faster."

Sweat dripped down my soaked back and I gulped large breaths of air. Owen smiled. The jerk wasn't even breathing hard. "You and your two animals!"

He raised an eyebrow. "Am I cheating? Do you think that not being able to beat me took away from *your* run or our enjoyment of the day?"

I scrunched up my nose. "Well, no. This was what I needed. I love our runs. And you know the idea that there are people who I can't beat amuses me. But this wasn't for a prize."

Owen winked. "Just something to think about, squirt."

Both our phones beeped. Pulling out my phone, I saw a message. Phoenix had been found, but not before his fall. Frustration and disappointment slammed into me, but I pushed through to read the rest of the message. They'd seen his fall and got there in time to heal the worst of his wounds. Jade was a wonder, and her epsilon ability to heal was one of a kind.

A shift did the rest. He would be okay.

Chapter 5 – Oblivious, Yet Always Aware

On the morning of the big day, I felt almost as nervous as Jade. I'd slept in her room with her, Brooke taking my guest room.

"Rise and shine, kitty-cat," I teased, the smile on my face so big it hurt.

"Gods, no." Jade glared at me, but it didn't hold much heat. "Bevin tried that after I'd first gotten bitten, and I said no then. I'm not changing my mind now." She sounded grumpy, but her glow and the citrusy smell filling the room told me how excited she was.

I flung my arms around her. "Okay, shower or bathe, I'll go get you some food and coffee. Breakfast in bed ... or bedroom at least, this morning. Then I'll get Sarah, and we'll start to get you prepared."

Jade slid from bed. "Yeah, okay. This keeping me from Brooke is ridiculous, you know that, right? I'm only putting up with it because it's a morning wedding. It's all just silly tradition."

After kissing her cheek, I went to the dining room and found Oscar and Tanner both cooking up a storm. "Hi, Tanner. When did you get here? And you're cooking? Don't you get a day off for good behavior? Did you not behave?"

He chuckled. "I couldn't let my brother have all the fun. He won't let anyone else help, but he can't stop me."

"That tracks. I need a—" A tray with two coffees and enough food for an army was handed to me.

Oscar winked. "I'll send one of the boys in with more coffee. This won't be enough."

Groaning under the tray's weight, I carried it towards Jade's room. Bevin saw what I carried and opened the door before I had to figure out how to juggle my load and enter the room without spilling the liquid gold.

He kissed the top of my head. "I'll get the next installment and Sarah. Be there in a few minutes."

I snorted and placed the tray on the table in the corner of the room. Jade joined me, her belly grumbling, and we both dug in.

A few minutes later, Bevin and Sarah joined us. Sarah held a tray of coffees, Bevin a second mountain of food.

Sarah's face glowed. "I can't believe you're actually getting married."

Bevin chuckled. "Me either. I think we made a bet back in high school."

"Oh, yeah!" Sarah's eyes widened. "That was before you started dating Piper. I had guessed in your forties, Bevin guessed never."

Jade snarled, but she was laughing. "You two are awful. I should grab Brooke and elope. I bet she'd be fine with heading to Vegas and avoiding all of this." She waved her hand to encompass all of Were House.

"You could," Sarah purred, almost as convincingly as one of the cats who ran around the house. "But then I'd track you down and you wouldn't enjoy that, trust me."

My sister scrunched up her face. "I dunno, it could be amusing."

Across from me, Bevin's smile kept getting wider. "If you get yourself injured fighting with your panther alpha, don't come running to me. That's all you."

Jade harrumphed and looked at her empty plate, confused, shook her head, and switched with a full one. "Whatever. You're both awful. I should switch to the Florida pack. Warm weather, panthers, and less harassment."

This was an old fight between these three.

"José would just come and collect you and then he'd be annoyed. Then I'd have to deal with his frustration at having to travel all the way to 'gater territory. Not worth it." Bevin shook his head sadly. "Otherwise I'd say go for it."

Jade laughed. "Ah, so I should stay for José? You'd be totally okay with it?"

"Yep. We don't want to upset *him*."

"You, who demanded we go to grad school together."

"Yep."

"And work at the same clinic."

Bevin nodded slowly. "You know. I may be getting sick of you. Florida is sounding better and better."

She threw a pillow at him, which he easily caught. He looked at it. "You still have your goose pillow. Will your wedding dress have a goose on it?"

Her eyes narrowed at Sarah. "It better not!"

When Jade was in high school she had taken a run along one of the bike trails near our house and had an exchange with a gaggle of geese who swarmed the path. To escape, she shifted to her panther form. The geese hadn't been impressed, and Jade leapt to the trees running above the gaggle. Afterwards, Owen convinced a very young me to give her a stuffed goose as a gift. Ever since then, geese-themed gifts had been a family joke. I think everyone had a goose somewhere in their room.

Jade glared at him. Then she leaned back and sipped her coffee. "Okay, tweedle-annoying and -annoyinger, how long until things start?"

Sarah snarled. "You know, I put a lot of work into the schedules I made. You could've at least pretended to look at yours once."

"I did," Jade protested.

"No, you didn't," Me and Bevin said at the same time. He smiled at me.

I narrowed my eyes at my sister. "You don't even know where the schedule is. I found it on the table in the living room and brought it in here on Tuesday."

"I know, I found it and checked it—"

"Nope," I interrupted her. "Then, thinking you'd hide it in your desk, I put it by your recliner in the living room. I noticed yesterday it'd fallen on the floor behind the chair, so I placed it back on the table. But then some of your books were stacked on top of it."

Jade opened and closed her mouth. "Fine, I didn't look at it. But if I had, then none of you would have any fun telling me where to go and when."

Everyone laughed at her unapologetic admission.

Finally, Sarah relented. "Okay, we should start to get you dressed and out to the back yard. The ceremony begins at eleven and Brooke will walk out to you."

Jade smiled. "I knew that much, just not the eleven part." She gazed at the ceiling. "No, I knew the eleven part, too, I'd just forgotten. Okay, time to get dressed." She sighed. "I like that Brooke is walking to me. I'd probably trip like last time."

Bevin's eyes widened. "You tripped at my wedding? Why didn't anyone tell me?"

I couldn't remember her falling and shrugged.

Jade winked. "Coach Nelson caught me before I toppled over."

"Why do you think we planned it this way?" Sarah stacked everything on the trays and headed into the closet to gather what we needed.

Bevin took the dishes to the kitchen, and Sarah and I helped Jade to dress for her wedding.

The dress Jade wore was fitted and sleeveless. Silk with lace to the waist with a jade green belt that flowed down the back in a waterfall of tiny silk flowers. The floor-length skirt allowed for her to walk but wasn't too billowy.

Sarah spent time pinning back her curls and weaving daisies and baby's breath into Jade's hair. Her makeup was understated.

Sarah and I dressed in matching asymmetrical fitted dresses that flared at our hips and ended just below our knees. They matched the jade belt in color, and we each had a white silk flower belt and hair clips.

We all headed out, and Mom rushed over, engulfing Jade in a hug. "My goodness, you look lovely."

José smiled. "Chica, you look amazing. Are you ready for this?" He wore a black suit with a pale green shirt. Like at his wedding, his jade green tie had a shadow of a wolf. Bevin's tie matched José's, but Owen's had a panther. Dad decided to get a goose on his.

"As ready as I'll ever be."

Dad kissed Jade's cheek. "You're perfect, Pumpkin."

Jade gazed at everyone's ties and smiled. "A goose, Dad?"

He laughed. "Someone had to. All your animals had to be represented."

The house was mostly empty. The guests were in the backyard, ready for the ceremony to begin.

Sarah nodded. "Okay, Jade, you'll walk down with your parents. Then me and Owen. I'll move to stand behind you, Owen will stand with Brooke. Pebble, you have the rings?" I nodded. "Okay, then Bevin and José will bring out Brooke."

Everyone nodded.

Sarah pulled her phone from a small pocket in her dress and tapped on the screen. A few moments later, the music began. Once Mom, Dad, and Jade were out the door, Brooke came out wearing a dress similar to Jade's, only hers was a halter top and the skirt was a bit fuller. Everyone hugged, then Owen and Sarah left. Finally, it was my turn.

I recognized a lot of the Wisconsin pack, my pack. They'd helped raise Jade and they were excited for her today. Not everyone had made it, but as many that could, had.

I stood proud, knowing that my people cherished former members even years after they'd left. That was important.

When I got to the front, I stood next to Mom, turning back to see Brooke walk down the aisle between Bevin and José. The three of them were stunning. The boys' black tuxedos with jade green ties. Brooke's white dress with its jade belt—which I knew from Jade's dress, flowed down the back—walked arm in arm with both of her alphas. A bit of the alpha mantle shone from both boys' eyes, giving the three a presence, a power, something everyone could feel.

Once they got to the front, Bevin kissed first Brooke's cheek then Jade's. "I bless this union and wish nothing but the best for you both."

A shimmer of power ran through the air.

José repeated Bevin's actions. "I, too, bless this union and see nothing but good coming from the joining of the two of you. Move forward in peace."

Again, the power of the actions and words could be felt, like a wave, through the crowd watching. At first I thought it was just me, but then I heard others behind me gasping in shock. The only time anything like this had happened before was at their wedding, and the only thing we could figure out was it had to do with mated alphas. There was power in that combination, as rare as it was.

The two alphas moved to the other side of the aisle as Brooke stepped up to stand next to Jade.

Aunt Allison tilted her head, gazing at Bevin and José. "Always something new with the two of you." She smiled and shook her head. Her words broke the shock from the wave of power, and everyone sat.

Mom grabbed my hand and gave it a squeeze. I leaned into her, excited for the ceremony.

Eyes bright, nearly glowing, Allison searched both Jade and Brooke's faces. "I have known Jade her whole life." A murmur went through the crowd. "My journey with Brooke may not have been as long, but that doesn't mean she doesn't hold as dear a spot in my heart. Over the last handful of years, she has proven again and again the type of person she is, the type of wolf she is, and the type of niece she'll be to me when she and Jade are married. I am excited to be part of this next chapter in both their lives."

Jade reached out and clasped Brooke's hand in hers. They both watched Aunt Allison as she spoke.

"I am here to bring the blessing of both Sonnara, the sun god, and Mondara, the moon god, to this union. As wolves, our dual nature brings strife within us, a fight, a battle. During the day, we wear the masks of humans, theoretically civilized. That union is simple and not always needed. Humans can be solitary creatures. But under the moon, when Mondara has us in her sight, we hunt as animals, we become pack."

For a moment I shut my eyes and thought about the gods, and how they formed the backbone of werewolf lore. The sun and moon, light and dark, control and wild abandon. After moving to Wisconsin, learning about the gods gave me peace, an understanding of what had happened to me. The werewolf wasn't a monster, but another aspect of who we were.

"We are drawn to connect with another," Allison continued. "It is with trust in our gods that we find that person who challenges us, trusts us, and supports us. I believe that Jade and Brooke have found that in each other."

Aunt Allison smiled first at Brooke and Jade, and then at the group witnessing their union. "Now, they each have something they'd like to say." She smiled. "Brooke?"

Brooke shook her head slightly as if breaking a trance. She glanced at me, and I stood and took a few steps to hand her a ring. Her smile lit the backyard, brighter than any star, and then she turned to face Jade, lifting her free hand and sliding on the ring.

By the time I made it back to my seat, they were holding hands. Brooke took a slow breath before she started her vows. "Jade, we've known each other for many years. If, when we first met, anyone predicted today, it would have been instantly followed with a snort and a laugh." There were a few snickers in the crowd. I didn't know them back then, but I'd heard a few stories. When they first met, Brooke was the mean girl, terrorizing the school and especially Jade. But now? I didn't think my smile could grow bigger.

As she continued, Brooke's voice softened. "For years I feared any real relationship because I thought anything that had real emotion would end up like my parents. And then you came around. I saw you struggle and fight and I knew if I could get myself figured out maybe I could be good enough for you. It took us a while, both of us with our demons, but I'm really glad we figured it out in the end.

"Longer than you've known, I've admired your strength, even when you haven't seen it for yourself. I know at times people wish that you'd be more careful or different, but if you'd listened to them, you wouldn't be you. It's your huge heart that will do anything for anyone that drew me to you, showed me the type of person I want to be, and the person I wanted to be with. I love you, Jade, and know that together we can build a love that will last."

I could see both of their eyes getting misty.

Aunt Allison smiled, then cleared her throat. "Lovely, Brooke." She turned slightly. "Jade?"

Once again, a glance told me it was time to do my part and hand Jade Brooke's ring. Finally, I could sit and just take in the ceremony.

Jade shut her eyes and slowly released a breath. Then she gazed up into Brooke's eyes. "Much of my life, I was lost. Especially when it came to matters of the heart. I clung to my friends because they've always been there for me and, as everyone here knows, will always be there for me. I have amazing people in my life. That doesn't mean I had things figured out." She looked up into the sky. A V-shaped gaggle of geese flew by, honking. Everyone laughed.

Jade turned to Dad. "Did you arrange that?"

I tried to hold back a snort. There was no way Dad could've gotten the geese to perform; the animals were feral ... and mean, but Jade was right, if anyone could do it, it was Dad. Or maybe Owen. Next to me, Mom shook with laughter.

Dad held his hands to the side and shook his head. "They came on their own, love. Probably wanted to say, we're always watching!"

Jade smiled, rolled her eyes, then looked back at Brooke. "When I was the most lost, in my darkest place, you came to me, a beacon, showing me a way home. Whenever I've been scared or in need, you were and are always there. You never judge me, never ask me to change, you just ..." She bit her lip, eyes misty.

"I love you, Jade. Those are the words you're looking for." Brooke smirked, leaning close. Then she rubbed a tear from Jade's face.

More tears slid down my sister's cheeks. "Right, love. I love you, too, you know. I never knew someone could see all of me and still love me. But you do. It's kind of weird, you know." She chuckled weakly. "I feel like I can be me, in all my aspects, and you'll love me. I don't need to change. And I see you, Brooke, and love the caring, accepting person you always tried to hide."

Aunt Allison sighed. "Okay, every wedding at this location is just going to be ... odd." She shook her head. "Before this goes on forever... By the power given to me by Mondara and Sonnara, I pronounce you wife and wife. You may kiss."

And they did.

Everyone around me cheered, but I leaned back, thrilled that they'd done it. My sister had found her happy.

After, there was food and dancing. Most people stayed for the night run, the second half of the wedding ceremony where the wolves honor the moon. It could be tricky with so many dominant wolves.

To help with the potential of in-fighting between the two packs, the groups split up with Mom leading one run and José leading the other. The property was big enough for two groups to run apart and sing to Mondara.

I ran between the groups, enjoying my last time as a wolf in California ... at least for a while. I loved the scent of eucalyptus and running in foreign woods. The sharper grass wasn't my favorite, but letting my muscles stretch as the warm air streamed through my fur relaxed me in a way I never fully relaxed in my human skin.

Chapter 6 – Downsizing

"**D**o you have everything you need, Applesauce?"

I looked around my room and then at the two suitcases and my bookbag. Everything that was my life as a werewolf was in this room. Near my bed was a book I'd spent years reading ... I wanted to bring it with me—it had always brought me comfort—but I couldn't.

The book used to be Jade's. It was a book on werewolf lore. The leather-bound tome was ancient. Mom explained it had been old when she'd been young. When I was old enough to read, I lost many nights of sleep to the stories about the gods, our history, and the classification of wolves.

The book hinted that the wolf spirit knew the needs of the pack, which is why we had an even mix of alphas, submissives, and others in between. Most new wolves were zeta, unclassified, only really figuring out their level after their first run once the pack's needs were understood. When the Stones first adopted me, that book gave me comfort and understanding of who and what I was. Its age and subject matter didn't belong in the dorms.

"I think so. I mean, if I need anything else, I can just call, right?"

"Nope, one and done, kiddo. We'll drop you off and see you in December." Dad kept a somber expression as he gave me this news delicately.

Mom scoffed. "Well, except for full moon nights, mandatory pack meetings, nights we miss you, and any other time you want to come home. The University of Wisconsin's Madison campus is close. Your dorm is fifteen, maybe twenty minutes away in traffic. It's walking distance from my office. So, except for all of those situations, yes, one and done."

With a deadpan look, I groused, "I know, Mom. I doubt I'll be spending much time in your office. It's even smaller than the dorms."

"Not by much," she teased.

With her being a professor at the college, there was a chance I'd run into her on occasion, but campus was big enough that the probability was small outside of planned visits.

"Well, yeah, except for those times," Dad said again with finality. "Besides that, no coming home until December."

I narrowed my eyes. "What about Thanksgiving? Should I call Jade and head out to California?"

Dad's eyes widened. "Don't you dare." He stomped to my bags, picked them up, and headed out. I could hear him when he opened the front door mumbling, "No more kids of mine are going to California. You're coming home for the holidays and that's that."

Mom's smile was small. "You know how much we'll miss you, Penelope Anne Stone." After calling me by my full name, something she rarely did, she wrapped strong arms around me in a familiar hug. "I can't believe you're all grown up and heading off to college. You were only five ... like, yesterday. And Jade was tromping off to high school, fighting with Owen. And now she's married with kids of her own. And so is Owen. I just ... all of you kids are so grown up now."

I squeezed her back. "It's okay, Mom. I'm staying close, and you can always visit the grandbabies."

I felt her shake with laughter, though she didn't make a sound. "Gods above, they're cute. And that pack has five of them to chase around. Five Stone rugrats with both Jade and Owen's curiosity and impertinence. I don't know that they understand what they've gotten themselves in for. They are going to have a time of it for the next few years."

"Sarah seemed happy when her parents asked to stay for the summer. They're back in town now, but a few weeks of help with that pack of young'uns..." I let my statement drop as Mom relaxed and pulled away.

Leaning down, I slung my bag onto my back, and we followed Dad to the car.

This was it, I was moving into the dorms. I'd moved the big things in the previous week, so this was just me, my clothes, and whatever I hadn't wanted to be without this last week.

"I can't imagine not being in the pack den, not having wolves around me all the time. Gods, Mom, I haven't been without family since I was five. This is going to be so weird."

She squeezed my shoulder. "You'll be fine. It'll be like a sleep over, every night."

"Or like when I moved into foster care after my parents died." I bit my bottom lip, scrunching up my nose.

Love emanated from Mom in a wave. "Not at all. You won't have those weird rules, and Dad and I will be close. Not to mention, you're older and you know your roommate. That's better than any of the older group did in their first year."

"Yeah, Hollis and I didn't want to play roommate lottery. I think we'll work well together." My shoulder muscles tightened. "Except the whole werewolf thing. Keeping the secret at school is one thing. Living with someone and keeping the secret ... it'll be a much different challenge."

We'd made it to the car, and we buckled in.

Dad shrugged. "I don't think it'll be as bad as you think, Applesauce. You'll see, before too long you'll find your routine, and everything will be fine."

The drive to campus and the dorms didn't take long. There were a lot of cars driving around, touring, dropping students off, or just getting lost in the maze of Madison streets. I got out of the car quickly with my things and waved goodbye. It was too much confusion to have Mom and Dad join me in my room. They'd done it at the last drop off. Today it was time to begin life as a college student.

Nervousness and excitement warred in me as I watched them drive off. Then I spun on my heel and headed in to face this new challenge.

Up in our room, Hollis was unpacking her things. She'd obviously recently redyed her hair because the blue and purple practically glowed under the bright fluorescent lights. *We need more lamps.* A poster and a few pictures already hung on the wall.

Closets on either side of the door created a small walkway. Our room had two beds, one on each side. At the end of the bed were built-in desks. Under the window stood the small refrigerator Hollis's parents had gifted her for good grades her senior year.

"Pebble! You made it despite the overwhelming odds!" She laughed as she hung up a dress.

"I know, right. There are so many people. The parents of all the students are making it so much worse. I just sent mine home."

We hugged and I got to unpacking. "How was your summer?"

She flopped onto her bed. "Good. The trip was amazing, and I can almost speak Spanish fluently. By the end, I wasn't getting looks of utter confusion or people immediately switching to English. I think that's the best part."

"Nice. Does that mean you'll focus on a different language?"

"Maybe. I'm still taking Spanish, but I think I'll pick up French or maybe German." She got a far-off look. The idea of all those languages didn't seem as exciting to me. Give me a science or history class any day.

She shot up and turned until she spotted my second suitcase. Once she got it on her bed, she helped me to get my stuff sorted. "So, what about you? California? Did you meet the man ... or woman ... or person of undefined gender of your dreams?"

I slid my empty suitcases under my bed and sat. "No, but I did have fun at Jade's wedding. It was beautiful. Just like it was supposed to be."

"I'm sure. Where are the pictures?"

I flipped open my laptop and navigated to the page. I had to enter a few passwords to get through the security. Hollis searched the pictures, smiling. "Everyone looks fabulous, and I love the flowers down the backs of Jade and Brooke's dresses. So pretty."

Hollis had met my sister and Brooke a few times when they'd visited Wisconsin, but she didn't know them well. Not being a werewolf, her interaction with any of my family was what any friend would have with older siblings. She knew Owen and Sarah better since they had gone to college in Wisconsin.

"Oh! Look at how handsome Owen looks. I always forget he cleans up well. And of course Sarah—she'd look like a model in anything."

I laughed. "I know. Can you imagine having to stand next to her?"

We both laughed.

As Hollis continued to scroll, I debated telling her more about my trip and discoveries. Outside of pack and werewolf topics, I'd never kept anything from her.

We'd talked a bit over the summer, but our schedules hadn't matched up well, so we agreed that most of the bigger things would wait until we moved in. *Now that the time is here, what should I do?*

I opened the front section of my bookbag and pulled out the literature Milo had given me at the Youth Outreach Center. I'd read over it a few times, and it had given me a sense of peace and hope. When Hollis finished and saw what I was holding, one brow lifted in question.

With a shrug, I tilted the pamphlets towards her. "One of Jade's friends works at a Youth Outreach Center. The two of us went there while I was visiting. Anyway, they gave me these. It helped."

Hollis took the papers and flipped through the top one. "Oh, this is great." She slowed down and seemed to read some areas with more detail than others. "Can I ask what you figured out?"

I scooted on my bed until my back rested on the wall. "I always thought I was weird—"

"You are weird."

"No," I chuckled. "Well, yeah, but different from anyone else. Like, no one was like me."

"Oh." Hollis came over and sat next to me. "I'm really sorry, Pebble." She rested her hand on my thigh. "I just always thought you were asexual and probably knew all about it. You seem to know a lot about everything."

Her words caught me off guard. She knew my secrets, but this wasn't something we'd discussed. "I don't think that's quite right. I wouldn't mind dating someone ... just, not until I really know them first."

"Huh," Hollis said. She squinted up at the ceiling as if rearranging pieces of a puzzle. "That's interesting. Have you ever found anyone you wanted to date?"

I laughed. "I thought at one point maybe you, but then ..." I paused, uncertain what to say.

"But then we kissed during that game of spin the bottle in eighth grade." She laughed. "Man, that game really figured a lot of things out for everyone, right?"

"Like, that we were great friends and nothing more?" I asked.

"For starters. It was good. I was starting to like girls, and it was good to know my best friend was just that, my friend." She smiled at me.

Amusement bubbled within me, glad we both had had the same epiphany. "Then there was John and Tim. They started dating that night and were together for like two years."

"Right!" Hollis agreed, head bobbing emphatically. "I don't even know if either of them were out of the closet before then."

When John had spun the bottle and it had landed on Tim, everyone had razzed them. Both boys just shrugged and decided they'd play along. A vanilla scent of attraction pooled out of both of them, quickly followed by the gingery scent of shock as the kiss must have been electric. Besides them, I was the only one who knew the progress of those emotions. Even if people knew I could smell emotions, it wasn't my story to tell.

I shrugged, playing off Hollis's words. "I don't know outside of asking them if we'll ever know."

Hollis knocked her shoulder into mine. "Okay, so, best friend for life. What did all this," she waved the pamphlets, "tell you?"

I gazed at the flapping papers, then a small smile tugged at the side of my mouth. "I think I'm demi."

"Romantic or sexual?" A slight woodsy scent of determination came from Hollis. She wouldn't stop until she figured me out.

"Yes? How about we take all of this one step at a time?"

She gave me a quick hug. "Sounds great. Now, we need to get you a flag for above your bed."

Chapter 7 – A Few New Friends

"Score!" Hollis yelled.

We were in a bowling alley at the Memorial Union with a ton of other first year students.

I shook my head. "Hollis, I don't think that's what you say when the ball hits the pins, especially since you only knocked down four of them."

"Look, girly, you're missing the point. I knocked down *any* of them." She swung her hips and retrieved her ball to take another go. Once her ball was launched, she walked over to sit next to me, ignoring the outcome. "Have I ever told you the story of when my family went out bowling two years ago?"

"Look, I love this story, but if you remember, I was there. You'd invited me because your cousins were there and they're all in bowling leagues."

Hollis laughed as her ball went into the gutter. "Oh, my God, that's right. The night was so fun ... except."

"Except you scored a twenty and your family will not let you live it down."

Hollis harrumphed. "A twenty-three, I'll have you know." A laugh came from one of the players on the other bench. "You know, those three points probably made all the difference."

Eyes alight, Hollis shook her head, finally having a fresh audience. "Half my cousins had more than that in their first boxy-thing."

I looked across the automatic scorekeeper to the two people we were playing against. One of the two was up and bowling. The other, a sandy haired young lady with gray-blue eyes, snorted. "I bet they did."

I waved. "Hi! I'm Pebble, this is Hollis."

She got up and came over to shake our hands. "I'm ... um, well, I'm Fern." Her accent told me she wasn't local ... somewhere south of Wisconsin. She wore some kind of woodsy perfume that I really liked. It hit me deep in my soul and I felt my shoulders relax despite the number of people bowling. In the awful smells of old burnt oil, unwashed used sweaty shoes, and stale beer, not to mention the sounds of the bowling alley, it reminded me of running through the woods, the wind in my fur ... though the scent was the wrong woods.

Attached to the lapel of her—their—shirt was a pin that said they/them and realized I needed to be more aware. Using my nose, I could tell more about them than they'd probably like, so I tried to ignore everything except what I saw.

"Hi, Fern. Are you new to Madison? Or are you from the area?"

They sat and watched the ball their partner threw zoom down the lane. I watched too and sighed. "I should probably play."

Fern nodded. "Probably. I'm from a small town in Kentucky. How about you two? And Pebble? Is that your chosen name or one you, um ... did you change your name to that? And what are your pronouns?"

I smiled. "Give me a minute." Hollis answered Fern's questions as I got up and selected my ball from the ones in the return. My first shot knocked down seven pins. The second wasn't a gutter but also didn't hit any pins.

Hollis replaced me as I sat and watched Fern. They did well. Six on the first, the remaining four on the second toss. Hollis's first attempt went right into the gutter, so I focused on the new person.

When they sat, I said, "My full name is Penelope Anne Stone. When I was young my Dad gave me the nickname Pebble. It's stuck. It was given to me because ... well, it matches my eyes."

Fern smirked. "I see it. That's cool. Your name sounds nonbinary."

"Is yours?"

"Yeah. It's ... I switched to Fern this last summer. My parents ... my mom is okay with the new name, but my dad doesn't like it. I've had to go back and forth a lot this last year, so it still feels really new."

Hollis returned and it was my turn to bowl. The bowling alley was so loud that while I bowled I barely heard anything. It made it easier to tune everything else and focus. I had to wait for Fern's partner to bowl in the lane next to mine before I could take my turn. She was good, and she smiled after getting a strike.

When it was just me and Fern again, the noise made it almost like we were alone, in private. I asked, "Is it just the name ... or everything that your parents are struggling with?" I waved my hand to indicate their body. Fern's eyes widened and their jaw dropped open. I realized I'd made a mistake. Fern presented feminine. The only reason I knew more was because of scent, and that wasn't anything I could explain to them. Quickly, I said, "You know, being nonbinary. Are they okay with that?"

They looked from me to Hollis and back. "Oh! That. I just." They shook their head. "Sorry. For some reason I thought ... but it doesn't matter. Yeah, they had an easier time with that. It was something they'd heard about with a distant relative."

I nodded, glad I hadn't made Fern uncomfortable. "I have a few friends, family friends, who are nonbinary ...

and trans. It's something I've grown up with. My family all seems fine with it too. I'm glad yours was accepting of that."

"Me, too. If only I can get Dad to figure it all out." Fern shrugged. "One day."

From the other bench, Fern's partner said, "Fern, you're up!"

Fern's head jerked towards the woman, and they smiled. "Thanks."

The rumble of balls as they rolled down the aisle and the crash of the pins as they fell filled the air. I placed my hand on Fern's arm. "I don't know how, but if I can help, let me know."

They smiled. We both got up to take our turn.

Hollis pointed at the line. "God, Pebble, that line will take forever." She sighed dramatically.

One of my brows rose. "Do you have someplace you need to be? It's a beautiful night, the lake is reflecting the sunset, and at the end of the line is ice cream. I fail to see what the issue is."

"Fine." She somehow made the word two syllables.

Behind me, Fern laughed. "You two act like sisters, did you know that?"

"Yep," we said at the same time.

Fern shook their head. "At first I thought you were dating, but now..."

"Eww," I said and faked a shiver. "Gods above, take it back!"

Hollis rolled her eyes. "You kiss a girl once in eighth grade and it's a complete fail and now it's nothing but drama. Look at what that spin of the bottle saved me from."

After a snort, I punched her in the arm. "I think I was the one rescued that day."

"Siblings," Fern said with a chuckle. "I almost think seeing you two kiss would be weird."

Hollis linked her arm in Fern's. "What about you? Boyfriend? Girlfriend? Themfriend?"

"No. I had a girlfriend in ninth grade, didn't work out well for either of us. She went on to date ... others. The school I went to was small and being ... well, queer, wasn't very accepted. I haven't dated since changing my ... name and pronouns."

"I'm shocked." Hollis narrowed her eyes, looking Fern up and down. "Someone as stunning as you and no dating? You're as bad as Pebble."

"You know, Hollis," I said with a droll tone, "some of us actually go to school to learn."

Fern looked at each of us. "What are you two here to study? I'm wavering between undecided and vet sciences. I just love animals. But so many classes."

"I'm studying languages, probably something with international business or something. Not sure." Hollis took a step as the line slowly moved forward.

Fern smiled. "I bet that will go great with the blue and purple hair."

Hollis blushed. "I doubt I'll keep the color past graduation." She lowered her chin towards her chest a bit and softened her voice. "Do you like it?"

Fern nodded. "I do."

I tried to see how many people were left until we reached the end. "I'm studying Psychology. I'll figure out a focus later."

"Excellent. Maybe Hollis can learn how to speak to animals, I can heal them, and Pebble, you can understand them on a deeper level."

I choked out a laugh. Understanding werewolves on any level was absolutely the goal of this degree. "Sounds like a plan. Though, if you like animals, we should go to the zoo. My aunt works there, so we can get in to see things most can't. She's a vet."

Fern's eyes widened. "That would be amazing."

We were making our way to the front of the line. The call of the ice cream was loud in my soul. I may not have liked it as much as my sister did, but it was close.

Ahead of us, maybe ten to fifteen people, a pair of students started complaining.

"What do you mean you're out?" I couldn't see who was speaking, but she sounded angry.

"What kind of school is this?" A second voice carried over the conversations happening on the terrace by the lake.

A cinnamon scent took over most of the people around us. Everyone was annoyed. I was annoyed with the audacity of assuming the school would provide for the thousands of people who stormed in for free ice cream. There had to be more than the invited first year students. And this group up ahead was yelling, not at the organizers, but the volunteers who were there to help out. Gods, that was obnoxious.

Two young women stormed away, one with light red hair and a second with brown hair in a bob.

"Come on, we'll get ice cream on State Street. There will be fewer of the," the brunette's voice took on a sickly-sweet tone, "'excited for college to start' crowd."

The cinnamon scent turned spicy as people's annoyance turned to anger. I couldn't blame them. Those two were obnoxious.

As I turned to ask ... something, my foot caught in a lifted stone, and I toppled over. My head hit the corner of a brick half-wall as I fell and my vision momentarily darkened.

The clothes in the closet are mine, but none of them are the ones I want to wear. Frustrated, I turn ... and see the phantom of a person. They're standing in the room. Once I acknowledge them, one of their arms lifts. There is urgency. Whatever they want, it needs to happen soon.

"Pebble, are you okay?"

I shook my head, then immediately regretted the action as a drum line started pounding away. "Gods ... ouch. Yes, I'm fine. Just tripped."

"And nearly brained yourself." Hollis's voice was full of worry. "Are you sure? Should we find a medical person?"

Both Hollis and Fern helped me stand. Their arms wrapped around me, supporting me.

Despite the scents of the terrace filled with hundreds of college students, once again Fern's perfume seemed to center me. I'd have to ask them what they used ... when I was feeling better ... because I had a feeling about this one.

"No, but I think I may be done for the night. I know you wanted ice cream, but maybe tomorrow?" I knew I sounded desperate, but suddenly I just wanted to go to bed. My body ached for rest and my room at the pack den, but I had to get used to the dorm being my new home.

"Should we call someone, your parents, take you to a doctor?" Fern held me securely.

A chill ran down my spine and I bit back a groan. I knew they worried about something bad, but going to the medical center wouldn't help. "No, I'm fine. I didn't really hit my head that hard. I'm more tired from a long day. I'm not used to peopling this much."

Fern and Hollis looked at each other and nodded. Fern said, their voice tight with concern. "I can help you get Pebble back to the dorms. Which one are you in?"

Hollis gazed down the street. "We're close. Chadbourne ... so close."

"Oh!" Fern perked up. "I'm in that one too. Seventh floor."

"We're on the ninth."

With a bit of help from a new friend, I got back to my room and into bed. Hollis brought me water.

Fern narrowed their eyes. "Are you sure you're okay. I'm worried about a concussion."

"Yeah, I'm fine, just a long day."

There was real concern in their gaze.

I pushed myself up to sitting and looked between Fern and Hollis. "I'm pretty resilient. You can ask Hollis. Nothing really holds me down."

Fern gazed around the room, then paused. "Okay, but when you're up to it, can you tell me why you have a goose pillow and mug? Like, if you like them, that's fine, but they're mean birds."

A laugh burst from me. I hadn't even realized the two items were in my stuff. Between Owen and Dad, everyone had goose paraphernalia. "Yeah. A story. It's short." Despite my head, I quickly told her about Jade and the geese. It was worth it to see the amusement on both Fern and Hollis's faces, though Fern looked like they were trying to hold their laughter back. After the ice cream being out and my fall, we all needed a bit of humor.

"Go ahead, laugh; everyone does. Anyway, the story is pretty notorious at this point. So, now that the bedtime story is done ... let me sleep?"

Hollis and Fern left the room to talk. It was still early, though I had had enough excitement for my first day in college.

Chapter 8 – For the Win

The coffee in the cafeteria was going to be my death ... or at least my not awake. As I sat and sipped the sludge, I wondered why I wanted to live in the dorms. I could've lived at home and driven in each day. Parking would be hell, but I'd have figured it out ... learned a system. What was the big draw of living in the dorms?

Hollis set her tray down across from me. "God, this coffee is horrible. What should we do? Suffer? Get a coffee maker for our room? Find a café? What's the plan, Pebble?"

"Uh," I grunted, not ready for words.

She snorted. "Your shirt is making a nice statement. Is it new?"

I gazed down. It had a dragon sitting on a pile of books. It said: *Books, Coffee, and Mythical Creatures. Don't mess with my hoards.* A phoenix was on the back, flying up from an explosion of fire. "It was a gift from Jade."

"I like it. Dragons are always a great look."

Fern walked up with their tray, their woodsy perfume cutting back the awful scent of unwashed students and sludgy coffee. A happiness rolled through me at the thought of hanging out with them. "Do you mind if I join you two? I don't really know anyone, and my roommate has a group of friends she knows from high school who all live in our wing. She's nice, but, well, I don't know if we'll be more than two people sharing space."

Hollis blushed, which finally cleared the sleep from my head. My bestie *never* blushed. *Hollis likes Fern!* I nodded. "Yeah, of course. Join us, my friend. Save me from this chosen sister of mine. She's chipper," I said that with all the disgust I could muster.

Fern chuckled as they sat down. Despite what I said, we were quiet for a few minutes as we ate. Then Fern narrowed their eyes. "Please tell me you think this coffee is awful, like, this isn't what people in Wisconsin think is good, right?"

"Really?" Hollis retorted. "You're from Kentucky. You're not going to claim life is that much different ten hours away."

"Seven and a half hours," Fern said, with a wink.

Hollis shook her head. "You are trying to lord your coffee over us and it isn't even a double digit of hours away by car?" She sounded indignant.

Before the conversation could disintegrate, I waved my hand. "Why don't we go down State Street? We can find a place to get coffee, maybe even a pastry if we're lucky. Have a bit of a tour. Fern, have you been?"

"No, not yet."

"Great." I finished my eggs. "We'll show you a bit of campus, maybe find a place with cheese curds, and then head back."

"Find some what now?" Fern narrowed their eyes. "Like, curdled cheese? Are they lost? Do you often have to locate a place to put them?"

Hollis stood then yanked on Fern's arm. "Come on, new kid. You have a lot to learn and apparently we're the ones who have to teach you."

After Fern learned the joys of fried chunks of breaded cheese, we walked to the stadium for day two of first year activities.

Today was more active.

I knew I could probably win at most of the events, but I chose to watch Hollis compete in the various field games instead. Fern chose to be a cheerleader with me. *If only we had pompoms.* Even without, we had fun watching Hollis. She was having fun and doing well. Her biggest competition was a redheaded girl. I thought I recognized her.

"Fern." I tapped them with my elbow as Hollis ran across the field with two spoons trying to keep a balloon from touching the ground. "Is that girl, the one four down from Hollis, the one from yesterday?"

Fern leaned forward squinting. "Which girl ... oh, the ice cream one? No, she's the friend. If you look over there," they pointed to the onlookers across from us, "there's a brunette, do you see her?"

I scanned the crowd, then saw someone intently watching the redhead. "Oh, yeah, I see her. She's very invested in this race." *Wow, these girls are competitive.*

"I believe she's the one who was really upset about the ice cream. The one racing was with her though. My guess is they're friends."

"Wow. I'm usually good at picking people out of a crowd, but, yeah, that was impressive." I wasn't used to people being better at identification than me. As I looked at the brunette, I realized she was sitting next to a student with blue hair and what I thought was a Bears jersey. Daring at a Wisconsin school. The Illinois football team was the natural enemy ... well rival to the national

Wisconsin football team. She must really come from a family of Bears.

I scooted in closer to my new friend. Blocking out all the people took work, and it was easier when I could focus on one person. I didn't know Fern well, but I knew them better than anyone else around me. Then there was their perfume, an added bonus I would've never predicted.

There were so many people in the stadium, it felt like thousands ... and there probably were. The university admitted close to ten thousand freshmen, and though they didn't all join in these welcome activities, even ten to twenty percent was a lot.

As we watched Hollis run, her blue and purple hair flying out in waves behind her, she was one of the first to cross the finish line. We leapt up and cheered.

After we sat and the cheering around us died down, Fern shrugged. "I've always been observant. It's helped me stay out of trouble. You know, a small town safety trait."

Fern's words brought me back to our conversation. "Got it." In the back of my mind, I filed that away. Having smart and observant friends was a bit dangerous as a werewolf. I had to be super careful about what I did and said around them. "If we're ever in class together, I'll know who to copy notes from."

Fern smiled as we shifted to the next challenge.

The next event was an egg-throw. Hollis partnered up with one of the people who hadn't been eliminated earlier on. This station was open to anyone, so Fern and I went to the losers' end and started tossing.

It didn't take long for Fern to drop the egg. Laughing, we headed over to watch.

"Look, Hollis is with the redhead." Fern shook their head. "I'm guessing the big prize will go to one of them. They both look super serious."

"There aren't many people left." I searched the competitors. "Maybe two other pairs."

As I watched, the two stretched their distance in the egg toss far enough to secure the win.

At the start of the games, I'd focused on blocking out the sensory overload of everyone in the stadium. Because of that, I'd missed what the prizes were for the day.

I decided looking like an idiot didn't matter. "What will they win?"

Fern dragged their eyes from the last two competitors, a smile brightening their face. They really were pretty. "Um ... I think they said third place gets free meals from the cafeteria for a semester, second a free iPad, and first place gets both."

My eyebrows rose. That wasn't bad, and Hollis could use both things. "Go, Hollis!" I yelled.

When it was clear she and the redhead were the last two standing, the organizers collected them, and the two who were in third and fourth place. They gave them each a spoon with an egg on it and had them start at one end zone. Whoever got the furthest the fastest without dropping the egg won. The rest of the places would follow.

I saw the redhead talking. Focusing, I could just make out what she said. "Like the wind, girly. No way you're going to win."

Hollis laughed, her voice light. "Whatever. This is for fun. Lighten up."

The other person rolled her eyes.

The two guys, who were in third and fourth place, snorted. "Like a couple of girls will beat us."

That got both Hollis and the redhead rolling their eyes.

"Okay, this will determine who gets each prize," the announcer said over the system, his voice reverberating throughout the whole stadium. "From the previous five competitions, we've determined who will be in first or second place ... one of the young ladies. And who will be in third or fourth place, one of the young men."

The guy who'd trumpeted his superiority snapped his head towards the speaker. "What? I thought I could win this thing. No way a couple of girls are gonna beat me."

The master of ceremonies continued, ignoring him. "Go!"

Caught debating the rules, the guy was left behind as the other three took off, leaving the sexist complainer behind.

Hollis was fast, but so was the other girl. I had run with Hollis on track, and I knew how fast she could be, but they had the full field to run.

The redhead sprinted. Her speed was ... I'd only seen one non-Olympian person run like that, and Jade wasn't fully human. That didn't mean anything, but it did pique my curiosity. The redhead dropped the egg just past the fifty-yard line, and her friend, sitting just down the row from us, let out a disappointed sound. The blue-haired girl next to her laughed. "She'll at least get the iPad. It's not like she needs the free meals, it's fine."

I saw when Hollis realized she could win. The other runner glared, but there wasn't anything she could do. The stadium was ablaze with yells and people stomping their feet. Red school banners waved, and it was all almost too much. I took a slow breath and readjusted my blocks.

The moment Hollis passed the fifty-yard line and continued, a wave of cheers erupted everywhere.

The announcer's voice cut through the noise. "Do you think she'll make it to the end zone?"

Unintelligible noise surrounded me.

"Well, I think if she does, we should increase her prize. What do you think?"

Louder cries and stomping reverberated throughout the stadium as Hollis continued to run.

"Let's say, from here on out, every ten yards we'll give her another quarter of free meals. She has thirty to go for her touchdown. That will be a year of free dining *and* an iPad."

The crowd of first years were too loud for even the speaker to be heard after that.

Hollis ran.

When she crossed the end zone a mass of students crowded her, lifting her up and tossing her in the air.

When Hollis finally joined us again, her face was flushed, and her eyes were bright. I caught her as she collapsed into my arms, laughing. "That was so fun! Can we do it again?"

The announcer called for her, and she ran back into the mob, yelling she'd be right back.

The redhead came over and watched Hollis getting all the attention. "Whatever. She probably needs it. She looks like a charity case."

I glared. "Why would you say that?" This girl had no right. Hollis had scholarships, and though this would help her, she didn't strictly need it. I had no idea about Fern, but I certainly didn't need any monetary help.

"Just look at you three misfits. It's obvious." Her chin was lifted so she could look down at us.

Before I could sputter out a response, she walked away, hips swaying. I wanted to run after her and ... I don't know, do something. Fern put a hand on my shoulder. "She's not worth it. People like her put others down to feel better about themselves. She's like a bird, flapping her wings and squawking. All flash, no substance."

I relaxed. Fern was right.

When we finally got away from the stadium, Hollis was elated. "I can't believe I won. I can't believe they upped the prize. I just, I can't believe any of it. That was fantastic!"

Fern laughed, giving her a half-hug. "I'm glad you won. It was fun watching you. It looked like you had a blast."

"Oh, my god, so much fun."

We were outside the building and about to cross the street when a goose flew across our path, honking at us.

The three of us stopped and watched as it flew off in apparent anger.

I laughed. "Geese are always mad, and scary, if you ask me."

"I do not like the cobra chickens," Fern said gravely, watching with wide eyes as the bird flew off.

I doubled over laughing.

Chapter 9 – Let The Lessons Begin

I woke up Tuesday morning ready to begin classes. We started after Labor Day, so the week was short. I found a shirt in my dresser which had a rhinoceros on it. Underneath read, *Save the chubby unicorn.*

Hollis smiled wide, pushing up from her pillow to gaze at me. "We have statistics together, right? Is that still the only one? We discussed History, but ...?"

"Not until next semester. And stats is at two twenty-five ... tomorrow. It's Tuesday, my friend."

"Oh! Yeah, so, class together on Monday and Wednesdays. Coolio. Okay, I'm going back to sleep."

"Right, okay, I have bio every day at nine-fifty-five, so I'm out. I don't know why or how you don't have an earlier class. When is Spanish?"

She groaned. "Right, I should get up. See you later and we can discuss classes."

"Hurry if you want coffee ... or what passes for coffee." I winked.

"Sounds good ... wait, no, sounds awful, but needed." She flopped back down.

In the cafeteria, I grabbed a doughnut and coffee. I was ready to join the police force with this breakfast of champions, but I figured I'd find something healthy later on. My phone buzzed and I had a text from Mom. *Call when you get a chance.*

Seeing her text brought a sense of pack and connection, warming me to my toes. There was a half-hour to get to biology, so I downed the sludge, dropped the tray at the window, and carried the pastry out with me as I walked towards class.

After tapping Mom's contact, she picked up on the first ring. "Hi, Pebble. Are you ready for your first day?"

"I am. Is that why you wanted me to call?"

"No, I just thought ... well, no. Dad and I have something we'd like to discuss with you this weekend. Any chance you want to come home Saturday?"

My head dropped back, and I looked up at the cloudy sky. A couple of geese flew by, honking. *Huh, it must be getting close to when they migrate south.* "I guess, but the full moon is next week, so that's two visits home in just a few days. My friends will think I'm seriously homesick."

Mom hummed. "Well, this could wait until the full moon, I just ... I would rather not wait that long."

"It's okay, you can pick me up. I'll just tell Hollis you're taking me out shopping for a coffee maker for our dorm room."

"Oh, is the campus selection that bad?"

I groaned. "So much worse. She'll understand if the reason is our morning salvation."

A laugh floated down the line. "Sounds good. I'll search over the next few days. Maybe I can have one waiting for you so we can have our discussion and not have to rush."

"Can we have a small run, too? After a week with this many people, I really want to stretch."

Mom sighed. "It's a hard line you have to walk being in college. Okay, sweetie, I'll see you Saturday. Have fun in all your new classes."

"Thanks, Mom, you, too!"

Mom grunted, and I hung up, slipping my phone into my pocket.

It takes pressure to create gems. It takes time to build roads.

I stopped two doors down from the biology room. *'You know that doesn't help me, right? Cryptic messages aren't helpful!'*

I could almost feel my wolf's amusement. Something about the words felt ominous, like they weren't going to help me today ... just an overall reminder of something I needed to know. I really wanted someone to translate all this for me, but over the years I'd mostly grown used to these.

I arrived at the biology lab early. The room was set up with lab tables, and I selected one at random. A few other students sat around the room, and the professor set up in the front. The information about the class portal was projected on a screen.

Nerves danced within me ... this was it. I was a college student. I hadn't felt this giddy since my first day in public school. I got prepared for class, pulled out my notebook and laptop, logged into the course portal, and looked over the different bits of material as the other students filed in. I didn't really pay attention to them. I wanted to be ready for class. It wasn't like I'd know anyone.

I guess there could have been people from my high school—it was a popular college for my classmates to attend—but I liked to imagine I was a pioneer, exploring new frontiers, and not about to run into the same people I went to school with for the last several years.

Once the room was full and the professor started, I realized the redhead was in my class a couple of tables over. *Gods above, can't I get away from this person? She's everywhere. Well, she's at a different lab table. I doubt I'll have to interact with her.*

Most of the first day involved going over the syllabus, important dates, and course expectations. It was nothing much beyond high school, though the professor highlighted the different expectations for lecture, lab, and discussion. This class would take up many hours of my week. I liked biology ... mostly, and hoped I still liked it come December.

"Okay, class. On the side table are boxes with slides. I'd like you to use a microscope and sketch ten different slides, five animal, five plant. The sheet I'm handing out has a place for your sketches as well as room for lists of five characteristics that all the animal slides have in common, five characteristics the plant slides have in common, and three that differentiate the two groups. You can work alone or with a partner."

Next to me sat a heavy-set boy. Before I could say anything to him, he slunk off. With a sigh, I shrugged and went to collect my own items. It took me just over half an hour to complete the assignment and hand it in. Though the lab went longer, the professor let us go early. When we had a full lab, I'd have an hour between class and Intro to Psychology. I was excited to see what that class had to offer. Today, I had an hour and a half to have lunch. Curious about why she'd called, I texted Mom to see if she was in her office.

She was available. I stopped at one of the cafeterias and grabbed a sandwich, chips, and a soda, and headed up to her department. When I got to her office, she smiled, and it warmed me to my toes. "Shut the door, sweetheart. It's nice to see you. I know it's only been a few days, but I've missed you."

I placed my bag on her desk and headed over to give her a big hug. "Missed you too, Mom." It hadn't been long, but I was touch-starved for pack.

We sat and I opened up the sandwich. I definitely should've had a bigger breakfast. My class hadn't been intense, and I was still this hungry. On a busier day, I'd be shaking.

"Are you okay, Pebble?" The warmth in her voice released a tension within me, and I smiled up at her.

As alpha, she could sense more about the wolves in her pack, intense emotions and such. I knew I would learn more soon. Ever since I started training to be alpha, she'd lost her mental connection to me. It was both good and bad. While I was connected to the pack, she wasn't as attuned to my emotions as she used to be.

"Yeah, I'm just adjusting. It's all new, but my first class got out early and I thought I could spend some time with you."

"I'm glad. Are you and Hollis doing well together?"

"We are. But can you give me a heads up about this weekend? I don't want to be fretting all week. Too much else to think about."

She finished warming up her cup of soup and smiled. "Okay. I have class this afternoon. We don't have a lot of time." She took a bite of her soup. "A young lady came to town, Trista May. She's a bit older than you, but not by much. She's from ... I can't remember, it was either

Tennessee or Florida. Anyway, she decided to come up here because she didn't have the best origin story. She wanted to get away from where she first learned about wolves. At first, she thought about being a lone wolf, going to school at Madison College, taking classes in culinary arts, and avoiding everything relating to pack. When she checked in and thought about next week's full moon, she changed her mind."

"Whoa." I held up my hands. "We have a new wolf in town, a *new* new wolf, and she wants to be a loner?" My head started to hurt. "More than that, she's what, nineteen, twenty? A new wolf who's a kid wants to do it on her own?"

Yep, this would be a full-on head-pounder. Not only did it sound like her introduction to wolves was bad, she needed to be trained. That was usually my job. More than that, if she pushed to be a lone wolf ... gah, that was such a hard path to take. Did she know what she was asking for?

A warm smile spread across Mom's face, making me feel better. "She's going to be there on Saturday, sweetie. It's why we wanted you to come home. We want to offer her a connection with you. Your first pack member. This will get you adjusted to being alpha slowly and let her feel like she isn't being thrown into the larger pack. We think this will make her feel better. If she prefers, or you prefer, I'll take her. I know you have a lot going on with starting college."

A coolness washed through me, battling the homey feeling I'd started having when I'd first seen Mom. "You want me to *what* now?"

"You heard me." Her voice was soft, and she reached out to squeeze my hand. I relaxed with the sensation of pack. "Now, I need to get to class by noon and I want to make sure the class is prepared, with all the electronics working. Come and give me a hug, and I'll see you Saturday."

Mechanically, I stood and did as she asked. Then I went to the building of my next class, about a block away. I had an hour, but I could read. Having a book on my phone so I could read anywhere without having to carry anything was amazing. Instant escapism. Despite that, my alpha training this weekend continued to niggle at the back of my mind. I was excited, but also terrified.

What will it be like? Will I be able to filter her out or will she take over, like what happened with Jade and Piper? When Jade accidentally picked up a ghostly impression of her ex-girlfriend, she couldn't control what information she got. But Jade isn't an alpha. I am. Right? But ... am I good enough to be an alpha?

I shook my head, I couldn't let myself think that way *... Focus on classes now, let the werewolf drama wait for the weekend.*

At one, General Psychology started. Just like biology, the professor focused on the syllabus, requirements, important dates, and expectations. She added that there would be a few group projects and, since we were first year students and in college, she would be putting together the groups.

Since I didn't know anyone, I didn't really care. I hadn't even looked at who was in the class. Again, there could have been people from my high school, but it wasn't too likely.

"I'll end class with the groups you'll be assigned for this project. If you end up liking the people you're with, let me know and you can continue to working together for the remainder of the semester. I like to switch things up for each project, otherwise." The professor announced. "Spend the last few minutes meeting your group members, exchange contact information, and making sure you know who will be partially responsible for helping you complete this assignment."

Each group was named and the professor pointed to an area for the students to meet once she was done listing everyone off.

As I looked around the room, I realized I did know a few people, some from school, some from my floor in the dorms, and, once again, that redhead. She was popping up everywhere!

I wanted to snarl, but there were other people around and I knew the sound wouldn't be natural.

Finally, I heard my name called. I tried to think back on the last few people I heard. "Marc, Pebble, Luna, and Kenny V. meet by the far window."

Once she was done, I gathered my stuff and moved to the windows. I shouldn't have been surprised when I saw the redhead heading in the same direction.

"Gah! I can't believe that person!" I stormed into the dorm room, hoping to vent to Hollis. She sat on her bed. Fern was sitting at her desk. They both slowly turned to gape at me, eyebrows raised in question.

"Ah, Pebble, you okay there? It's only the first day." Hollis smiled, then patted her bed.

I sighed, shut the door, dropped my bag by my desk, then crawled to sit next to her. "Yeah, I mean, mostly."

"Well, start from the beginning."

My back hit the wall as I blew out a sharp breath. "We were assigned groups in General Psych." I rolled my shoulders back as I tried to relax. "I'm going to be working with that girl, you know, the one from the stadium?"

Fern barked out a laugh. "You mean the jerk who claimed we were all paupers who needed government help to make our way through college?"

"Yeah, that one."

"Wait." Hollis shook her head. "When did that happen?"

Neither Fern nor I had discussed keeping that from Hollis, but I hadn't gone out of my way to bring it up. Apparently, neither had Fern. I looked between the two of them. "When you were being tossed around like a rag doll and being celebrated for winning. Luna—that's her name—she was just full of sour grapes, that's all."

"Pretty much," Fern said in a droll tone. "She just squawked and flew off in a hissy fit."

I waved my hands in the air. "Anyway, she's in my group with a couple of guys. We were given like five or so minutes to meet, exchange contact info, and all that. I started off, but Luna cut me off. 'I'm Luna, here's my info, and I'm out. Contact me so I have yours, see you Thursday.' She didn't even stay long enough to get the other two guys' names, like she was so much above us."

Hollis placed a hand on my leg. "Did *you* get the other group members' names?"

"Yeah, but we were all so dumbfounded we didn't do much else. It was just ... obnoxious." With a snarl of frustration, I stomped over to my bed and hugged my goose pillow. It wasn't pack but it reminded me of them.

Fern leaned forward, resting their elbows on their knees. "Just remember, it's one person in one class. You won't have to worry about Luna after this semester."

I wanted to snarl.

They smiled and I started to relax. It was similar to when I talked to Jade. Fern was a great misfit to add to our island.

Chapter 10 – A Proposition

Wednesday morning, I decided to head to a local cafe, Electric Brew, for coffee. I needed something more powerful than what the dorms provided before my bio lecture. I went to the cafeteria for breakfast because I decided I couldn't spend a day in classes without food, but the dark sludge they called coffee wasn't going to cut it today, focus was also important.

A hidden shadow is an obstacle found.

I wanted to gnash my teeth. I was too tired for my wolf's puzzles. Second day of school and I already had three ... not to mention the recurring nightmare. I may need to get a dedicated notebook for my premonitions if this continued. I usually didn't have them stacking up like this.

There was a line at the café, but the wait didn't take long. I ordered a large coffee, sweetened, with a splash of milk, and an apple muffin. Though my parents could afford to send me to college, I'd worked summers during high school and could afford extras like this on my own. After my order came up, a couple left a table, and I actually got to sit.

I had twenty minutes before I needed to leave for class, and I debated what to do. It didn't take long to decide to read a bit from a book I'd recently gotten addicted to. I'd picked up *Legacy Bound* by Elizabeth Daly and was loving it.

It took a moment to navigate to the story and then I took a sip of my coffee. My body sang with the intensely wondrous flavor of something it had missed for the last few days. *Gods above, I will not survive on the dorm's swill.*

My eyes slowly closed as I took a few more sips of coffee.

A low chuckle drew me out of my moment as my eyes snapped open. An older man, thick with muscles, stood across from me, hovering over the table. His warm brown eyes and easy smile looked familiar, but I couldn't place him. His face mapped years of laughing and life.

I squinted as I tried to figure out why I knew him. Then the scent hit me ... cat ... panther.

"Do I know you?"

"Can I join you?" He deflected my question with his own and held up a coffee and a small white bag. "I have a class in fifteen minutes, but I saw you sitting here and hoped we could talk. I'm Kal, we met years ago ... I believe. You're Pebble, right? Jade's younger sister? Hazel's daughter."

My muscles relaxed and I leaned back in my seat. Years ago, Kal had been the one to gift my sister with her panther. It had been a misunderstanding during a spring break trip to Florida, where I thought he lived.

I waved my hand at the other chair. "Yes, please, join me. It's been a long time. Didn't you return to Florida?" I thought for a moment to try to pull his daughter's name up from my memory. "Is Dayo in town as well?"

The cafe was full of people, and everyone was having conversations. It was almost impossible to hear what the next table was talking about. We leaned in and spoke quietly. If we hadn't been wereanimals, we wouldn't have been able to hear each other. We hadn't said anything sensitive yet ... but between two wereanimals meeting in the wild, it was bound to happen.

"No, she graduated years ago and got a job in New York. She's a big city gal now." He sipped his coffee, then dug a sandwich from the bag. "I really liked my time here and when I saw an opening, I applied. I've been working here for just over five years."

"Huh, does Mom know?"

"She does, but your pack doesn't really have reason to know about a panther in town."

Without Sarah, Jade, or Owen around, he wasn't wrong. He was probably the only werepanther in Wisconsin. No reason to out him, though any of the wolves would smell the cat on him. If they passed him on the street, they *may* think he just had a pet, or a bevy of cats, but since our pack had lived with werepanthers, probably not.

My wolf's words echoed in my mind again ... a hidden shadow is an obstacle found. I smiled at Kal. "I know that you've been solitary most of your life, but are you opposed to running with wolves?"

"Well, I guess not. I just go to the arboretum when I want to run. I've never thought about running with your parents' pack." His brows knit as he thought. "You know my kind isn't tied with the moon, right?"

"Well, yes, I wasn't thinking about those runs. I was thinking about doing some training sessions ... if I could come up with something new and exciting. Our group hasn't had many since Jade, Owen, and Sarah moved to California. If you joined us, we could play a version of hide-and-seek." I waggled my eyebrows, trying to sound enticing.

He nodded. "That could be ... fun. Training games. Interesting. I'll give your Mom a call and see what we can arrange."

"Awesome." I finished my muffin and checked the time. "Gods, the time flies. I need to get to class. I hope to see you soon and maybe your cat."

"You too, youngling."

As I ran to class, I texted Mom to give her a heads up on my meeting with Kal.

I got to biology and found a seat alone. One of the kids from my psychology group, Kenny, sat next to me.

"Hi, Pebble, right?"

I nodded. "That's me."

"If you forgot, I'm Kenny." He was heavy-set, with wavy black hair, and a hesitant smile. "I don't know anyone in class, and since we're partnered up in psychology, I just thought it'd be okay if I sat next to you in here? Are you okay with that?" He'd ended his statement sounding meek and lost. "I mean, we're going to be spending a lot of the semester together. Hope we don't get sick of each other."

Snorting, I shrugged. "Sure, why not." I held out my hand. "Kenny, here's to being class friends."

He took my hand and gave a small smile. Shoulders relaxing, he seemed much more at peace after that.

The professor started class. There was some basic class information, but most of that was left for the next lab. Once that was done, it was all notes—hard and fast for an hour.

I had fifteen minutes to get from biology to English class. Hollis was in this class with me, and I saw her approaching the door from the other direction. We both smiled and I smelled the bergamot scent of relief on her that I felt. It was really nice and comforting to have a class with not only someone I knew, but my best friend.

The room had tables so we could sit in groups. This didn't necessarily bode well, but at least I'd know someone in my group as long as we weren't moved. We chose a table in the center back and watched as the rest of the room filled. About five minutes later, Fern walked in, and I felt a lightness. Two people to look forward to.

Fern's expression transformed into one of joy, and they joined us at our table. "Oh, my goodness, I am so happy you two are in this class. I get that college is about meeting new people, but these big lectures with so many students, it's overwhelming. It's nice to see a friendly face."

I smirked. "And in lieu of that, us? Or should I ask, which one of us is the friendly one?"

Fern laughed.

"Oh, it's definitely you," Hollis said. "Aren't you always the nice one? I'm just here to be pretty."

"Exactly!" Fern agreed, then they blushed. "Not that you're not ..."

"Stop." I held up my hand, stopping them before this got out of hand and laughed.

The professor handed out the syllabus and began going over the same song and dance every other class had done. His special addition was which books we'd be expected to read, the number of papers we'd be expected to write, and what the final project would look like. The books sounded interesting, and I filled out my calendar with notes about when I'd need to start writing out the papers. If I finished writing my papers early, Hollis would edit them. She'd been helping me out for years.

Once class finished, we headed to lunch.

"I have two more classes, stats and English discussion. Hollis, did you get the same English discussion as me or is yours on Friday?" The pizza was good, but the fries weren't—too soggy. *How do you mess up fries?*

"Nope, different discussion. Once we're done with stats, I'm heading home and collapsing. All these classes are making me tired. Too much thinking for one day." Hollis sipped a soda.

Fern pulled out their phone and checked their lock screen. "What stats class are you in? There are several."

"Um." I showed Fern my schedule and where the class would meet. They showed me their schedule.

"We have two classes together? That's amazing."

We made it to stats class early enough to sit together. Hollis sat in the middle, grumbling the whole time that this class would be impossible. Afterwards, the two left me to find my English discussion.

By the end of that class, it was only four-twenty, but I felt beat. As I trudged back to my dorm room, I saw a flyer for a campus job to become a tour guide. It would work around class schedules, and I'd get a nifty shirt.

I took a picture, thinking I liked the idea.

When I got to my room, my feet hurt, and my body ached. All I wanted to do was collapse on my bed. Swinging the door wide, I opened my mouth to say ... something, but my throat clamped shut, eyes widened, and I gaped. Fern and Hollis sat on Hollis's bed, kissing.

Dumbstruck, I forced my feet to backtrack, as I pulled the door shut behind me.

Chapter 11 – Fireworks

The phantom was behind me. I now knew the room was my room, my dorm room ... or one similar. Its arm rose. It wanted, no, *needed* something from me.

With a small growl, I forced myself awake. I was tired of this ... whatever. The dream didn't feel like a premonition. In the past, they'd never happened during my sleep or when I was knocked out and it made no sense. I'd have to talk to Mom and Dad about it when I went home this weekend. Whatever my wolfie was trying to tell me, I needed to get to the bottom of it.

My small clock said it was just after five. My class wasn't until nine-fifty-five, but I didn't want to go back to sleep. Dragging myself from my warm covers, I grabbed my shower caddy, robe, and flip flops, and made my way to the shower. It was early enough that there shouldn't be a line for the shower. I could take my time.

The warm water felt good. I turned the heat up and let it seep into my skin, washing away the stress of living in tight quarters with so many strangers. I hadn't let myself think about it, but the pressure had been building. Going home for a few hours Saturday and then for the full moon next week would be good.

I quickly washed my hair, again grateful for the short cut. After I added some conditioner, I let it sit while I washed. Then I went back to letting the water flow over my head and body, the heat as high as I could stand.

The image of the phantom came again and all the muscles in my body tightened. My sense of it was a bit different this time. *Is that because I'm awake?*

I wasn't in my dorm room.

The person squatted, facing away from me. The focus was on ... I wasn't sure.

Suddenly, I realized there was pressure in my head. This wasn't the phantom. My arms began to shake as I realized this wasn't the recurring dream. This was a premonition.

Focus Pebble, wake up your sluggish brain and think! I threw my hands out to the walls to hold myself up.

The misty shape of a person, blurry like an apparition, suddenly had a burst of red fireworks explode from their center, raining down on them. They ran as the fireworks colored the air around them.

My heart beat a fast staccato as the images faded. On the walls of the shower, my hands trembled. Despite the heat of the shower and the steam all around me, I felt cold. I shivered with a chill that would take more than a few minutes to warm.

Once my breathing had evened out, I straightened, turned off the water, and dried off. I wrapped the robe tightly around myself and made my way back to the room. It was nice to have werewolf eyesight, so I didn't have to turn on a light to find clothes.

Jeans, a t-shirt, shoes, my school bag, I was set. I made my way back to the Electric Brew. They had so much I wanted, but I limited myself to the largest coffee they'd make me, a breakfast sandwich, and an apple muffin. There was a chance that, if I'd selected everything I wanted, I'd upset the workers. *Maybe I could've told them I had friends coming.*

The place was mostly empty, so I found a table and texted Dad about the premonition. I told him I'd call him at lunch when we were both more awake and able to talk.

Once I'd eaten everything from my first round, I ordered another sandwich, refilled my coffee, and read my book until it was time for class.

Dad had replied to my text agreeing to wait until my lunch to talk. Usually my premonitions could wait a few hours. They rarely were *that* urgent.

The biology professor handed out a flier for a winter field trip. He was planning on taking a few students with him to Colorado for his research on pronghorns, an antelope type beast. He wanted to tag a few to track their migration behavior with the warmer winters. He would also take some blood samples.

Sign-up was due by September twenty-fifth.

I really wanted to go. It sounded amazing. Once I became alpha, travel would be hard. This would allow both travel and study. The challenge would be to convince Dad it was a good idea. Technically, I was an adult, but try to prove that to my parents.

"Now that we've gotten the paperwork out of the way, it's time for us to get better acquainted. I want you to form groups and start to get to know each other," Professor McCrea said, pacing the front of the lecture hall. "Say your name, where you're from, and one boring fact about yourself. For instance, my name is Randy McCrea. I'm from a town near San Francisco none of you have probably ever heard of, and I had oatmeal for breakfast." He smiled wide. "Then you'll introduce each other to the class. I'm going to have the computer put you into groups of three randomly. It will appear on the screen up front. These will be your partners for your first group assignment. I'll randomize the class differently throughout the semester, so if you can't think of something boring now, just wait for the *next* challenge question."

It took a few minutes for him to log in, but then our names started to fill into a table, three names per box. I finally saw my name. Pebble Stone, Dayna Briggs, Luna Zweck.

A second class with groups? Gah, not again! And the teacher was selecting the students again? Seeing the names made it all so much worse. I slumped.

The universe, my own personal whatever, was determined the two of us would come together at every opportunity. If I believed in magic or superstition, I'd be reading more into this than there was.

The three of us gathered in a corner. Dayna was tall with short, spiky blond hair. The sides were buzzed short and dyed blue. She wore a Chicago Bears jersey. I recognized her from the stadium with Luna's friend, or who Fern and I thought was Luna's friend. It amused me that she wore such a controversial shirt, once again.

With a forced smile, I held out my hand. "Hi, I'm Pebble."

"Dayna." She smiled wide, very different from how Luna had been every time we'd met.

Automatically, I moved my hand over to Luna, who I hadn't really introduced myself to the day before.

Luna—whose hair wasn't really red, more of a dark auburn—crossed her arms and raised an eyebrow. "You know me, we've met. Can we just get this over with?" Her expression told me she wasn't impressed that we were matched up again. I let my hand drop, realizing she wasn't going to shake.

I would love to get this over with and I don't really know you, I thought. But I kept my opinion to myself and my face blank.

Then she turned to Dayna and smiled, an actual warm smile. "Hiya, Dayna."

"Hi, Luna. Look at this, we're in the same group. Will I ever get time away from you?"

Funny that—I had the same exact thought!

"Don't know, but I'm glad there's at least *one* other intelligent person in this group. I don't have to drag two people along to get a decent grade."

I clenched my jaw at her accusation but kept my face blank. My family had taught me well. Then I smiled again, knowing it probably looked fake. "So, you two know each other?" I could hear the edge of exasperation in my voice.

Dayna shrugged. "We're on the same floor in our dorms. Okay, let's do this. I'm Dayna Briggs, I'm from Chicago ... if you couldn't tell," she waved down at her shirt, "and I was named Dayna with a 'y' instead of Dana, the boring spelling, because I was supposed to be born at night, but instead I was born in the day, so my parents put the 'day' into my name."

I narrowed my eyes. "That's actually kind of interesting."

A smile spread on her face. "Fine. I think the coffee in the cafeteria is awful."

"It is," I chuckled, "and I don't know if that's a boring fact or just a fact fact. But, if that's been your only source of caffeine, I guess I can't blame you." I smiled at her.

She winked. "Well, I've given two, so I'm done. What's your boring story?"

"Well, I'm Pebble Stone. I'm from right here, Stolzburg, Wisconsin. And I woke up at just after five and took a really long shower this morning ... completely alone. It was glorious. And if you want two for two, I got coffee at the coffee shop down the street, with a refill. No dorm swill for me today. Be jealous!" I whispered the last two words and winked, giving Dayna a real smile as she laughed.

"Oh, I like you, you're sassy."

Luna rolled her eyes and shook her head, as if my details were well below her. Then she sighed. "This is so dumb. I'm Luna Zweck. I'm from Maine, and I always put my right leg into my shorts or pants before my left leg."

I narrowed my eyes at her. "Really? Gods above. I'm going to have to think about that. Like, do I do it a specific way? Do I mix it up? I may start asking people. I've never thought about that before. I never knew a person could or *would* think about it."

Her face hardened. "You really are slow, aren't you? You're investing too much into this. It's just something boring." She huffed in annoyance.

"But *is* it a fact?" I pressed.

"Can we be done?"

Dayna's smile seemed more forced. "I think it's time to do the introductions. I'll do Pebble's, Pebble, you can do Luna's, and Luna can do mine. I think that will be best."

Imagining what Luna would say if allowed to introduce me almost broke my blank face. Dayna's plan made sense and I nodded. And when we were called on, Luna presented like a professional spokesperson. My jaw dropped. Quickly adjusting to her different personas, I introduced her, then Dayna ended with me.

After the other students had introduced each one in their trios, and one quartet of people, we were released. I had an hour before General Psychology, so I headed for lunch and called Dad.

"Hiya, Applesauce. How is your first week of classes?"

"Good. I think I'll enjoy the semester. Or have a brain aneurysm. You know, one of them."

He snarled low. "So, your text, tell me about it."

"The premonition early this morning. It was weird."

After I'd given him the details, we talked about what everything might mean.

There was a stress in his voice, and I envisioned him pinching the bridge of his nose. "Tanner is on a big case with his other job. I'll tell him to wear a bulletproof vest. I think that's what the fireworks are. If not ... I don't know, we'll have to keep digging deeper."

When Tanner wasn't Dad's right hand man, he worked as a bounty-hunter. Though he was good at what he did, it was a dangerous job.

Over the years, Dad and I had been working and training to get better at deciphering what I saw and felt in my premonitions. He was really good at puzzling these things out. Being alpha, he also knew what most of the pack was up to, which also helped. He was probably correct.

"Okay, I'll keep working on it during my free time, but I'm banking on your instinct."

There was a moment of silence, then he asked, "Anything else up, Pebble? You sound ... off."

I released a quick burst of breath. "Yes and no. It can wait until I'm home on Saturday. I can tell you and Mom together."

"Are you sure?" The concern soaked into me, even over the phone.

"Yeah, I'm sure. It's nothing big, just not phone worthy."

"Okay, I'll be at your dorm at nine."

"Have Mom pick me up at seven, I know you won't be up that early. I need better coffee and a decent breakfast."

He chuckled. "I'll let her know. Love you Applesauce."

"Love you too, Dad."

Chapter 12 – Brain Games

"Gods above, this coffee is good." I drank from a travel mug Mom had brought from home. "I could almost swoon."

Mom chuckled. "I'm glad you're enjoying it, sweetie."

It didn't take long in the car to feel like college had been more like a camp than my new way of life. That, or I was leaving a strange dream and Mom was bringing me back to reality.

"Was Dad up when you left?"

"Dad? Awake? You're kidding, right? We'll head home and have breakfast. I invited Aunt Allison to come over this morning. With a new wolf, I thought she'd be a nice calming influence. So, she may be there. I doubt you'll see anyone else before ten."

I leaned back, watching the homes and trees stream past as she drove. "Is ... what was the name of the new wolf?"

"Trista?"

"Yeah, her. Is Trista staying at the pack den?" I rubbed my legs nervously. I hadn't been able to talk to anyone about this. I could've called Jade or Bevin, but I didn't want them worrying about me. They had a mini sports team of babies to watch over, their own pack, and jobs of their own. That was more than enough distraction. Anyway, I could always call them later if I needed to.

"No, she decided she wanted to stay at a hotel until she figured out if she really wanted to join the pack. We don't live very close to Madison College, so she's looking for an apartment over on the east side of town." As Mom spoke, she navigated the mostly empty roads.

"Weird." I shook my head. "I get she doesn't know us and all, *and* that we're not exactly on the east side of Madison, but doesn't free room and board account for anything anymore?" I flung my free arm to the side in question, then sipped the magical elixir.

"No prejudging her, Pebble. Let's just get home and talk about how you're enjoying classes. I promised your dad I wouldn't get any real school details from you before he could be there too. He is excited to see you." The drive from campus to the pack den was short and Mom soon pulled up to the house, not bothering with the garage.

The pack den was big ... like really big. It may not have been as big as Were House in California, but it wasn't anything to be ashamed of. The first time I'd come, I'd only been five and I thought we'd arrived at a hotel.

The first floor had a massive living room that opened into an industrial sized kitchen. The pantry alone was bigger than some small apartments in New York. All of the family's private rooms were on this floor. The second floor had rooms for pack members, a library, and Dad's office. Mom used the room as well, but she had enough office time at work.

In the basement was a study room, a huge room for the kiddos, and a few more dorm-like rooms for sleeping. There was also a second kitchen. Everything you'd need to spend a fun-filled evening while parents were out wolfing it during the full moon.

Inside, we headed directly to the kitchen. I sat on a stool at the counter. Mom handed me onions and peppers to dice. She turned on the oven, then began prepping the rest of the ingredients for a skillet-type breakfast: sausage, cheese, eggs, and hashbrowns. When the oven dinged, she pulled a coffee cake from the fridge and slipped it in. Then she started making hashbrowns and sausage.

My body settled into the familiar routine and scents of pack den. There weren't any pack members living here currently besides immediate family, but that was okay, the den was ready when needed.

I heard a car driving up, and smiled when Aunt Allison walked in. I stood, embracing her when she got to the kitchen.

"Pebble! I'm so glad to see you. How is college? Your classes? Any new friends? Boyfriend? Girlfriend? Themfriend? Are you and Hollis doing okay as roommates?"

I laughed. "I don't know if I even remember everything you asked. I'm going to need a lot more coffee. I'll start there. The school's coffee is bad. Just awful. I will not survive on the stuff."

Mom just made a face at my dramatics. "Look on the dining room table, sweetie."

I did. Sitting there, all snug in its box, was a French press and three bags of ground coffee. I went over and sniffed the bags, marveling at how good they smelled.

Curiously, I held the box up, wiggling it towards Mom. She winked. "I know the rules, and that is allowed. It makes excellent coffee. All you need is boiling hot water, which, if you look, we got you a kettle as well. That would be good for coffee and tea. All your warm liquid needs."

I sighed contentedly. "Okay, this will work. We can pick up more when we run out. Hollis's parents got her a small fridge, so we can pick up milk, and sugar is simple. Suddenly college is looking feasible."

"Such a drama queen." Dad's tired voice came from down the family hall, followed by a yawn. "Speaking of coffee ... more needs to be made if I'm going to be conscious this early on a Saturday."

"Dad!" I ran towards his voice until I saw him in his pajama pants and an old t-shirt with a griffon on it. My hug should've knocked him down, but it was hard to unbalance a werewolf. His strong arms wrapped around me, making me feel young.

"Heya, Applesauce. Let me wake up, then we can discuss the day."

It didn't take him long, and while he showered and dressed, Mom made four stacked plates of a sausage-veg mix, topped with hashbrowns, then cheese, and finally sunny side up eggs. I found a watermelon and cantaloupe on the counter and cut them up. As I put the chunks in a bowl, Aunt Allison added grapes and strawberries.

We all started digging into our skillet-inspired meals.

Dad made a content sound. "Hazel, this is excellent ... or should I say egg-cellent?"

"No," I groaned. "You shouldn't."

"Ah, you missed me." His smile grew. "Anyone else need a refill on coffee?"

I held up my mug and Aunt Allison nodded. Once Dad returned, he narrowed his eyes on me. "Okay, my brain is reconnected. Tell me about your classes. Have you met any new friends?"

For the next half-hour I told them about Hollis and Fern and everything that had happened over the previous week.

Dad smiled. "Oh, before I forget, Tanner called. Your premonition helped. He wore a bulletproof vest, and it saved the day."

I closed my eyes, thinking about the image of the darkness and fireworks. *At least one of my visions made sense.*

"Anything else up with you, sweetie?" Mom asked. "I feel like there's something you're avoiding."

My face scrunched up, then I leaned back, hugging my warm mug of coffee to my chest. The recurring dream only happened a couple of times before school started and hadn't seemed important enough to tell my parents. But now ... too much filled my plate. "There is. But it isn't new. Since ... let me think. California, maybe."

"What?" Dad leaned forward. "There's been something going on that long and you never told me? Us?"

"Well, yeah. I didn't think much about it, but ... well. Some mornings when I'm waking up I have this sort of waking dream. I'm searching my closet for an outfit, but the clothes aren't really mine ... nor was the closet. Well, I didn't think it was, but now I realize it's a dorm closet ... it could be mine, but they all look the same, right? Anyway, I turn and there's this phantom of a person who reaches for me. Over the last few weeks it's happened a lot more and the phantom, well, there's a desperate urgency."

"Hmm." Aunt Allison tilted her head. "Do you think it's a premonition?"

"It's hard to tell. Since it starts while I'm asleep, I don't have the initial pain in my head or anything else. But the room, it confused me until I got to the dorms ..."

Dad nodded slowly. "That's when it clicked. Your premonition has to do with someone at college."

"Yeah, well, if it *is* a premonition. Sometimes I wish I could talk to my wolf the way Jade does. I can sometimes sense things and talk at her, but the conversations Jade has ... I can't do anything that elaborate."

Mom laughed. "I think we're all a bit jealous of your sister, now that we know it's possible. I keep asking her to write a book, but part of me wonders what's the point. The likelihood of another epsilon is very low. And what would the other wolves think? The book will read like fiction."

We all laughed.

Dad looked at his watch. "So, when are the others coming?"

"Trista will be here soon. She's coming over to meet Pebble before the training games."

Excitement bubbled in me. "Training? Did you talk with Kal?"

"I did." Mom nodded. "He said you two spoke. Dad was around when Kal called so the two of them made plans."

The thought tickled me. When I looked at Dad, the mischievous smile told me he was as excited as I was about the whole thing.

Aunt Allison rubbed my arm. "As fun as this afternoon will be, should we discuss Trista?"

Apprehension quickly replaced my joy at the idea of searching for a panther hiding in the woods. I licked my lips and turned to Mom. "I know we've talked about this, but are we sure I'm alpha level? With José and Bevin it was obvious right away, but with me ... I mean, it wasn't. What if we do this and I'm overwhelmed? What if something like what happened to Jade happens to me?"

Dad rubbed my arm. "You don't have to do anything you don't want to do, Pebble, but you definitely have the alpha mantle tucked deep inside of you. From what we can figure, being bitten as young as you were, your wolf protected you. It wasn't until you were willing to go out and hunt on your own and embrace the full you that the wolf released all of her and your strength."

I took a deep breath. We'd discussed this before, but I needed to hear it again. The touch of pack, of alpha, and of Dad helped, too. "Okay, yeah, you're right. I did put Tanner on his butt when I dropped all holds on my power, opening up completely. I guess that's a thing?"

Aunt Allison chuckled. "It is, and something I enjoyed watching. There are so few wolves stronger than him. He could've become alpha level if he'd wanted, but I think he likes having others above him. It allows him to snarl more ... it's his love language, you know."

A laugh bubbled out of me. "Gods, I never thought about it like that, but you're right. Snarling and cooking."

The doorbell rang. I'd heard someone approach, but the conversation had been something my inner self needed, and I hadn't wanted to waste one second on the person coming to visit.

Mom stood. "I'll get it, I'm sure it's Ms. May."

"Pebble, why don't you go to the living room while me and Allison clean up in here?" Dad leaned over and kissed my forehead.

I nodded and moved the few feet to one of the larger couches. I hadn't even sat when Mom came in with a teen about my height with sandy blond hair and blue eyes. She stood tall, but her shoulders were a bit hunched.

"Pebble," Mom said, "this is Trista May. She just moved up from Tennessee to go to culinary school at Madison College. Trista, this is our daughter Pebble Stone."

Trista's eyes widened and her jaw clenched, as if she didn't want to gape at me. Then she took a few quick breaths. "You named your daughter Pebble Stone?" Then she shook her head holding her hands, palms out, towards both me and Mom. "I'm sorry, that was rude."

The situation was just too funny. "It's okay. I'm adopted, and my full name is Penelope Stone. Pebble is my nickname and what I'm used to. It was from before my adoption."

"Oh!" Her eyes widened and a smile spread across her face. "Gotcha." Trista seemed to relax. "Actually, Pebble Stone, I really love that."

Well, at least she had good taste.

Mom had a satisfied look on her face. "Okay, Trista, are you ready for this?"

"Well, yeah, that's what I'm here for, of course I am." She had a bit of a southern twang, but not much.

A sour, nutty scent came from her. She was stressed and nervous. I walked over to her and rubbed her arm. "When you were in Tennessee, were you part of a pack? Is this new to you?"

"No, it isn't new. I've done this before, totally." She bit her lower lip, then shook her head.

I sighed. "Okay, listen, I don't know your past. I'd love to get to know you better, learn all about you. Let you learn about us. I want you to know you're safe here. The best way we can help you is if you're honest with us."

"I *am* being honest." Her words spilled from her quickly as her focus bounced between me and Mom. "Why don't you think I'm..." She trailed off as she finally looked at the floor.

I rubbed her lower arm. "We can hear lies. You should be able to as well. If you can't—" I caught her gaze which snapped up at my words, the gingery scent of shock filling the room, "—we'll teach you. That's what we're here for. Pack. Family. Teachers."

The muscles in her arm relaxed and her head bobbed. "Okay, yeah. I'm sorry. I just, I don't want you to kick me out. And ... I'm a bit scared."

I leaned in towards her. "So am I."

After a moment, she smiled at me as if I had told her a joke.

Before I figured out if I was ready for this big jump in my life, I wanted to know more. "Can you tell me a bit about yourself?"

"Sure." She sounded uncertain. "What do you want to know?"

There was so much I was curious about. "Let's start easy. How old are you?"

Her smile lit up the room. "Nineteen."

The two of us smiled at each other. "Ah! A baby."

Her brow furrowed. "A baby? How old are you?"

I snorted. "Eighteen."

As I hoped, her whole body shook with her giggles. In my periphery, I could see Mom smirking, amused at my antics.

Once Trista stopped laughing, head shaking at me, I asked, "How long have you had a wolf?"

Her body froze, but then she blew out a breath, as if remembering we were in a safe place to discuss the mythical creature. "This will be my second full moon."

. "Well, how did you become a wolf?"

"Heh, that's a ... um, a funny story." She balled her fists then, relaxing her hands, rubbed them down her legs. I was about to tell her she didn't have to share, when she started to talk. "This is going to sound like a fiction book, but I was on vacation in Florida with my family." She barked out another laugh. "You know, camping. The site was close to where I grew up, a favorite camping spot, you know the kind of spot."

"So, you're from Florida?"

She paused for a moment to gaze at me. "Yeah. Anyway, I um, wandered into the woods, following, um..." She looked up to the ceiling. She wasn't lying. The story was a true tale, but the way she spoke was so halting. Maybe she just felt uncomfortable about it or telling a couple of strangers. "Sorry, I haven't really told this before, it's just really hard ... emotional, you know."

I wanted to hit my head. If it had only been two months, and she'd lost both her parents, of course she was emotional. "You don't have to continue."

"No, it's fine." She wrung her hands together. "I followed a lightning bug. It was the craziest thing. I got it into my head it would be good luck to catch it. It was late, and I must've made noise. Anyway, a wolf attacked me and my parents. I was the only one who survived." She shook her head then bit her lip. "It was awful. I thought I was going to die, but somehow I survived. Mom and Dad didn't." Her voice softened and she licked her lips. "Anyway, I have some relatives in Tennessee who I went to live with after that. I was shocked when, at the next full moon, I shifted." She shivered, eyes wide.

Whoa, until the end, that could've been a version of Jade's story. It was like she was just retelling it with a few minor detail changes. I squeezed my eyes shut. *Stop putting the cart in front of the horse, Pebble. Lots of weres have similar stories. Don't be an idiot!*

Mom leaned forward. "That's when Kendall and Iris found you, right? The Tennessee alphas."

Trista nodded slightly. "Yeah. It was good. I was scared. The last wolf I'd met had attacked me and killed my parents. But they were really nice."

"And do you think, despite all of that, you are ready to join a pack of wolves?" Mom's voice was soft, comforting.

Trista's eyes widened, "I think so."

"Good," Mom said. "Do you have any questions?"

She shrugged. "There aren't a lot of people here, so pack doesn't have to live in the pack—" she bit her lower lip as her head swiveled. "Den? That's what you call this place?"

Nodding, I tried to see my home, my safe place, as it would look for the first time. When I'd been five, everything had been larger than life, but now it was just home. "Yes, this is the pack's den. As alphas, we live here, though really, anyone in the pack is more than welcome to stay here. Most choose to live in their own homes, but there is enough space here if you want to pick a room."

She shook her head. "There's so much more than just becoming part of the pack, isn't there?" Her arm lifted. "Your touch ... it calmed me. And this home. Family. You said that, but that word, it has a deeper meaning to you, doesn't it?"

A giddy hope rose in me as I nodded. "Yes, it really does."

Mom placed a hand on her shoulder, and I saw Trista relax even more. Then a small smile played across her face as the citrusy scent of hope poured off her. Mom asked, "Trista, do you want to join our pack?"

"I ... um. Yeah, I do." Her words were hesitant, but she sounded determined.

I smiled. "And you're ready?"

There was a pause, then she took a deep breath. "I am." She nodded, then said, more slowly, "I am."

I licked my lips. "Now, here's a big decision. You can join through Mom or me. I'm eventually going to be the alpha, but right now it's still Mom and Dad. Do you want me to take the reins?"

Her eyes widened. "I have no idea what you're talking about. You seem nice, so sure?"

I took both her hands. "Okay. You don't need to understand, just know you'll be part of our pack and welcome."

In the back of my head, my wolf was trying to tell me something, but there was too much emotion. She'd get me the message later; she always did. If it was really important, I was sure I'd be in the middle of a premonition.

"Pebble, you know what to do." Mom's voice soothed me.

Trista's face paled. "Will this hurt?"

"No." I shook my head with a small laugh. "Not at all. You shouldn't feel a thing."

I put the base of my hand on Trista's forehead, letting my fingers lightly fall into her hair. *Okay, wolf friend. It's time for us to start our alpha life. Who are we bringing in?*

The name 'Elizabeth Trista May' floated through my mind. *Huh? She goes by her middle name ... interesting.*

I licked my lips. This was it. No more delaying. "Elizabeth Trista May—" my voice sounded strong and clear; it had a power I'd never spoken with before, and when I first said her full name Trista jerked. Despite that, our connection never wavered, "—welcome to our pack."

And then all that which was Trista hit me, and I understood.

Chapter 13 – Into The Woods

My body trembled as I slowly backed away from Trista. I tried to keep the shock from my face as a part of my brain was given over to her emotional state. She was scared and nervous, nothing new. Her mind whirled with anxiety and fear, hope and ... there was something she was hiding. I debated following that, but then I realized I had secrets, and it wasn't my place to pry.

If I want to know her, I should do it the same way I learn about any other person ... talk with her over coffee and preferably something chocolate.

I shifted my foot, and my heel knocked into the couch. With a start I realized I'd backed up to the couch. Smiling shyly, first at Trista, and then at Mom, I sat.

Trista's eyes narrowed. "What just happened?"

"Can you sit?" I looked up at the ceiling and raised my voice. "Dad, can you bring me ... us coffee? Or hot chocolate? Or both? Or cake?"

His laughter came to me as I lowered my chin and saw Trista take one of the recliners. She kept her eyes on me. A cinnamon scent came from her. She was skeptical of the situation.

Mom sat in the love seat. "Trista, would you like something to eat or drink?"

"I could eat, and I prefer tea ... or hot chocolate."

She didn't drink coffee? My mind whirled, but then I decided to give her a chance anyway.

"I'm making hot chocolate now," Aunt Allison said. "River is getting a tray of food."

Once I'd centered myself, I said, "We're connected. What that means is, if you have any intense emotions, I'll be able to feel them." Trista opened her mouth and eyes at the same time as her scent shifted to the sweet scent of fear. I lifted my hands to stop her from asking what everyone assumed. "No, before you ask, I can't read your mind. And yes, that is everyone's first question. Emotions, I can feel the intense ones. Also, if I focus on you, I should be able to figure out what direction you are from me. So, if you get in a jam, I'll be able to find you."

Jam ... toast with jam would be good. Toast and jam, and cheese and sausages, and that hot chocolate. Gods, I was hungry.

Once I finished, her scent shifted to a light chamomile of acceptance, then became more neutral.

"So, you can feel me in your head?" Trista's question pulled me from my food musings.

"Um, yes. But that's it. And only if I focus on it. It isn't like I'm watching the Trista show."

Her eyes closed, then she curled her legs under herself, crossing her arms across her chest. After a few seconds, she looked at me, confused. "I can't feel you. Nothing feels different to me."

"You won't. The touch of pack will help soothe you better, and when we run in wolf form we can connect, but beyond that, there shouldn't be any difference for you." I watched her closely to make sure nothing freaked her out.

She nodded and looked at Mom. "So, you have all these wolf emotions in your head? Like, all the time?"

Mom nodded. "I do. When you're alpha, you get used to it."

Dad walked in with a charcuterie board with crackers, cheese, and meats. In his other hand was the fruit bowl I'd helped make. Behind him Aunt Allison carried a tray with the hot chocolates.

"How are you doing, Applesauce?" He sat down next to me, placing a hand on my knee. The contact relaxed a tension in my shoulders I hadn't realized I'd been holding.

"Good, but the hot chocolate is probably more exciting than the food."

He chuckled.

"Applesauce?" From across the room, Trista's brow dropped. "Did he just call you ... Applesauce?"

I snorted. "Yeah, he did."

"Okay." She leaned forward, taking one of the small plates in the center of the platter and filling it up. "I get nicknames, but Applesauce?" One of her brows rose in question.

Her citrusy mint scent filled the room. She was amused and confused. Come to think of it, so was I. "Yeah ... um, I have no idea." I looked back and forth between my parents. "Dad, why *do* you call me Applesauce? I just," I shrugged, "you've always called me that. It never occurred to me to question it."

Both my parents, as well as Aunt Allison, looked ready to burst. Dad said, "Gods above, it's been years. When we adopted you, we had a few interviews with child services. During one of them they asked if we'd love you as much as our biological children. I told them, 'like the apple of my eye.' Owen snorted and said, 'More like applesauce.'"

Mom couldn't hold back her giggles. She covered her mouth as she laughed. Next to her, Aunt Allison caught a case of the giggles with her.

Dad shook his head. "Anyway, you apparently hadn't had applesauce or didn't remember having it because after that you asked what it was. For some reason you connected our love with applesauce, or you just decided you loved it. For the next month—"

"Two months," Mom snorted out.

Dad sighed. "Two months you demanded applesauce with every meal. The name just followed."

My mouth hung open and when I turned, Trista's hands were over her mouth and her shoulders shook with her amusement.. I snapped my mouth shut, then started to laugh. It *was* a bit funny. "You named me after a snarky comment Owen made?" I demanded, giving each of the adults in the room a mock-glare. The idea actually warmed me to my toes. I loved my brother.

"And ... that ..." Mom could barely speak over her laughing. "*You* wouldn't ... stop eating." She fell into Aunt Allison who was also laughing.

"Gods above. I'm getting marshmallows. You all need to get yourselves together."

When I reached the pantry, I heard Aunt Allison say conversationally, "Aren't the marshmallows stored next to the extra jars of applesauce?"

I wasn't going to tell her that that helped me to find the pillowy treats. I always knew where the applesauce was. Apple was one of my favorite flavors.

Back in the living room, I put some marshmallows into my mug. "Trista, do you want any?"

"No thanks, I don't like them." No coffee *or* marshmallows? This person was *very* suspicious.

I sipped the warm treat. "You said that you moved in with your Tennessee relatives. Do they know anything about the werewolf? Did they see your shift?"

Inside my head, I could feel her discomfort with the question, but I was going to go by her words, not my inside track to her emotions. "No, I had been taking a hike by myself. Those relatives hadn't ever approved of me or my parents ... the shift gave me a reason to leave."

Maybe that was the spike in emotions I felt—first losing her parents, and then unsupportive relatives. Gah! Trista hasn't had an easy time with any of this.

Before I could ask anything else, I could hear a few cars driving up.

I took a plate and started filling it with food. "Sounds like it's time for some training."

"Training?" Trista's heart rate increased.

Trista and I sat on the back porch. "A werepanther? There are more than were*wolves*?"

I hooked my arm in hers, hoping that my touch would calm her. "Yep. And we're going to train with him. Hide and go seek."

"Okay. Yeah. Sounds good. And also the rest of the pack?"

"Yep. We'll introduce you to the wolves that come today, which won't be everyone. On Thursday, during the full moon run, you'll meet everyone else."

Trista seemed to blanch. "Gotcha."

I know she hasn't had much experience with good wolves ... I hope she realizes soon that our pack is great.

We stood, and I introduced her to Kal. She visibly trembled. "Hi, you smell of cat ... like a really big murder mitten."

He laughed. "Yes, well, that is probably a good description. I'm going to go change so you can see my black panther. I promise not to bite."

Trista laughed a bit manically.

After that, I introduced her to Uncle Jackson and Tanner, who had shown up just after Kal. José's family, Clare, Alejandro, and Estrella came next. Estrella was in grad school studying linguistics and economics. She planned on taking over the pack finances from her mom. They were closely followed by Bevin's family, Fred, Janet, and Hannah. Bevin's other sister, Heather, had moved to Colorado for work. Hannah had mastered the fine art of computers, IT, and hacking ... she was the one who'd taught me everything I knew.

There were a few more, but Trista waved her hands, saying everyone was blurring together.

By the time she'd met as many of the pack as she could, Kal had time to shift. He came from around one of the privacy walls, black and sleek, like Jade. I worried

Trista would crumble to the ground. The sweet scent of her fear perfumed the air.

"It's okay, relax. It's just Kal. As dangerous as you are as a wolf."

She took a deep breath and slowly calmed. Kal circled the backyard, meeting everyone. By the time he got to us, Trista was breathing calmly, and her scent had shifted to a nutty nervousness.

Afterwards, we all found places to shift, and Kal ran off into the woods.

Trista was a tabby-colored wolf with black markings on her paws and snout. In wolf form, Trista strode around the yard, head held high. She even approached some of the pack she hadn't met before. Her confidence impressed me.

I couldn't seem to gauge her level. *Can she hide her power? We'll have to test her against Clare and Tanner, the top two wolves outside of me, Mom, and Dad.*

Dad circled the wolves present. "Okay, we're going to get into groups of three. Tanner, you'll be with Allison and Jackson. Fred, Janet, and Hannah. Clare, Alejandro, and Estrella. And Pebble, you'll run with Trista and Hazel. Each group will race to find Kal, who is currently setting false scent trails."

The fact that Mom and I share a group means none of the others can beat us. I smirked, not that it translated with a wolf snout.

Dad gazed at each group. "From what I can tell, Tanner, Clare, and Hazel are our best noses, though

Pebble is a good seeker. Hannah has been catching up. Sorry, Fred, you can glare, but your daughter outclasses you." Fred's tongue lolled out in a laugh. "Janet or Fred could swap with Hazel to even out the groups or we could leave them as they are."

Fred and Janet gazed at each other and seemed to have a conversation. Only Jade had the ability to speak in pack members' mind—being epsilon—but married couples always had their own unspoken communication. Though I didn't date, the idea of having a special connection with another person intrigued me. Finally, they both gazed at Dad, unmoving.

"Very good. We'll give Kal five more minutes, then the race is on."

Once the time was done, we took off. Mom led, with Trista in the middle. She didn't know the woods like we did. Kal's scent was everywhere. Barely into the woods, I knew Mom was heading in the wrong direction.

I growled low and Mom stopped, staring at me. I pawed the ground twice with my right paw. Her eyes narrowed, her red fur waving in a cool breeze. Again, I pawed the ground.

With a snuffle, she changed directions. We were off, and Trista and I followed. After a few minutes, we were off course again and I signaled Mom again. The third time she pushed me to lead. A warmth suffused me, and I ran, pushing the others to keep up with me. I loved stretching my legs and feeling the wind brushing through my fur.

Though Kal's scent permeated the backwoods, I could still smell the birds and a few foxes that had traveled through recently. We never got stray cats on our property, but most other animals found their way to our sanctuary.

A few minutes later, we stood under the tree my gut told me was the right one. It had nothing to do with what my nose told me, but something deeper. As one, we all gazed up. Kal blinked. We turned and headed back to the house.

Halfway to the backyard, the premonition of the phantom rushed me, knocking me to the ground. I whimpered as I saw myself sorting clothes, turning, and the person lifting their arm. Nothing had changed.

Like someone turning the volume on, I suddenly could hear ... cars? in the background. Honking. Was that traffic? And the person, so desperately reaching for me, drawing me towards them, finally spoke.

"Find me!"

Chapter 14 – Crashing The Party

Tuesday night, Hollis, Fern, and I went out for dinner. We decided to go to a Mexican restaurant just off State Street for a taco Tuesday extravaganza. They had a party-platter special with a dozen tacos, rice, beans, and chips. This place understood students.

Fern sighed as they ate their first pork taco. "This is good. I know it's only been a couple of weeks on campus, but real food, my friends, real food."

Hollis leaned over, bumping shoulders with them. "I know, right. Pebble headed home for a day, so this isn't as big a deal for her, but I agree." She took a bite of a steak taco. "Are you treating, Pebble? Didn't you just get a new job?"

I smiled at them. "I did, but I don't start work until next week."

"What's the job?" Fern asked.

"I'm going to be a tour guide on campus. I saw a flier and applied. I think they hire anyone. Anyway, they work around student schedules. I know the campus pretty well since my Mom works here and I've been hanging out in downtown Madison most of my life."

Fern narrowed their eyes. "Don't the tour guides walk backwards to face the people they're speaking to? Does this mean you need some sort of eyes in the back of your head?"

A laugh bubbled out of me.

Hollis sipped her soda. "No. You can't convince me to walk around campus backwards. It's not happening."

"Just because you'd end up falling on your butt is not my fault, friendo." I waggled my eyebrows at her.

Fern laughed. "So, you're telling me you're going to be a xenagogue."

I narrowed my eyes at them. "A what now?"

"Duh!" Hollis made a face at me. "A xena ... oh! You're Xena!"

"Yeah, I see that." I shook my head. "I'm not buff enough to be the warrior princess from that TV show. Not to mention, my parents are the only ones who think I'm a princess."

Hollis shook her head. "No! Hear me out. You have the dark hair, and you're totally strong enough. We just need to get you a costume." Hollis leaned forward, pointing her taco at me.

I snagged it and finished it in one bite. It had been the last pork one, and it was good.

"Hey! That was mine!" she snapped, narrowing her eyes at me.

"Want it back?"

"Children." Fern put up their hands. "My goodness you're awful." They waved their hands until we both leaned back, smiling at their antics. "A xenagogue is a guide who leads new arrivals. At least I think that's what it was. It's been awhile. Though, Pebble, you being Xena is also a fun thought. How are you with running through the woods and being powerful?"

It took all my training not to groan. To hide any reaction, I rubbed my face. "Yeah, tour guide." I picked up my soda, took a sip, then selected my next taco. "We need to find something better after this. I mean, this is amazing, but ... hot chocolate, shakes, muffins ... I don't care, as long as it's sweet."

Hollis nodded. "Now you're talking."

We focused on eating for a few minutes.

"So," Hollis tapped her finger on the table. "Tell me about these bad dreams you've been having."

I continued to eat my taco, looking back and forth between Hollis and Fern, wondering what dream she meant. It occurred to me they were both staring at me pointedly. A chill ran down my spine, and I placed my taco on the plate. "Dreams?"

"Come on Pebble, we share a room. Like, maybe four or five times you've had a bad dream. You groan and start to thrash in your bed. You don't seem happy. I'd have to be deaf and blind not to notice. Or not caring. I don't think I'm any of those things."

"It's okay," Fern's voice soothed me. I hadn't realized how tense Hollis's words had made me. "You don't have to tell us, or if it's me, you can speak with Hollis later ... or your parents, but I think you should talk to someone if the dream is disturbing."

It was like when Jade or Bevin speaks to me—the stress just melts away. I rubbed my face. Despite the calm, I couldn't believe the broaching of this topic with non-pack.

This isn't happening. Gah! "Actually, I have talked to Mom and Dad about this, last weekend when I went home."

"Wow, you really do tell them everything." Hollis sounded hurt.

Slumping, I rubbed my forehead. "It's not that ... it's—" I took a moment to gather my thoughts. "The dream has been happening since I was in California. I ... it's nothing. I don't think of it as a nightmare. I'm shuffling through a closet, but the clothes aren't even mine. I turn and there's a person reaching for me. And then I wake up. That's it."

Fern's head tilted. "Not your clothes? Whose closet are you in? Are you at home?"

"No. I'm in the dorms. I didn't realize that until we moved in."

Hollis leaned forward. "Are they *my* clothes? Are you trying to steal my style?"

Closing my eyes, I tried to think about the dream. Beyond not being my shirts, I never really thought about the clothes. "I'm not sure. If and when the dream happens again, I'll try to focus on the exact wardrobe. You know, because *that's* what's important."

Fern laughed. "I'm glad you said this started this summer and it wasn't connected to us dating. You really are okay with that?"

The subject change was more than welcome. I popped up from my slouched position, unhappy to realize how much I'd folded into myself. "No, I mean, yes, I think it's great if you both are happy with it."

"So far so good," Hollis said. "But we decided to do everything slow."

I raised an eyebrow and gave my friend a challenging look. "Do you know how to do slow?"

Hollis threw a napkin at me.

We'd finished the platter of food, and while gathering our stuff to leave, Luna sat at our table.

All my muscles tensed. Hollis's mouth pursed tight together and one of Fern's eyebrows rose.

"What do you want, Luna?" I asked.

"Yeah," Hollis snapped. "Are you here to express your assumption that we're all paupers again?" Hollis's eyes widened. "Or is this charity? In an altruistic act of goodwill, do you want to offer to pay for our dinner since we obviously can't pay ourselves?" She sneered. "Wait, that involves goodwill, forget it."

I saw Fern place a hand on Hollis's arm to try to calm her.

Luna rolled her eyes then rotated so she only faced me. "Look, Pebble, our first bio assignment is due on Friday. We need to meet Thursday. Dayna is available. Eight. At the library."

She made to stand up. I barked out a laugh. "You are too much. No. Just no."

"What?" It was like she'd never had anyone talk back to her before.

"Look, I'm busy Thursday night. I can meet Wednesday if you want, but I have plans on Thursday." Anger boiled in me. This person was so self-centered. She just assumed everyone would jump through her hoops.

I saw Hollis's face scrunch up as she tried to figure out what I was doing, but she wouldn't question me with Luna at the table.

Luna huffed. "What are you doing Thursday? Move it."

"None of your business, and no. You're not my boss or in any way in charge of me. Thursday is out." I wanted to throttle her. Very few people caused so much negativity in me.

"Gah! Fine. I'll talk to Dayna about moving our Cards Against Humanity game or skipping it this week. Tomorrow, eight, library." Before anything else could be said, she stood and sashayed out.

My brain stuttered at the mention of the card game. *A card game! She demanded I rearrange a schedule—not knowing what I had to do or how important it was—for a card game.* I wanted to scream.

My hands ached from making fists at my sides, and my shoulders rose from the tension building in them. I shook out my hands and forced myself to relax. "So, how about chocolate shakes?"

Both Hollis and Fern looked at me, the sandalwood scent of concern coming from both of them. Hollis smiled wide. "Yes, but only if we find a place with more than just chocolate. Your obsession is too much, my friend. You do know there are other flavors, right?"

"Gods, no! Say it isn't so."

Chapter 15 – What's Not To Love

Wednesday was my long day. Bio lab, English, stats, then English discussion. When classes ended and I got back to the dorm, I rested for a few minutes before starting homework. I had to have dinner and be at the library by eight to meet with my bio group.

The room was empty when I got there, so I lay down to rest. My head began to ache, and I knew a premonition was starting. I wasn't sure if it was college or what, but I felt like more visions were invading my mind, like my wolf was handing in extra credit.

A bear roared, running past me. For a moment I tensed, but then I realized it almost looked amused. Wolves ... everywhere. A sound of birds in the sky, but when I looked up, there was only one. I squinted, was that a black swan? The shape wasn't quite right. As I tried to identify the bird, the vision faded out.

"What the hay," I mumbled to myself as my eyes opened and I gazed up at the ceiling. A conclave of wereanimals and shifters? We just had something similar to that in California. One of Jade's work colleagues was a werebear, so even that had been covered. Were my premonitions shifting to something that looked both backwards and forwards? Was that even a premonition or just ... something else?

I debated calling Dad, but the door opened, and Hollis walked in. "Hiya, Pebble. Are you sleeping?"

"No, just debating when to head down for dinner." I pushed myself up to lean on the wall.

"Oh, how about after we talk?"

I stilled. "Everything okay? This sounds serious."

"Yeah, I mean ... um, yes. I just wanted to figure some stuff out, and you know me—how do I know what I think until I hear what I have to say?"

I laughed. That had always been her motto. "Okay, my friend, talk. I'll be your sounding board."

She sat on the edge of her bed facing me, but scooted back, mirroring my position, then lifted her knees, hugging them into her chest. "I'll start with: I told Fern I'd probably discuss all of this with you. They know. They also said they thought you might know but weren't sure. So, when we're done, we'll have a discussion about that, too."

One of my eyebrows lifted slowly in question. I had a guess but wasn't sure.

"Okay, you know me and Fern are dating."

I sighed. "Yes, and I told you it's fine. We're all friends. I think they'd be chill even if the two of you broke up."

Hollis waved her hands. "No, that's not it. It's just, did you know Fern is trans?"

There was a tightness to Hollis's body. She'd always been a lesbian. I closed my eyes and took a slow breath. "Yeah. When we first met them ... I had a feeling. I wasn't one hundred percent sure but wondered." At times like these, I never knew what to say to my friend. Should I say yes, I detected ... something, because I knew several other trans people, so my unintentional detective skills were fantastic? Or, the truth, I smelled it on them. Yeah, that last was probably a bad idea since it was connected to my werewolf. I had no idea.

"But how?" Hollis said, a whine to her voice.

My head fell back, hitting the wall behind me as I tried to come up with something ... not wereanimal related. "I just ... I don't know. But does it matter?"

She stared at me for over a minute, thinking about the question. "I don't think so. I really like Fern. They're amazing. Like, the perfect person. And though they're nonbinary, they present more feminine than masculine and are so pretty."

I smiled, a happiness filling me. "Well, then, I think you've figured it all out."

She bounced. "It wasn't that big a deal after all." She patted herself down as well as any cop. "I need to text Fern. Let's go get pizza."

The weather was nice at a quarter to eight at night in late September in Wisconsin. A cool breeze blowing in from the lake combed my hair, feeling similar to when I was a wolf. I breathed it in as I walked to the library. It was easy enough to find the group. Dayna's navy blue and orange Bears jersey stuck out like a sore thumb in the sea of green and gold for the Wisconsin Packers and red and white for the UW Badgers. I wondered how much razzing she got for wearing Bears paraphernalia every day.

Before I even sat, Luna started talking. "We have a few options for our project ... which is due next week Friday, but we have to have our choice handed in this week with an outline."

"Right, we all know that." I couldn't keep the exasperation from my voice. She assumed everyone was dumber than her. "Pick an animal—"

"I think we should do the pronghorn and its migration cycle within the borders of Colorado."

I held up my hands. Luna's constant interrupting, first in class and now here, was going to make me snap, and then things would get ugly. Possibly ugly enough that Mom and Dad would need to send in a clean-up team. This person just rubbed me the wrong way. "Stop interrupting me. I know you want this done—"

"And you can't meet tomorrow," Luna mumbled.

"Can you stop talking for a minute?" I snapped. "My gods, I've spent a life working in groups, and you are awful … maybe the worst, and that's saying something. Let a person get a full thought out without interruption or a snide comment. Is that a possibility?"

"Yes, Mom." She rolled her eyes … again. I think that was the fifth or sixth time I'd seen it today, and I'd barely spent any time with her. She couldn't be much more obnoxious.

Dayna leaned forward. "Did you say, 'gods'?"

I released a sharp breath and slumped, deflated. "I did."

She smiled. "Coolio. So, are you against the pronghorn, or just Luna being Luna?"

That amused me. "Oh, I have no problem with the antelope type creature. They're artiodactyl, right? Hooved? They're what the professor is focusing most of his research on."

Luna's face hardened. "Right. Good. Not an imbecile. That's good."

"Well, no." I shrugged. "I mean, I have my moments, but I didn't get to college on my looks alone."

Dayna smirked. "I like you. You're fun." She indicated Luna with her head. "Luna will grow on you. By the end of the semester, you'll love her."

I gave her the best smile I could. Despite the pep talk, I highly doubted it.

Chapter 16 – For Mondara's Sake

"And to reiterate, get into your group, outside of class, select one of these topics to study, then create a presentation." The psychology professor handed out papers to the end of each row. "The presentation will need to have aspects from each member of your group. I would suggest a slide show or some other visual aid to help explain to the class what you're trying to teach. You will have just over two weeks to complete this."

She walked back up to the desk and threw the extra papers near her bag, giving the class time to pass the assignment out.

"Okay," her voice snapped out. "You have about three minutes until class is over to arrange a time to meet and start working. I would, as always, suggest one of the libraries." She paced across the front of the room. "Don't plan on class time to work on this. Once you've figured things out, you are welcome to leave. Have a great day, great weekend, and I'll see you all on Tuesday."

I packed up my bag and stood. Marc, Kenny, and Luna were over by the window, so I headed over to them.

"We can't tonight," Luna glared at me. "Pebble is busy ... apparently."

I tightened my jaw and counted to three ... five. "If I wasn't busy with a personal appointment, we'd be busy with our bio group. Tonight would've been out no matter what. Don't make this sound like it's all on me. Hell, I have an hour right now, if you really want to get something done immediately. I'm in." I raised an eyebrow at her.

Marc held up his hands. "Whoa. Hold up. I have a job I need to get to. I work until nine tonight. I'm available tomorrow."

I shrugged. "Works for me."

"Me too." Kenny's voice was timid, like he wanted to be anywhere but with the three of us. He kept glancing at Luna then dropping his gaze to the floor.

I wonder if he spent time around other fighting people and learned to disappear? My hackles rose and I wanted to protect him. Slowly, I moved to stand between the two of them.

"Friday night? Really? All of you losers are free? Wow. Welcome to college in the Midwest." Luna shook her head as if disappointed. "Well, I for one don't do homework on Friday nights."

A bark of a laugh burst out of me. She was so full of judgments and rules. "Does that rule extend to Saturday nights as well?"

"More or less. We need to have some fun, though it doesn't seem like there's much to do around here. I'm debating a trip to Chicago tomorrow, not that it's any of your business. I'll be back by Sunday. We can meet then. Bio in the morning, psych in the afternoon."

Both Marc and Kenny gaped at her, the minty scent of confusion coming from both of them. Marc got his voice back first. "Biology?"

Luna patted his cheek. "Not you. I have to suffer Pebble in two groups. So, let's say library, one-thirty. Sound good?"

Marc's face hardened. "I'll be there, but do remember, this is a project done in equal parts. You aren't the leader."

Before Kenny or I could answer, Luna shrugged. "Whatever. Enjoy the rest of the day." And she flounced off.

I watched her go. "Are you two really okay with one-thirty on Sunday?"

A small smile flitted across Kenny's face. "Yeah, that works. I hadn't realized you were in her group in bio too, that's awful." He grimaced in disgust.

With a shrug and a sneer, I gathered my stuff. "It is what it is. One project, right? We'll probably have different groups next time, right? And she's only in my classes *this* semester. There are so many sections of each class, and I don't think we're studying the same thing, I probably won't see her much after finals."

"True. I'm so used to high school. Mine was small. You always ran into people all the time." He gazed off for a moment, then shook himself. "What *is* her focus, anyway? Do you know?"

I paused, then scoffed. "You know, I have no idea. For some reason, the getting to know you part of the program has never gotten that far with her."

They both chuckled as the tension released.

As I walked from the class, my phone buzzed with a text. Checking, I saw a text from Trista. *I got out of class early. Want a ride home?*

I checked my watch. Two-twenty. *Sure. Do you know how to get to my dorm?*

Yep. The reply came quickly. *Be there in a jiffy.*

As I headed back to the dorm, I contemplated the word 'jiffy.' Did people really say that word anymore?

Once in my room, I tried to decide what I needed. There wouldn't be time to do homework, but I didn't want to have to stop here in the morning to grab my bag before class. My bio material replaced the psych stuff. With a glance over my shoulder at my closet, a shiver ran down my spine. It was the same motion as my dream, but in reverse. No, I had clothes at home ... pack house home not dorm home, so I didn't have to worry about that. Just the school stuff.

At Hollis's desk I found a small pink piece of paper and wrote: *See you tomorrow after class. Stay safe!* ~P

Back out in front of Chadbourne, I found Trista in her car, an older model red Kia Rio. I slid into the passenger seat.

"A friend of mine said I had to see State Street. Can we take a driving tour?" Her eyes widened in excitement.

"Well, no."

"What?" Her brows furrowed in disappointment. "Don't we have time?"

I smiled at her. "We do, it's just that you can't drive on it. Only buses and cabs are allowed, but if you turn over there and look for parking, we can walk down a bit of it. We have time for that."

It took several blocks of searching to find a spot, but we weren't too far from State Street and there wasn't a meter. Free parking. *Score!*

Once we got to the street, we headed towards the capital. Trista beamed, and her joy swirled within me. "It's so great. I mean, some of the stores are chains, but so many are local." She grabbed my arm and dragged me to a window. "Gah! Look at those dresses, and necklaces, and shoes. It's all so pretty."

For a moment, I let her joy wash through me. Since I'd connected with her, this was the biggest spike of emotion she'd experienced. There was a lot of information coming in. *Does proximity intensify this?* Not only was I picking her up as alpha, her citrusy scent blanketed the area.

For a moment, everything else around me faded as all I knew was Trista and her elation. My hands trembled as I gazed at whatever part of State Street she was focusing on.

Taking a slow breath, I built up my walls, trying to block most of it out. I'd been a werewolf my whole life, I could do this. I was alpha, I had an alpha mantle of power. *Just tap into your power, Pebble. Control what you're experiencing; do not let her take you over. Remember, Trista isn't in danger, and you don't need to follow her emotional tsunami.*

Turning quickly, Trista pointed. "And smell the food from that restaurant. Do you think it tastes as good as it smells?"

With a shake of my head, I settled her emotions into a manageable headspace. My hands still trembled, but it wasn't anything I couldn't handle.

"Better." Her eyes widened, and I chuckled at her reaction.

Before she could bruise my arm with another grasp, I linked my arm in hers and led her towards the capitol.

Eyes narrowed, she looked at the majestic white structure. "Why is there a building in the middle of the street?"

I snorted before I could stop myself. "Sorry, that building is the capitol of the state of Wisconsin. It's pretty impressive inside. We don't have much time now, but you should check it out when you have time. Maybe some weekend I'll take you."

After nodding, she slipped from my arm and spun. "There are just so many different places. That other end, that's campus, right? Where I picked you up?"

"Yes. If you stay in Madison for any time, you can experience any or all of these places."

"Food, and theater, shops and a small park, this is ... I see why that girl from my class told me to come and check this place out. She said it would give me a better idea of the flavor of Madison." Trista's eyes never stopped moving around every inch on the street.

Excitement built in me as we walked to the end of the street and turned back towards campus. My blocks started to slip, and I realized her emotions were so intense, they were almost becoming mine.

"What else is down there besides your dorm? It's rather distinctive, you know."

"It is. Library mall, my dorm, and the rest of campus." I laughed. With her emotions adding to mine, I couldn't remember the last time I felt so light and free.

Despite Trista's joy, it was a full moon night and time was limited. When we returned to the car, Trista sighed. "That was amazing."

"I'm glad you liked it. I enjoyed your enthusiasm, it was fun."

She sat, hands on the steering wheel. "Pebble, can I ask you a question?"

A tension began to build in the car from my nervousness. *Did I mess up? Does she want out? Is she feeling hampered by my parents? The pack? Me?* "Of course. Anything." *Just please don't leave the pack. At least not yet. I don't want to fail in under a week.*

"I know this is going to sound dumb, but I've heard people in your pack say ... um, Mondara? Or something. Can you explain that to me?"

In an instant, the tension left my shoulders, and I slumped. "Oh, yeah, of course. Most werewolves believe in a set of twin gods. There is a moon god: Mondara. They protect the animals of the forest, watching over the run and the hunt. They oversee the darker impulses of the wolf. We shift at least once a month, under the full moon, and sing in love and acceptance to them as one of our gods and our animalistic side."

Trista nodded. "Okay, a moon god. And this god has a twin?" As we spoke, she started driving towards the pack den.

I smiled. If I were to be honest, in a lot of ways, I wouldn't call myself religious, but discussing the twin gods and teaching about them made me happy. "Mondara's twin is Sonnara, the sun god. Sonnara oversees the day and the lighter side of the werewolf ... our humanity."

"So, more of the human side and less violent impulses?" Trista asked, a quizzical look on her face.

"Yes, dual gods for our dual nature."

As Trista's face scrunched up, then relaxed, I could feel her determination. She continued to drive, leaving campus and heading onto the main city streets. Halfway to pack house, a smile spread across her face. "I like that. Is there any literature on the gods? Anything I could read?"

"Yeah, I think I can find something for you at home."

"Thanks, Pebble. You're really amazing, did you know that?"

A sense of peace and acceptance filled me as we continued our drive home.

Chapter 17 – A Strange Divide

It was just after four when Trista and I drove up to the pack den. There were several cars, but it looked like not everyone had arrived. I pointed to a place Trista could park and then we headed in.

I guided Trista into the living room. Fred sat on one of the couches with his wife, Janet. Trista knew both of them from the training game and smiled with a wave. On the other couch sat Piper, Julez, and their two-year-old child, Spruce.

Speaking as quietly as I could, I leaned into Trista and said, "Do you know Piper and Julez?"

She shook her head.

We walked over to them. "Piper, Julez, this is Trista, our new pack wolf."

Trista gave a small smile and held out a hand. They both shook in turn. Julez shifted a bit, getting Spruce more comfortable. The toddler was fast asleep. "This is our child, Spruce. We're trying to keep them gender neutral until they can tell us what they prefer."

After a moment to consider, Trista nodded slowly. "I've heard about that, but you know your child's sex, right? You change the diapers?"

Julez's body stiffened. "Well, yes. We know what's between their legs, but that's not the full story. You should do some research."

"I'm just asking. This isn't anything I know about." Trista's hands flew out to the side. She seemed to want to understand, just wasn't sure what was going on. I could feel her confusion start to cycle through me.

Julez shook her head. "Well, we aren't the encyclopedia or a website. Do your own learning from somewhere else." Her voice was cold and dismissive.

Trista took a step back. I placed my hand on the small of her back. "It's okay, Trista. Let's go to the kitchen, see if we can find something to eat."

She shook her head. "I'll go, say 'hi' to your parents. You can follow after you spend some time with your pack mates."

I watched as she walked away. Once she was out of sight, I squatted, my face hard. "She's from a small town, doesn't know much about what you're doing or about us. She's trying."

Julez scoffed. "She sure is."

Piper smiled at the double meaning.

I wanted to howl, but I kept my voice low since I didn't want to be overhead. "Why didn't you ... why *don't* you give her a chance?"

"I get impressions of people, Pebble. I always have. I just ... I don't know, don't get a good impression of her." Julez shrugged.

My jaw clenched. Ever since visiting California and Julez had been attacked and turned into a werewolf, she had been lording all that she knew over everyone. She'd come home to learn everything she could from Mom. The relationship between her and Piper grew to the point that the two had become inseparable.

Originally, Piper wanted to follow her friends, my sister and crew, to California. After Julez's shift, they both decided to stay in Wisconsin because they had family here. Even though Piper was Jade's ex-girlfriend from high school, everyone remained friendly. More than that, the two had always been really nice to me. I thought they'd be my biggest supporters as the next alpha ... not this. It felt like a betrayal.

"Well, it doesn't really matter *what* impression you get. She's my first official pack member, and I'm going to go check on her."

They both paused. Piper leaned forward, eyebrows raised. "Wait, you mean she went to you, not Hazel?"

I straightened my back, proud of my new position. "Yeah. They're starting me off with one person, getting me used to holding wolves. She's my mini-pack."

Julez snarled, glaring in the direction Trista had gone. "Why didn't your parents just give you us? We'd love to have switched over early. Then you'd have two of us."

Though her words warmed me, I didn't like how they'd treated Trista. "I love that idea, and you're welcome to talk to Mom about that, but I really wish you'd give Trista another chance. She's part of the pack."

They both shrugged and Julez rolled her eyes, jaw clenched. Then she shook her head and gave me a bright smile. "Yeah, whatever. Another chance. Heard, boss."

The title made me laugh. Owen used the same one for his alphas. After giving baby Spruce a kiss on the forehead, I headed into the kitchen. Mom and Dad weren't there, though Trista sat with Hannah, Bevin's younger sister, and Chloe, a daughter of two of our submissive wolves. Chloe never became a wolf and decided she didn't want anyone to bite her. She still came to the pack house each full moon to watch over Spruce with Piper's mom Helen.

Trista smiled and I could feel her contentment settle within me. I waved a finger from me to her in a question and she shook her head as Hannah said something and all three of them laughed.

In a flurry of action, a couple of pack wolves cooked, Tanner and his son Easton. Gods above, that family could cook—dinner would be fantastic. No wonder Easton wasn't visiting with Spruce. Though Spruce was fully Piper and Julez's child, Easton had donated to help them get pregnant. He loved the kid, though he wasn't an active parent by the mothers' request.

Since Trista didn't need me, I hunted for my parents. There was a question I'd been needing to ask them for a few days, and if they weren't surrounded by other pack members, now may be perfect. Checking the areas around me, they weren't in the dining room or the basement. Next I searched the family hallway with our bedrooms and knocked on their door.

After a pause, Mom said, "Come in, Pebble."

In their room, they had a small round table with five chairs. They sat drinking coffee. I sniffed ... tea. I shut the door and sat in one of the remaining chairs.

Dad smiled. "Hey, Applesauce. How are things?"

"Good. I'm excited to get out and run tonight. I just forgot to talk to you about something on Saturday and wanted to bring it up sooner than later."

Dad leaned back. "Should I be worried?"

"I don't think so." I sighed. "It's just ... my biology professor, he's doing research on pronghorn—it's like an antelope, though it isn't. Anyway, he's bringing a group of students to Colorado for a week between Christmas and New Years to help him tag some animals and collect labs. I was hoping to sign up."

After sipping his tea, one of Dad's eyebrows rose. "Do you need parental approval to sign up?"

"Well, no. But—"

"Then I think we're done here." Dad slapped the table and stood.

My mind whirled ... completely confused. "That's it? I heard the stories of what you put Jade through to go to Florida."

"She was fifteen, and I was right. You're eighteen and I'm expecting you to behave on this school sponsored trip and to return as you are." His face hardened with his words. "No more kids with more than one animal. I have one with three, one with two, and you have one." He winked. "One each. I'm good."

A laugh exploded out of me. "Yeah, sounds good to me too. I also plan on telling Heather so she can let her pack know I'll be in the area, though I don't think I'll be that close."

Mom nodded. "Good, I'm glad we didn't have to remind you." She stood. "Now, dinner and a run."

Back in the kitchen, Easton set platters out with something that smelled amazing. I waved my hand. Easton nodded. "Piri piri chicken, bunny chow, Cape Malay curry, chakalaka and pap, jollof rice, and malva pudding for dessert."

I moaned. "Why don't you two cook every month?"

Easton chuckled. "Too bad Mom is busy tonight. She's really better at helping Dad than I am."

"I'm not complaining." Taking a plate, I signaled Trista, then took some of everything they'd made. Wanting to get out of everyone's way, I went and sat down in the dining room. Slowly, the room filled as others got food. I saw Trista sitting back down with her new friends in the kitchen, joy filling me that she'd found people to connect with.

Everything tasted as good as it smelled.

Dad leaned back, a smile of contentment on his face. "Have you had the dream again?"

"No. Not since Saturday. Though, Hollis said she can tell when I'm having the nightmare. She and Fern had an intervention."

Mom smiled and Aunt Allison laughed.

Tanner's brow wrinkled. "Tell me about this premonition dream."

Once I was done, he nodded. "Do you think the person is someone you go to school with? Maybe a wolf about to come out? Someone you know?"

Piper leaned forward. "Maybe it's Hollis." Her eyes were wide, and she looked excited at the story. "Could she be a werewolf in hiding all this time?"

I tried to think if she and Jade ever shook hands. My sister's epsilon abilities were amazing. It was a shame she was the only one anyone knew of. *I don't know which one I'd want more— healing, picking out wereanimals with a touch, or talking with my wolf. Probably that last. It would make understanding my premonitions so much easier.* "I don't think so. I'm almost positive Jade would've had some reason to shake her hand at some point ... right?"

A low chuckle came from the other end of the table. Shifting, I saw Tanner shaking his head. "How many times have you been at Hollis's house, Pebble? If Hollis is a wolf, at least one of her parents has to be one. You'd smell it there. You have a brain, child, use it."

My cheeks heated, and I went back to eating.

Piper gazed up at the ceiling. "What about that new friend, Fern?"

I rubbed my temples. "Stop. I think this conversation is going a bit far afield. Next you'll be pointing at each person in my working groups, which includes people I'll happily not think about as being pack. So, instead, we'll eat wonderful food, then go and run. That seems like a much better plan."

Everyone laughed, and conversation shifted to other people's lives.

As soon as everyone finished eating, it was time to run. Mom stopped me at the door to the backyard. "Piper and Julez mentioned switching over to you to give you more practice. I'm game if you are."

Her smile reached her eyes, and I could smell the jasmine scent of pride coming from her.

Closing my eyes, I thought about the emotions I'd been juggling since I'd taken on Trista. Couple that with having a pack of three where the trio didn't get along. In my heart, I wanted to be alpha, taking on Trista had proven that to me, but starting off with such big emotions ...

When we'd discussed my mini-pack, I hadn't imagined Julez and Piper following through this quickly, but we'd always been close. After Jade had left and Piper had wolfed out, she became one of my sisters. Julez loved and supported me, too. They'd always had my best interests at heart, even when they weren't the best at presenting their thoughts. Gazing into Mom's eyes, I nodded. "Yeah, that sounds ... great."

Mom chuckled. "Okay, let's get them moved over and then run!" Her eyes almost glowed with her excitement for the hunt. This close to the moon, our wolves rode closer to the skin.

We found Piper and Julez in the basement hugging Spruce. They ran over to a box of duplex Legos and began to play.

Mom approached them. "Now, are you sure you want to do this?"

Piper slouched into herself, looking smaller than her normally small self. Julez had mostly broken her of the habit, but it came back when she was nervous or didn't want to hurt a friend's feelings. *Ah, she doesn't. Julez is pushing her into this. I get it.* Piper lifted one shoulder. "Does it mean we're out of the pack? Will it hurt?"

Mom's head dropped back, and she laughed. It was so reminiscent of Owen, I smiled. "Oh no. You are still very much part of our pack. We're just a three-alpha pack at the moment. It happens in times of transition. It isn't common, but it also isn't unheard of. It's a training exercise."

Piper's eyes widened and a small smile played across her face.

Julez bumped shoulders with her. "See, I told you. Nothing to worry about. We're just helping Pebble out. This way her only pack person isn't Trista. I want her to have good people in her head."

My jaw clenched, but I stopped myself from reacting.

Mom's face tightened slightly, but you'd have to know her to see it. She didn't like the way Julez spoke about Trista, either. "Right, if you're all ready."

They both nodded. I approached Piper first, she was closer. I put the base of my hand on her forehead. The connection gave me her name. "Piper Brittany Schneider, welcome." The emotional onslaught rushed through me, but I didn't have time to process it. We had a run to get to.

I moved to Julez. "Juliet Roby Lolite, welcome." What came with her was much more intense, and it took me a moment to get it all settled in my mind. Finally I shook my head. "How many people do you hold?" I asked, turning to Mom.

She chuckled, then rubbed my back, leading me to the backyard. "You did great, sweetie."

Behind me, I heard Julez whisper, "I don't feel any different. And how did she know my full name? I remember Hazel asking me."

Mom rubbed my arm, letting me know it was fine.

In the backyard, everyone else had shifted. Watching Trista as she stood at the edge of the yard, I could feel her walls strongly in place. Was she hiding something? *Is she hiding her power?* I still wasn't sure that was a thing. I'd have to ask my parents or Tanner later.

Mom approached Trista, signaling for Tanner to test her dominance. He did, gazing into her eyes. It took a moment, but she backed down. *Is that an act? Is she pretending to be weaker than she really is?*

A snarl bubbled up in my belly when I realized I'd let Julez's words sink into my head. With a shake of my head, I forced away the thoughts. *Stop presuming things! This is your first run as alpha. Focus on that, not on making mountains out of someone else's imagination.*

Mom continued to call wolves up. I moved behind a privacy screen to change. When I was done, everyone, including Mom, was ready to dash to the woods.

Mom and Dad led as the pack spread out to stretch our legs, let the wind ruffle our fur, and howl to Mondara. Though I wasn't leading, I kept track of my three mini-pack charges. Trista ran near me. It took a moment to find Julez and Piper in the mix of wolves, but their joy in the run was on the other side of the group, following a few paces behind.

There were some paths, especially near the house, but soon enough the woods opened up, thick foliage all around, the scent of peat, wildlife, and a lake nearby.

I leapt over a fallen tree. I felt more than saw other wolves making the jump. The exhilaration of my small pack thrummed through me, and I howled with the knowledge of fulfilling my purpose.

We ran. A branch scratched down my side. Far off, the scent of rabbit perfumed the air, but it wasn't time for the hunt. We followed our main alpha. Joy bubbled within me and my wolf that one day the pack would be mine and we would lead the moon run. But for now, it was Mom.

Eventually, Mom stopped and signaled for us to all hunt on our own. No group hunting tonight.

I turned left and took off towards the rabbit smell that continued to tease my snout. The hours of running had built up a hunger, and I was ready to eat. It didn't take long to feel others with me: Trista, Julez, and Piper. My pack.

We ran for maybe ten minutes until we came nearly to the edge of the woods. We found several plump rabbits. Both Julez and I pounced and each caught one. Julez gazed at me expectantly and I nodded. We each took a couple of bites and stepped back, letting Trista and Piper have some.

After that, I decided I needed sleep before school and headed back home. I dove into the lake on the way, the cool water washing the woods from my fur.

At home, I leapt up to my old treehouse, the habit long ingrained in me. Piper and Julez followed. The minty scent of Trista's confusion filled the small area as she followed as well. The four of us dog piled up to keep warm.

Surrounded by my pack within a pack, sleep quickly found me.

Chapter 18 – A Night On The Town

I flipped through the clothes in the closet. I needed to find … no, they weren't my clothes. I turned. The phantom stood, arm reached out towards me. In the background cars honked … or was it just one car? The sound was reminiscent of … gods, what did it sound like? My mind searched.

"Find me!" Desperation dripped from the person.

"Who are you?" I sat up, bleary eyed, in the treehouse. The other three still slept. There were robes hanging on the wall. I slid one on and headed into the house to shower and dress. Piper's mom was cooking breakfast for the hoard of hungry wolves ... bless her.

"Morning, Pebble. Coffee now or after you're dressed?" She held out a mug.

"You are a saint. Both?" I took the mug and dragged myself down the hall to my room.

Once clean and dressed, I returned to the kitchen, got more coffee and added a plate of food. I trudged to the table and sat to eat. It didn't take long for the rest of the pack to slowly wander in.

Trista sat next to me. "Do you need a ride back to campus? I could take you."

Just then Mom flew by. "Ten minutes. I have someone coming into office hours."

I gave Trista a small smile. "No, I'll go in with Mom. No reason not to. We're both going to the same place." I could see the disappointment cross her face. After a moment of consideration, I asked, "Have you seen much of Madison since you've relocated up here?"

Trista shook her head. "Not really. I moved up just before school started and I don't really know anyone."

I took a bite of the scrambled eggs and sausage mix that Piper's mom had made. So good. "If you want, my classes end at a quarter after three today. Want to go on a driving tour of the area and then get dinner? You could see more than just State Street and the pack den."

Her face lit up. "That would be amazing. I'll pick you up outside your dorm at three forty-five? Is that enough time to get back and change or whatever?"

"Yeah, that will be perfect."

In the car, my thoughts whirled, a twister in action. Campus wasn't far, so I pulled up my proverbial big girl panties. "Mom, can a wolf fake a dominance test?"

Traffic cluttered the roads, and she focused on driving for a few moments. "Not that I've ever seen. You may look through the pack library, but besides a new wolf being unready for placement, in wolf form, the wolf doesn't understand human need for those types of games. It's why we test in our animal form."

"Is that why Julez is prickly to Trista in human form but when we ran everything was fine?"

Mom sighed. "That woman. Ever since she had Spruce, she had become more opinionated and headstrong. She's great to have in your corner, but once she has made up her mind ..." Mom shook her head. "You handled it well. They're adults and it isn't your job to fix everything. You're alpha, not a parent or boss. If they ask, maybe, but unless their wolves fight, let them be."

I knew that. It's why I'd probed a bit, but hadn't stepped in.

Despite being tired from the late night, my classes went by quickly. It was like the professors wanted the weekend as much as we did. Before I knew it, the drudgery of taking notes was done.

"So, what are our plans?" Hollis put her arm around me and Fern. "We have a whole weekend ahead of us."

We walked towards the dorm. "I have plans for tonight, but tomorrow morning we're going to the zoo, right? Fern, you still want to meet my Aunt Allison?"

"Yes! That sounds fantastic. I love zoos and all the animals." There was a tone of jubilation in their voice.

"Well, good. As for tonight," I slid out from under Hollis's arm to get the door to Chadbourne, "someone is picking me up soon for dinner out."

Hollis almost screeched. "What?!"

I made it to the elevator before answering. "It's nothing like that. A family friend is going to school at Madison College. She just moved here from down south. I thought I'd give her a driving tour of Madison and we could get dinner."

Hollis leaned in. "Maybe we could do a double date. Fern doesn't know Madison either."

Fern leaned down to kiss Hollis's cheek. "You're right, I don't, but we have plans. We're going to watch that movie tonight and order in pizza." They slipped an arm around Hollis's waist. "Just the two of us."

The words seemed to electrify Hollis. "That's right. Oh! I've been wanting to see the movie. Yes, yes, yes. Pebble, go, get scarce. You're no longer wanted."

I laughed. The elevator arrived and we all got on. In our room, I dropped off my bag and grabbed my purse. While I hugged Hollis goodbye, she said, "Be careful, don't stay out too late, and remember you have my number."

"Yes, Mom." I dragged out the second word.

On a whim, I gave Fern a hug as well. They hugged me back. "You have my number, too. So you're doubly covered if you need anything. Though I won't know where you are, how to get there, or anything else. I will try if you need me, though."

I smiled wide at that. "That's good to know, my friend." One more wave, and then I left.

Trista waited for me by the front door, the windows of her red Kia rolled down. I got in and began directing her. We drove around campus, then around the west side of town.

"You're living and going to school east of here, right? Would you rather I show you around over there?"

Trista shrugged, slowly starting up as the light ahead turned green. "I don't know. It's nice knowing where the big hospital is. We could turn around and head that way, but I've seen a bit between school and my apartment. As you said, I'm living over there, it might be nice to see what's over here. To be honest, I could go for an early dinner. I don't know that I've eaten enough today."

I nodded. "Turn left up ahead. You shouldn't let yourself get hungry. It isn't safe."

"I know. It's one of the first lessons I learned. No more worrying about what I eat."

Amusement filled me. You'd think everyone would love that, but for some reason, half the time, people sounded sad.

"Okay, turn right into that parking lot. There's a hole-in-the-wall, all you can eat sushi restaurant, with conveyor belts. It's amazing and no one will really know how much we eat.'

Trista perked up. "Oh, that sounds fantastic." She parked and we walked in. It was early enough that we were seated right away. There were three other groups, two eating at the conveyor belt, one ordering from the menu.

As soon as we sat, and ordered water and hot tea, we started selecting plates. Each plate had one or two pieces of ... well, everything. Pieces of sushi, edamame, crab Rangoon, spring rolls, even dessert, though we decided to wait on that until closer to the end.

Every few minutes a server would come around and clear the plates, fill our water and tea, or just check to make sure everything was going well.

I narrowed my eyes at the latest selection Trista took from the conveyor belt. "Are you purposely taking sushi with cream cheese?"

"Oh, yeah, that's my favorite."

"Gah! That's it, out of the pack, back to Tennessee with you. First coffee, then marshmallows, now this. It's the last straw. Executive order time."

She laughed. "I'm not the one who's taking all the crab Rangoon and sesame balls, even though we're not at the dessert course yet." She raised an eyebrow.

"But ... sesame ball. Have you tried one?"

"You made me, like twice. Where have you been, Pebble? Yes, they're good, but I'm guessing the table behind us may want one or two as well."

I sagged. "Fine, I'll let some go, but if any of that yellow cake comes out, I don't care, they'll have to fight me."

This time she threw her head back and laughed.

It warmed me to see her so relaxed and happy. I tilted my head. "Are you enjoying your time in Wisconsin? Madison?"

Her eyes narrowed as she considered the question. "I am. For the most part, the pack seems really accepting. I know that Julez doesn't really like me. I messed that up, but I'll fix that mistake. Don't you worry."

I wasn't sure of her chances of success, but she was confident, so I smiled.

It took a while, but we finally were full, and I paid the bill. After a loop of the highlights of Madison, we headed back downtown. Trista parked near the capital, and we walked down State Street again, enjoying the hustle and bustle, as well as the sights. I heard honking above and saw a v-formation of geese flying south.

Trista pointed. "Fascinating birds. Did you know that they mate for life and protected their young fiercely?"

I smiled. "I knew the second. My older sister was attacked on the running trail once. As for mating for life, no, I didn't know that. Maybe the creatures can be nice to someone—or rather, to each other."

"Yep. Like Julez. She's nice to Piper, even if she's not nice to me."

"But Julez is a person, not a bird."

Trista winked. "As far as you know."

"No, I know. Trust me." When Jade healed Julez after her attack, if there had been a shifter bird in her, Jade would've found out.

Shifter geese. I shivered, what a terrifying thought.

Chapter 19 – Calming The Beast

It was always exciting when I woke up and realized I hadn't had my morning dream ... or nightmare ... or premonition, or whatever that thing was. Once again, I wished for my sister's ability to really sit down and have a long talk with my wolf. It was great that I got these insights from the wolf, but if they didn't make sense, what use were they?

Hollis was still asleep. We weren't getting picked up to go to the zoo for almost two hours. I slipped on my shower shoes, robe, and grabbed the shower caddy. In the bathroom, I brushed my teeth then set the shower to the warmest temperature I could handle. After I'd shampooed and put conditioner in, I heard movement in the shower room. I tried to hurry the process before my body started to tense.

There was something enjoyable about meeting so many new people in the dorms ... the shared bathroom wasn't it.

Once clean, I dried my short hair as well as I could, wrapped in my towel and robe, and made my way back to the room. Hollis was up. "Hey, Pebble. I'm going to quickly shower, then we can get breakfast. Your aunt is picking us up at nine?"

"Yep. Have you texted Fern?"

"Yeah, they'll be down in the cafeteria at a quarter after eight." The words sounded like she dragged them out, she was so tired. "Shower now."

My first objective was to make a couple of mugs of coffee. The new French press thrilled me every time I depressed the plunger. We'd get some at the zoo, but Hollis seemed desperate. Then clothes. I found a shirt with a stylized black panther on it. My friends wouldn't know it was in honor of my sister, they'd think it was for the area my aunt worked. I matched the shirt with black jeans and black sneakers.

When Hollis returned, she groaned at the scent of coffee filling the room. Once she'd had her first mug, she got dressed. Her outfit was similar to mine with jeans and a snarky shirt that read *You think I'm condescending? Do you even know what that means?*

I loved that my friend wore sassy shirts like my family.

Once we got to the cafeteria, we each grabbed a tray, filled it with food, and found Fern.

"Morning, sunshine." Hollis leaned down and gave Fern a quick kiss.

Fern sniffed. "You had good coffee before coming down, cheaters."

I laughed. "You should've met us in the room."

They narrowed their eyes. "Watch out, I may just do that next time."

After we ate, we headed out to meet Aunt Allison. Hollis knew her, but when she pulled up and they got in the car, I made sure to introduce Fern.

Aunt Allison looked through the rearview mirror at them. "Welcome, Fern. It's a pleasure to meet you." She pulled away and headed towards the zoo. "I hear you want to be a vet."

Fern smiled. "I am. I love animals, helping, and science. It just seems like a logical step."

"Well, I think that's great. I love that you're coming to visit me at the zoo."

After that everyone got quiet for a few miles. Then Aunt Allison asked, "So, Fern, where are you from?"

"Kentucky, ma'am."

"How did you end up here?"

Fern leaned back. "My mom went to school here. She loved it. I thought it would be nice to go to a school that had good memories for her. My dad also liked the idea of my coming here. He has opinions ... but that's a long story." Fern paused for a moment, then shook their head. "I also wanted to move away from my dad. I love both my parents, but I make them uncomfortable."

Aunt Allison sighed. "That's rather unfortunate. Is it because you're nonbinary?"

Fern paused, gazing out the window. "Yes, well, no. That's part of it, most of it. They just ... I'm not what they ... or he, wanted for a child."

There was a pause, but Aunt Allison had the decency to blush. "I'm sorry. I shouldn't have pushed. Today is about having fun."

"It's fine." There was a tone of resignation in their voice.

Hollis groaned watching out the front window. "Ugh, roadkill. Is that a possum?"

Fern leaned forward. "I do believe it is. Why, are you hungry?"

"Gross! Are you saying you'd eat roadkill possum?" There was a silence after Hollis's question, and I gaped at Fern. Hollis gave them a similar look. Hollis said, voice a bit frantic. "Have you eaten roadkill possum?"

"No, not roadkill." They sounded thoughtful. "The meat is good otherwise. Now, roadkill deer, that's another story. I'll make you something sometime. Would you rather have a roast or chili?"

Hollis's mouth just hung open.

Aunt Allison chuckled. "I would prefer the chili. I'm always curious about other people's recipes."

I've had deer in wolf form, but never human. I should talk to Mom and Dad about that. Maybe it's good.

"Next time you have deer meat, let me know." Fern sounded excited. "I haven't had good chili in a long time."

Eyes narrow, Aunt Allison glanced at Fern then back at the road. "Does it have to be roadkill?"

A pained sound came from Hollis, and I laughed.

We pulled into the zoo's small parking lot, cutting off the end of the conversation. Part of my mind thought about shifting to wolf. Most of the time we came to the zoo was to go to the field and woods in the back for training. Today was not going to be a wolfy day.

We walked through the wide walkways, admiring the animals. Hollis loved the pink flamingos and penguins, always her favorites. Fern wanted to visit the lions, elephants, and big cats.

When Aunt Allison heard that last, she got a tiny thrill. "Oh, I can introduce you to some of our panthers. They're my favorite. My office is near their sanctuary."

Fern stopped walking. "Really? We can meet some of the spicy kitties?"

Aunt Allison laughed and wrapped an arm around Fern. "You know, I think we'll get along just fine, you and me. Let's go meet the cats."

Hollis and I followed, appreciating the rest of the park. Somehow it felt like we were enjoying it on a different level—tourists but we also had the inside scoop.

When we got to Aunt Allison's office building, next to the cat sanctuary, we all stood and watched two light brown panthers play. Aunt Allison said she had to get something from her office and asked us to wait for her as she slipped away.

"There you are!" Julez's voice pierced the relaxed atmosphere my group had created.

I turned to see her and Piper approaching with Spruce. The child walked between their two moms, though Piper pushed a stroller as well.

Spruce pointed to the panthers, "Cat."

"Excellent, Spruce."

The smile they turned up to Piper was angelic.

Piper picked Spruce up so they could get a better look at the giant 'cats.'

"You were looking for me?" I gazed at them, confused.

"Yes." Julez came over to give me a hug. Then she hugged Hollis. "Long time no see."

Hollis narrowed her eyes. "We met a couple of times at Pebble's place. You and Piper were dating ... and now you two have a baby." She smiled then turned to me, leaning in. "Isn't Piper your sister's ex?" Her voice was low, but not low enough that werewolves wouldn't be able to hear her.

Hollis and I had been friends for about eight years. Despite that, she hadn't been to my house all that many times. Bringing norms to the pack den was tricky. In the few times she'd been there, she had met Julez and Piper. Their story was an easy one to share.

Remembering every person in and out of my home would've been almost impossible. I didn't talk about most of the pack people. It would make me sound insane.

"Oh, yeah. Yes, I have a baby with Piper," Julez answered, ignoring the fact she shouldn't have been able to hear Hollis. "Anyway, I needed to talk to Pebble about her new friend Trista. Trista is bad news, I know it, and I just ... well, I needed to tell you before it was too late."

I sighed, then searched for Aunt Allison to ask her to take my friends ... anywhere, but she wasn't back yet. *Darn it!* "Now isn't a good time, Julez," I tried to subtly point to Fern and Hollis with my eyes and head, "and Trista is fine. Don't worry about her."

"I'm not worried about her. I'm worried about you. You went on a date with her last night."

Hollis squealed and Fern looked interested.

I wanted to throttle Julez. "No!" I faced my friends and tried to speak clearly. "I didn't." Then I turned back to Julez. "Not everything is about dates."

With an exaggerated roll of her eyes, Julez shook her head. "You're awfully naive to be—" she gazed at Hollis and Fern who were listening in. *About time you notice them.* "—planning on taking your mom's place. A tour of the city and dinner, Pebble, that was a date. Did you two kiss?"

"Julez," I hissed out. "It wasn't a date. I was ..." How did I explain that I was her alpha and responsible for showing her around and making her comfortable when Hollis and Fern were here. "You know why I did it."

"No, Pebble, I don't."

My jaw hurt from my constant clenching, as did the muscles in my hands. I was going to have bruises on my palm. "As my parents would do to show hospitality, I did for her last night, that's it. And no, there was no kiss!" I could feel myself tensing as my voice got louder. I had to calm down.

Julez's head tilted. "Is that what Trista thinks?"

I wanted to scream. "She knew we weren't on a date. We're friends. That's it. Gods above, what's gotten into you?"

Before either of us could say more, Fern came up and placed a hand on my arm. I breathed in deep, the woodsy scent calming my heart and relaxing me. "Hey, everything okay here?"

My breathing slowed. "Yeah, we're fine. I just ... no, we're fine."

Fern smiled at Julez. Then they held out their hand. Julez took it and even she seemed to relax ... maybe she could smell Fern's perfume with its outdoor scent and remember, at heart, we're wolves, pack, and above all, friends. "I know change is hard. Some change more than others. I don't know this Trista person, not yet. If I'm to be honest, I don't even know Pebble all that well ... *yet.*" They emphasized the word as if to say they were here for the long run. "I'm getting there. I really like her and Hollis and plan on making it my semester project to become the third in their musketeer group. If you'll trust me," they looked at Hollis, "*us,* we'll watch over Pebble. We see her every day. No more ambushing her when she's off doing something else and having a good time, okay?"

Julez took a deep breath and smiled. "Yeah, okay. But you have to promise to watch out for Trista; she's not trustworthy."

Piper came up and rubbed Julez's back. "We came, we gave our message, I think it's time for us to go, love. Not to mention, Spruce wants to see prairie dogs."

Spruce squatted down, draping their arms over their head, then popped up, jerking their head left and right with a giggle. "Danger!" Then they made themself small again.

"Okay, fine." Julez gave me a dazzling smile. "No hard feelings, okay? You know this is all coming from a place of love, right?"

"I'll talk with you later. Bye, you two." They finally headed off and I wanted to sag.

Fern closed the space between us and wrapped an arm around me. "You okay?"

I rested my head on their shoulder. "Yeah. I just wasn't prepared for a confrontation. Thanks, by the way. Your defusing of the situation ... that was ... thank you."

Fern smiled wide. "It's really nice to feel useful. Like I said, I like to help when I think I can."

Aunt Allison finally returned. "I have one of the panthers sequestered. Why don't we head in, and I'll introduce you." She pointed to a door. Hollis and Fern lead the way. Aunt Allison held back, signaling me to stay with her. "That Fern kid, what they did to calm Julez, I haven't seen anything like that since your sister. I know they're not a wolf, we'd smell it on them. But, Pebble, what they did was amazing."

I took a moment to think about what Aunt Allison said. Were their actions so shocking?

Chapter 20 – What's Good For The Goose Is Good For The Gander

My morning premonitions seemed to be flip-flopping, as random as a roll of a die. Instead of the phantom reaching out for me, today I had a bear roaring at me and the wolves that surrounded me. The bird that was so like the swan, but not, flew above. It was too high in the sky for me to identify, not to mention ... bear! Outside of the roar, there weren't any sounds. At least this one was in the woods, all the animals seemed in good humor ... except maybe the bird?

When I woke, I decided I really needed to figure this out. It couldn't be about Jade's wedding.

I texted Dad to let him know which vision woke me. He had always been my trainer, even for my premonitions. With their new regularity, he was back on the clock, so to speak. If my guess was correct, he was keeping records. It was probably too early for him to be up, but he'd get to the statistics eventually and let me know.

I got to the library to meet Luna and Dayna for our bio project at nine on Sunday. We had a few hours to work. I had to search for them before finding them setting up on the second floor in a mostly empty room.

Luna sat at the head of the old oak table. After sitting across from Dayna, I pulled out my notebook and folder with notes I'd gathered on pronghorns. I'd handed in my application to go with Professor McCrea on winter break to Colorado, so learning about the creature became even more important than just this one project.

"Okay, let's get this over with," Luna turned to me and said with disdain.

I felt the muscles in my body tighten, then I forced a smile before facing her. "What did I do to you, Luna? Or are you like this with everyone? I have to spend the day with you, and I don't feel like dealing with your attitude without understanding why you're being such a pill."

Her face stiffened. "I don't know. You're just so ..." her hand waved in a circle, indicating all of me, "you." She shook her head. "But it doesn't matter, let's just get this done. Do you even know anything about pronghorns?" One of her eyebrows rose in challenge and she crossed her arms over her chest.

I sighed. "Yes, I've done a lot of research. I know this is a shock, but we're at the same college. We both got in, theoretically for grades and abilities. I know how to do my part of the work. Why do you think I'd slack?"

Before Luna could bark out any negativity—her constant attacks made me think of Jade's story of being attacked by geese—Dayna put up her hands. "How about a truce? At least until we get through this?" Though the words were spoken to both of us, she glared at Luna.

With a huff, Luna looked down at her stacks of papers. "Whatever." Then she looked up at me with a small snake of a smile. "So, what angle do you want to take on this project?"

I gave her a hard look back. "What was the initial cause of the pronghorns' slide to extinction and what can be done to help with their repopulation."

Both Luna and Dayna paused their shuffling of papers to consider. Then Dayna said, "It would include population, habitat, migration, history, and physiology. I like it."

Luna shrugged. "Whatever. It works. It gives enough for each of us to work on, assuming you can back your topic up with actual work."

"Again," I snapped, "what makes you think I'm less capable than you or Dayna? You said you just met her this semester. What did she do to win your frozen heart over?"

Dayna snorted, then covered her mouth as she laughed.

Luna just shook her head. "Let's just get to work."

Once the work was divided up, we each dove in. By eleven, we had most of the project done. Apparently, all three of us were efficient. All we had left was finalizing our stuff and making a slideshow.

Dayna leaned back. "Okay, I'm done. Why don't you both send me your things and I'll get the slideshow together?"

"Are you sure?" I put the books I'd found on a cart to be reshelved. "I don't want you to be stuck with extra work."

"It's fine. This is the only group project I have this week. You two have another one to meet with this afternoon." Dayna finished getting her papers in her bag. "By the way, we're off to get some lunch. What are you—"

"Pebble's busy." Luna narrowed her eyes at me.

I couldn't help it. The previous couple of hours had been peaceful. Then again, we'd all been quietly working on our own things. For a spell, I'd almost forgotten the time bomb of a group member. One of my eyebrows rose in challenge. "Oh, I am? Good to know."

Dayna opened her mouth, but I waved it away. "Don't worry, Luna needs to decompress. You know, too much time with me and her head may explode. Haven't you heard, I'm onerous."

"That's not it. And stop putting words in my mouth." The statement was spoken low and full of vitriol.

"Oh, like you did for me?" I would not let this person push me around. I could see her ready to explode. "Look, we have a couple of hours. I'll see you back here at one-thirty. Dayna, it's been a pleasure."

Before they could say anything else, I walked out. I texted Hollis. She said she and Fern could meet me for lunch. I would recharge better than eating with Dayna and Luna. I just didn't understand what was up with Luna. There was time during our studying that she proved she could be a decent person ... but when her guard went up ... gah! She was awful.

Imagining poor Dayna alone with Luna sent shivers down my spine. *Gods above, someone has to share a room with her!* I almost missed a step at that thought. Thank goodness for my friends and the time I had with them.

I arrived at the library at a quarter after one for the second meeting. After the first group project, I decided I wanted to be early.

It didn't take long for Kenny to show up. "Hiya, Pebble, how's your weekend going?"

"Good ... I mean," I thought back on the trip to the zoo then working on the first project, "yeah, good."

"Well, that sounds convincing." He laughed.

Bobbing my head, I smiled at him. "Well I went to the zoo with my friends yesterday, that was fun. But I had a run-in with someone I've known for some time. I don't know. She was being weird. And then I had the bio group meeting this morning."

Kenny's face scrunched up. "So, a full day with ... our bestie. Got it."

I pulled out my notebook and folder for psychology. "So, how are classes going for you? How about your weekend?"

He sighed. "Eh, fine. College isn't what I expected. High school was ... I don't know. Somehow I was in the popular group; things were easy. I forgot that when I started here no one would know me. You see, I'm from Wausau, and a few other people from my high school are here, but not *that* many. I feel lost a lot of the time."

His confession hit me like a truck. "You aren't doing well?"

"I mean, yeah. It's fine. The classes aren't hard ... but, the semester's young, right? I just ... I miss my friends and family. Most of my friends went to school in Green Bay, Stevens Point, or Milwaukee. I wanted to come here because I'm pre-med, but other campuses have pre-med, right?"

"Are you thinking about transferring?" He sounded really stressed and a sour scent surrounded him.

"No, I ... not immediately. I just need to find my people. I'm not used to being so independent or introverted. I'm sure I'll figure it out. I like that we'll switch groups after this project is done. I like you, you're nice, but a lot of people are really standoffish. It's like everyone already has their friend group picked out and we're only in the first couple weeks of school, if you know what I mean."

"I do." I thought of Fern joining me and Hollis and how hard that probably was. "It's a big campus."

"Yeah. I'm joining some groups this week. I'm sure that'll help."

I smiled at him. "I'm glad you're going to do that."

Before we could say more, Marc showed up. "Hey, guys. How were your weekends?"

Kenny slouched a bit. "Good. I studied a lot yesterday. You?"

"Amazing. A group of us went running yesterday. We then went downtown, bar hopped, met some coeds, it was amazing." Marc said. "I love college. I'm rushing this week. Once I'm in the frat, it'll be epic."

Kenny's face hardened. "Sounds fun."

Luna walked in and dropped her bag. "Can we get this over with? I'm tired of this place and I won't be doing any of your work, just so you know."

It was too much. "Luna, you've got to stop being such a condescending, arrogant, bully. We're all members of the same group. Grow up. We need to get this done and

I'm not listening to your assumption that we're somehow less than you and you're the leader."

As I spoke, her face scrunched up. "Why do you care, Pebble? Who are they to you?"

"They are people. People deserve respect. Don't you get that?"

"I get that you respect your family, even friends, but these two? You make no sense. Now, can we just do this?" I watched as she sat.

Marc didn't seem to care about the conversation Luna and I were having, but Kenny collapsed more into himself. He reminded me of Piper when she got nervous.

Marc had the assignment paper out. "Okay, which of these topics should we select?"

There were several to choose from, but most of them seemed too broad. "Since there are so many, can we narrow them down and vote?" I asked. "We can add more if you want, but the ones I like, in the order I like them, are: How media consumption has affected the development of youth—a comparative analysis of two decades pre and post two thousand; how psychology has evolved throughout the decades; and the emotional effects of literature and should there be an age limit on some books."

"I don't care," Marc said. "Just choose one and let's get this done. I have a date."

Luna scoffed. *Of course, she did.* "I like the last one. There, I've decided, it's done. Let's get to work."

Kenny cleared his throat. "I kind of like the first one, like Pebble. The comparison of say, the twenty-teens and maybe the nineteen-eighties could be really interesting. And why is your vote it?"

"Because it was a decision. They are always good. That one's dumb. Media consumption? How different is ten years ago to the nineteen-eighties anyway?"

I nearly guffawed. "You're kidding, right? Phones, computers, internet. It's so much different."

Marc raised one shoulder. "I agree. That's probably easier than a report on why we should ban books for kids."

Luna snarled but acquiesced.

We spent a few hours breaking the topic into four parts and doing research. We had a group document we could all add information to. I started a slide presentation and got the parts organized. By four, it was almost done.

Marc smiled a huge toothy grin. "That's fantastic. Do we even need to do more? It looks so ... complete. I don't know that I've ever completed something so fully in one sitting."

With a look that told a story of annoyance and disgust, Luna shook her head. "It's acceptable. We can do better, but it *is* group work ... with this group." She packed up. "I'll see you in class." Then she left.

Kenny visibly relaxed. "I really hope I don't end up with her again. You were a great buffer, Pebble, but she's awful."

Marc smiled. "At least she's nice to look at."

I took a calming breath. I could only face so many battles in a day. "Kenny, I'll see you in biology tomorrow. Marc." I didn't have more to say to him.

The cool air when I exited the library was a balm to my stressed body. I began my short walk to the dorms. Just as I thought I was over the hours of group work, a goose dive bombed me, honking its annoyance at my existence.

Chapter 21 – Personal Connections

Lunch on Mondays was always a quick turnover. Forty-five minutes between English and stats. I had just sat down when Fern slid in across from me. "Hey, do you want company?"

"Sure. Well I guess it depends on who. But if it's you, yeah." They looked pensive despite my teasing. "Is everything okay?"

"Sort of. You know my story, well, a lot of it, but I was wondering if I could share more?" Fern wrung their hands as they sat looking down towards their lap. The nutty scent of their nerves perfumed the air.

It troubled me to see my friend so broken up. "Of course. Is this something you've spoken to Hollis about?"

I started eating my ham and cheese sandwich while Fern sat mute. Finally they shook their head. "I will, eventually. I just, for some reason you seem like someone who I can talk to ... you know, about anything. I think Hollis would listen and try to understand, but ... I don't know, is this okay?"

"Yes." I reached over and rubbed the back of their hand. "This is your story, and you can decide who to tell and when to tell them. No judgment. Not from me. Just know, Hollis will be there for you, too, when and if you decide to tell her."

A smile blossomed on their face. "Yeah, I knew you'd say something like that, both about you and Hollis." They reached down and took a bite of their pasta, then sighed. "When I was younger, like six or seven, my parents went through a rough patch. They would fight. My mom wanted to go to counseling, but Dad refused. He was so angry ... like, all the time. I don't think it was me, but I was never sure. When they got a certain tone to their arguments, I knew it was time to hide in my room."

As Fern spoke, their voice got rough. There was a lie in what they said, though their emotions told me most of it was truth. I wondered what they were hiding. *Had they really seen it all?* "Were you ever afraid for yourself?"

"No, it wasn't like that. Not really." They looked up towards the ceiling for a moment, then shook their head. "It all came to an end when one day I heard something sharp and loud. A bang, so to speak. Being so young at the time, I didn't know what it was. I learned later that Dad slapped Mom in anger. He was so angry at himself that he agreed to counseling. Their marriage got much better after that. You have to understand that Dad wasn't violent by nature and the hit was really out of character. I think there were other things going on, but again, I was like six, and kids aren't told much of adult business." They smiled. "We moved a few years later and things got a lot better."

I understood being a kid of angry parents better than Fern knew. My biological parents fought, turned me into a werewolf, bit someone else, and ended up dead. They hadn't been good people. I wasn't upset that I didn't remember much about them. Ending up with the Stones had been one of the best things to happened to me. The path had been scary, the prize, wonderful.

"That's awful. I'm sorry you had to suffer through all of that."

"Thank you. In the end, my life got better for the therapy sessions." Fern went back to fidgeting for a few moments as I finished off my sandwich. Then they said, "I was on State Street yesterday, at the park halfway to the capital."

"I know it."

"There's a kind of private place to sit. I really like it. It's outdoors but semi-private. I can watch people without really being seen. A win-win, if you ask me."

I smiled. "I like studying outdoors when I can. My double indoor session yesterday was awful." I tilted my head. "So, this was after lunch?"

"Yeah, I took a walk and then studied. Anyway, a couple got to the park. It was otherwise pretty empty. They started to fight. It triggered some of my memories. His voice and tone of superiority were so similar to what I remembered from all those years ago." Fern shivered.

"The guy asked the woman if she'd done what he asked," Fern started off. "At first the woman stood up for herself. She got angry, said of course she had, he knew she had. Apparently, she'd been texting him updates."

With a shiver, Fern sipped their soda. "The guy got all indigent, rolled his shoulders and snarled at her. 'It took so long, Beth.'" Fern put their drink down and massaged their temples. "The way he spit out her name, like it was a swear word. Anyway, it took so long, they thought she'd bailed on them or switched sides. The utter vitriol made me shiver."

"She fought back though. I wanted to cheer her on, but I also didn't want to catch their attention. She explained she was in the group, but they'd made her wait for a new head. Apparently, that was one of the possible scenarios, so, no surprise." Hands trembling, Fern gently placed them on the table. "So, the guy scoffed. He said they just needed someone in the organization, a spy, someone to not only feed back information, but help affect policy. He wanted to know if she could do both, you know, get to the top of the food chain."

"The woman made an unhappy sound then defended herself again, saying she was doing what she came here to do. She was making nice with the new staff. It's her way in. She said in her own condescending tone, 'Danny, first I get her to like me, then trust me. That's how you get things done.'"

Fern's head fell back, and they looked up at the ceiling. "I know, this story isn't really important, but it was so intense, like my childhood, full of anger and words I didn't really follow."

Pebble reached over to squeeze their hands again. "No worries. Just say what you need to say."

Nodding, they continued. "Well, the guy, Danny, grunted, 'You're not here for friends, Be. We sent you in to let *us* know what's happening in there.' Even in her jacket, I could see her body tense. Then she said she knew and to let her do her job. He asked if she liked the new person, but she wouldn't answer. I'm not sure why. Then it happened." Fern's face drained of color. "He slapped her."

Now I understood why I was hearing the story. I moved around the table and wrapped them in a hug. "Are you okay?"

"Yeah, it was just that slap, it felt like I was being smacked back to my childhood. Unlike when I was a kid, that jerk is going to continue to be abusive, and I have no idea if the woman will continue to fight back or if he'll break her."

I gave an ironic laugh. "Well, it doesn't sound like either of them are pillars of society. Not that that makes the slap any better, but did you get a good look at them? Maybe we could go to the authorities. Stop him that way."

Fern slumped. "No, they both wore hoodies. I couldn't tell you anything about them. Average height, average build, hoodies, and jeans. Nothing."

"No worries. I'm more worried about you than this company they're trying to take over. I wonder if it's a chain or somewhere local. I didn't know businesses did that outside of movies."

Fern finally smiled. "I did have that thought, too." They looked at their watch. "But we should get to class if we don't want to be late."

"Gah! But this conversation is just getting interesting."

"We can talk after class. We have the whole evening."

"Fair."

As we headed out, I realized it was nice to talk to someone. It occurred to me I hadn't had a good conversation with either Owen or Jade in weeks. I shot off texts to each of them asking when we could have a phone call. I needed some good sibling time.

Chapter 22 – Weight Of Responsibility

The phantom reached for me. A shiver ran down my spine. A car outside honked. Was it just one car? Why was that important? The phantom stepped closer. "Find me!"

I sat up, shivering. I really needed to figure this out. This dream, this vision, this premonition, It must be figured out. It was getting more intense. *Maybe Jade could decipher it ... if she were around.*

No more sleep for me. I got up, sent Dad a text with which dream I had, showered, dressed, and headed to the cafeteria for breakfast. I ate slowly while reading my book. It was the silver lining to my early mornings.

My Dad's text interrupted my reading. *If you're going to be up every day, you should be doing daily exercise routines, not sitting on your butt. I'll get a book ready for you on your next visit.*

Rolling my eyes, I laughed to myself then responded, *Is this incentive to come home or are you trying to get me to stay away?*

I could almost hear his grunt as he replied with an eye-roll emoji.

After eating, I headed to bio lab. I was the first of my group there. I sat and pulled up the group document and slides for psychology. It looked like Kenny had finished his part and had cleaned up the formatting. There were some gaps in the information from the nineteen eighties, but most of the information from this century looked complete.

I added the last of my material and moved some things around, cleaning up the slides I changed. I got lost in the work until the class started filling with other students.

"What are you doing?" I looked up to see Luna standing over me.

Everything in me wanted to snap at her, but I knew that wouldn't get me anywhere. "I'm just cleaning up a few slides and adding some of the research I did over the weekend for psychology."

"And you say I'm trying to play leader," she snapped, walking across the room to a different lab table with Dayna.

I clenched my jaw, willing myself to ignore her. I looked around the room, but Kenny still hadn't shown up. Even though classes had only been in session for a few weeks, it was unusual. He was usually early to class, and we would catch up. When class began, I didn't have time to worry about him.

Once class ended, I grabbed a quick lunch before heading to psych.

Kenny always got to psych before me. When he wasn't in class, I finally checked my email. Nothing. I checked other social media, but I couldn't see any reason for him not to be in class.

The room slowly filled and then the professor started his lesson. It was an interesting hour plus of notes.

At the end, Marc came over, a wide smile on his face. "Did you hand in the project?"

"No idiot, we need to meet tomorrow night to finish it." Luna's words stabbed from behind me. I hadn't seen her approach.

Marc's face scrunched up. "But I thought we got it all done Sunday."

I sighed, but before I could answer, *Ms. Diplomatic* beat me to it. "We finished the majority of the research. We laid down the framework and outline. Gods above, it's people like you that make me hate group work. And where is the other numbskull?"

I glared at her. "Kenny didn't send me an email, so I don't know where he is, but he finished his parts of the slides and information on the document. I've also finished mine. Marc, some of your information has been deleted and messed up, you need to clean it up before tomorrow—"

"Okay, Ms. 'There is no leader.'" She used air quotes to get her point across. "We get it. You're organized. Tomorrow. We can discuss it all tomorrow. Are you always this ... you?" She waved her hand to encompass my whole body. The motion was getting old.

Marc shook his head. "I'll look at it tonight. We're meeting tomorrow?"

Luna practically squawked, "You need to listen to all the words, not just the ones that end in 'you getting a date.'"

His eyelids lowered. "Are you saying you want a date with me, sexy?"

I took a step back, just in case. Luna just swung away, bag on her back, and left the room. I thought I could see steam billowing from her ears.

Marc watched as well. "Do you think that's a 'yes' or a 'no'?"

"I would tell you to test the waters, but you wouldn't survive, frat boy. Steer clear of that one. Trust me."

The serenity of Electric Brew called to me, as well as their selection of coffees and pastries. I'd just finished my English homework when I received a text from Tanner.

We've found a dead body in a park on the near east side of town, not too far from campus. It's just off Willy Street.

Heart pounding, I gazed at the phone.

Questions piled up in my mind. *Okay, first off, were there wolf scents on the body? How did you find out about the kill? And lastly, why come to me?*

I sipped my coffee and debated if I was going to get any other work done.

Easton smelled wolf, looks like a rogue. He was there. This should answer your first two questions.

Ever since Easton had gotten a position on the police force he'd tried to get assigned to any weird murder cases, especially ones outdoors or seeming to involve animals. My jaw tightened. It was bad enough this wolf had killed someone, but rogue meant the wolf had a taste for people. Once a werewolf went down that path, they invariably attacked to kill and eat again.

Though my stomach twisted, I sent a thumbs up emoji.

Tanner continued. *As for why come to you, you're one of three alphas. You're up.* I could almost hear him laughing. *On call, so to speak.*

A chill, like icy water, shot through me. My first real duty as alpha. I really didn't want to mess this up.

Okay, if you can, double check the scent, it would be nice to have two people who know who we're dealing with.

It would also be nice to have someone who could be called in to help without having to take time off from a job.

Tanner was infinitely more flexible that way. As an independent bounty hunter, he was the pack's best security.

I'd like a nightly patrol with two wolves assigned in a three-block radius. You said it was near campus, but until we know if the person killed was a student or if they're targeting me, I'd like to focus on the drop zone and not school.

I closed my eyes to think of ways things had been handled in the past. Lone wolves attacking wasn't really that normal. I didn't want to leave anyone at risk. We didn't have teens in the pack, well, except for me ... wait, and Trista. But everything should be good with those measures in place.

Tanner finally texted back. *Anything else, boss lady?*

A boulder crushed my bones as I breathed through the weight of responsibility. I really didn't want to mess this up. *I'll talk to Mom and Dad about setting up pack check-ins, but not just yet.*

The pause was a bit shorter, but still longer than I'd expected. *Sounds great.*

I'd done it. My first real act as leader.

A moment later Tanner texted, *Are you using the bear soap?*

My only response was a thumbs up emoji.

Years ago, before my pack had met them, the werebears had developed a full line of bath products that neutralized most wereanimal scent. Shifters, like the swans, didn't need it, because they didn't carry a scent, unless they actively tried to use their bird abilities in human form. From what I understood, that wasn't a good idea. Prey animals in human form amplified both the scent and draw to predators. My sister found that out once, luckily she was with our brother. If it had been with someone more dominant, the wolf may not have been able to control themself.

After getting my acceptance to college, I had a long talk with Mom, Dad, and Tanner about living in the dorms. We all decided it was safer if I didn't smell like wolf. The likelihood of a lone wolf was small, but it would be nice to not have to deal with it head on if I didn't have to. Even with my alpha power, right now my focus needed to be on school, not territory.

I thought back on my decisions and, with a smile, I headed to the service counter. I deserved a slice of chocolate torte.

Chapter 23 – Sibling Bonding

Wednesday—my long day. My classes didn't end until almost half past four. Homework was piling up. The tour company had hired me, and my first tour was Saturday. After classes, I had a quick snack, then headed to the library for a couple hours of studying. Once I felt less behind, I stopped in the cafeteria for dinner.

The psych group was scheduled to meet at eight-thirty. Marc had fraternity business until eight and Luna couldn't meet earlier either. I still had over an hour to wait. There was a big open space outside the library, Library Mall, that had a water feature, paths, and green spaces. Students and locals walked through it, relaxed, and socialized there all the time. I went to sit and decompress for some alone time to recharge before meeting my group. I'd had very little since college had begun.

The evening was nice, and I could feel the tension oozing out of me as I tried to tap into some of Mom's meditative practices. I usually ignored them, but I would start to get headaches if I didn't unclench my shoulder muscles.

My phone rang. Checking the display, I saw it was Jade. I was both elated and at peace when I saw her name. This would be better than any breathing exercise. "Jade! You called."

"Of course I did, silly goose. How is college?"

"Lots of work. I'm enjoying it." I pulled my knees to my chest, imagining I was in the same room as her.

"You better be doing more than just studying." Owen's voice was only a bit softer than Jade's.

A small thrill went through me. I had both of them. I loved my siblings to the moon and back. Becoming the next alpha was going to be amazing. Not having Jade and Owen near was going to suck. The good and bad of life. "Heya, bro, who invited you to this convo?"

He laughed. "I'm always welcome, and you know it."

Giggles bubbled out of me. I tried to hide them, but knew he'd hear. "Fine, if you must."

"So," Jade said, "college?"

I filled them in on classes, my first charges, the dispute between Julez and Trista, and Luna. When it came to my life and my siblings, there wasn't anything I wouldn't tell them.

Owen sighed. "You're in, like, the fourth week of classes. Don't you know you're supposed to be taking it easy? That's a lot."

"I've gotten to know Julez over the years, Pebble. She seems like she has a good head on her shoulders. I've never known her to not like a person. Have you spoken to Mom or Aunt Allison about this?" Jade sounded concerned.

"I haven't. I thought this was something I should ... I don't know, figure out myself?" I curled up a bit more, glad neither of them could see my body language.

"Oh, Pebble, no. This is what people in Aunt Allison's position and Moms are for. You aren't an island."

I shut my eyes and thought about it. She was right. "Okay, I'll find a time to talk with Mom."

Then Bevin spoke up, and my joy rose. It shouldn't surprise me, Jade was probably in a common room, and wolves had excellent hearing. "I like that you have Hollis and this new friend Fern. They both sound great. But do you realize you're treating Luna like an ... employee?"

That gave me pause. "I'm what now?"

His low voice carried over the line, thoughtful. "You're guiding her to be a better version of herself. Letting her be herself but helping her to not be as mean to others. Be Luna but not shut others out or down. It's a very ... leader ... thing to do."

We were taught over the years to be careful what we said over the phone. We tended to not say anything that overtly hinted at anything wereanimal.

"Was it?" I scrunched my nose up. "I just saw it as trying to survive with a self-centered bully in the group."

"Is she a bully or just very confident?" This time it was José. "A person who knows their value and worth and is unwilling to let others bring them down?"

"I don't know, but if it's the second, she assumes everyone will bring her down without giving them a chance. It's obnoxious." I could hear the whine in my voice as well as the soft laughter from my family in California.

"Pebble," Jade took over again, "I know it's hard. It sounds like after this week you won't have to be in her groups anymore. It also sounds like you've been doing a great job. I'm proud of you." She paused. "We're proud of you. Now, anything else we should know about?"

Through the turmoil of emotions, I perked up. "I made my first executive decision as a leader."

I heard Owen wooting in the background as soon as I finished my sentence.

"Do tell," Jade prompted.

I told them about my text from Tanner and the choices I'd made, careful in the words I chose. After the debacle that was Luna, I was expecting good things from this. But, once I got done, the other end of the line went silent. It lasted long enough that I checked to make sure we hadn't gotten disconnected.

Then Jade cleared her throat. "Wow. Um, good job, sis. It sounds like you and Tanner figured it out." There was another pause and silence behind her. "It's getting late there, and didn't you say you had a meeting soon?"

"Wait. What did I do wrong?"

Bevin's warm voice replaced Jade's. "You didn't do anything wrong, Pebble. You're a new leader, that's it." I heard a scream in the background. One of the kids was in need of a parent and most of the parents were on the phone with me. Sarah couldn't handle all five kiddos. "Oh. I need to go."

I sighed. "Jade, there's something else."

After a moment of shuffling, she said, "Yeah?"

"I know we're not physically close so your friends can't talk with mine, but ... I've been having this ... dream. It's recurring. Maybe it's just ... nothing. But I don't know what it is. I thought you could help anyway."

"Tell me."

I did.

In the background, I could hear Owen muttering. "We'll talk with the bosses about this. See if they can think of anything." Knowing both Bevin and José would help with figuring this out settled something deep within me.

"Thanks, Owen, thanks, Jade. I miss you both. I love you."

"Love you, too," they both said.

Then Jade said, "We'll speak soon. It has been way too long between our talks. Let's figure out a time on Sundays for us, okay? Like when I was in college. Too much happens otherwise."

"That would be great." A sense of tranquility washed through me at her words.

I got off the phone and started to get my bag onto my shoulder and to head into the library. It was still early, but not too early. I took one more cleansing breath and started walking. Suddenly, my nemesis of a goose, the creature who'd seemed to be following and harassing me everywhere, flew low and honked. I leapt high, landing awkwardly, falling on my butt.

Now I'm being paranoid. There are probably dozens of the creatures all over campus messing with all the students. I wonder if there's a nest nearby.

Grumbling about geese and starting to agree with Jade—after her run-in, she never liked them—I headed to the library.

Marc was already waiting, playing on his phone. I sat down across from him. "Hi, how are you?"

"Good." He put his phone down. "You?"

I bobbed my head back and forth. "Not too bad. Classes are falling into a rhythm."

"Definitely. And the extras outside of classes, too. Joining a frat is amazing!" His smile lit up his face.

"What things does the frat do?"

"Oh, not just party, if that's what you're thinking. They help with school, too. Tutoring, mentors, everything. But partying is epic."

His smile stretched across his face, and I couldn't help but smile back. "I'm glad you're enjoying yourself."

Nodding, he got out his work. "Yep, I sure am."

I pointed at his things. "How is your part of the project going?"

His face scrunched up. "I ... I think I made it better. I spent like, a few hours yesterday working on it. Your stuff and Luna's and Kenny's was good. I don't think I messed it up."

A bit of worry wiggled through me. I pulled the laptop from my bag and opened up the group project. Marc had moved things around and changed a few words but mostly hadn't added anything. At least he hadn't deleted anything, either. I wasn't sure what he'd done.

"Um, what did you add?"

"Oh, add? I just ..."

Luna walked up. "Please say nothing. I want to pass, and I'd rather not have you messing up my grade, frat boy."

His mouth snapped shut. "I'm not a bad student."

"But you're not an 'A' student, are you?"

"Whatever. Don't we have to do a presentation?" he grumbled.

"Yes, and by the end of the night, you'll know what to say." The purr in her voice was scarier than the bark.

Before Marc could say more, I checked my watch. "Still no word from Kenny?"

Luna narrowed her eyes on me. "It's late. We're starting. If he doesn't show, who cares? He finished his part of the slide show and notes. He just needs to know what to do in class. We can email that to him."

That almost sounded like a compliment.

I thought my head was going to explode.

Chapter 24 – Consequences

I got to biology early on Thursday. I hoped Kenny would show up. I was getting worried about him. I'd sent him an email, but he hadn't responded. When we exchanged information, he hadn't shared his phone number. I hadn't thought about it at the time but now wish I had gotten that.

As more and more people came in, I kept watching for Kenny's wavy hair, but he didn't show up. The seat next to me remained empty.

"Okay, class." Professor McCrea walked into the lab and dropped his bag on the front desk. "Today each group will present your project. You will have five to eight minutes to show what you chose to research as well as your findings. Your grades on the presentation will be posted by next week Tuesday. You will be given the option to update your project and resubmit by next week Thursday or keep the grades you have. If you resubmit, you won't be able to do another presentation, so the updated grade doesn't have as many potential points as today's grade."

Professor McCrea gave us five minutes to get ready. Luna and Dayna came over to my table and we discussed which part of the project each person would present. There weren't many groups, but the waiting was horrible. A few of the presentations weren't bad, but some ... I wanted to poke my eyes out ... and my ears. I started to understand Luna's opinion to assume the worst and be surprised at competence.

Once we went up, I felt we did pretty well. The professor seemed to perk up, and he even smiled. I hoped he absorbed our commitment to the topic of pronghorns ... or at least mine. I really wanted to go on his research trip in December.

Lunch wasn't long enough, but with the presentations, the day wasn't too hard. I made it to psych and hoped

Kenny would be there. I hadn't seen him in bio during any of the presentations, but maybe he was sick.

Marc was early. "Pebble! I fixed my slides. I added things, like you asked."

I just nodded, more focused on the fact that Kenny wasn't in class. I was really worried about him.

Though this class had the assignments due, we only had to turn them in, not do a presentation today. As I thought about what we would be submitting, Marc's words finally sank in. I pulled out my laptop. I had to check our final assignment. *What if Marc messed things up?*

I also wanted to check my email.

To prove to myself I wasn't obsessing over what Marc had done, or acting like *the leader*, as Luna claimed, I started in my email. Nothing from Kenny. A knot of worry twisted my gut.

A new thought niggled at me. I opened up a news site. By now the name of the person from the park had to have been released. *Don't be Kenny, don't be Kenny, don't be Kenny.* I searched for articles and skimmed through them. I finally found a name. I nearly fell out of my seat when the person came back as a twenty-three-year-old from Janesville. Not Kenny.

When I finally checked in the documents, they all looked good. Again, I couldn't figure out what Marc's big changes were ... thankfully. *Did Kenny change something in his section since last night? Am I imagining things?*

I did one last look around the classroom, but I didn't see him.

The professor walked in. "Find your groups and take five minutes to make sure you're ready to go. If everything is set, submit your files to the classroom portal under any of the group member's names."

Both Marc and Luna joined me. Luna glared at Marc. "Like I said last night, you better not have messed up my grade."

He opened his mouth to respond, but the professor approached us. "I wanted to speak with your group before you turned anything in, or worried about your grades. I double checked attendance before class. I usually do before the first group project. I don't get messages when students sign up or drop out of my classes, but figured with the presentations coming up I should know if someone isn't here if there's a reason. Anyway, Kenny is no longer on my roster."

The news disappointed me. "Do you know if it's just this class?"

"I don't. I just checked my classes, not overall student standings. Even if I had, that isn't anything I would be at liberty to share. If you have his contact information, try asking him directly. Anyway, do you need extra time since he's not here? Are there holes in your document?"

Marc started to nod as both Luna and I said, "No."

I continued. "If it's all the same, we'd like to get this behind us. There's enough homework in college that having this on the to do list seems silly."

Luna sneered at me. "We finished the project. It is complete and you'll be impressed."

The professor nodded gravely. "So, you feel you're prepared to hand this in, even without Kenny?"

"He finished his part before dropping the class. We should be good." I shrugged, trying to let her know we really weren't stressing. Well, maybe Marc was, but I wasn't sure he knew what was going on.

The professor looked at Marc, then nodded. "Okay, then, it sounds like you have everything in hand."

Luna smiled. "We do. We're very organized in our group."

The look on Marc's face said he would be glad to be done working with the two of us. To be honest, the feeling was completely mutual.

During class, I got a text from Mom asking me to stop by her office today. I told her I could be there at about three-thirty. She said that would be perfect.

When I got there, the door was closed. I knocked.

"Come in, Pebble."

Inside, I found Mom, but Dad and Tanner were there as well. "Oh ... hi, Mom, Dad, um, Tanner. Why is everyone here? Why am I here? Am I in trouble?"

Dad patted the back of a seat near him. "Come on in, Applesauce. Sit."

"Okay, but is everything okay? Is *everyone* okay?"

"Yes, we just wanted to talk," he said.

Mom leaned back. "We thought we could take you out for dinner, but my office is oddly private for being on campus. So, talk first, dinner after. Maybe Thai food?"

My mouth watered just thinking about it. "Okay, you win, though you used unfair tactics. What's the torture?"

Tanner chuckled low and deep. Mom and Dad smiled. Finally, Dad said, "We wanted to talk to you about the decisions you made on Tuesday."

A wave of fear washed through me, though I tried to hide it. "Did I mess up? Was I too lax? Did someone else get hurt? Is there another dead body?"

A citrusy smell filled the small room from all three wolves. They were trying not to laugh at me. Behind me, Tanner said, "No one else is hurt ... at least as far as I know. We're still on the first situation."

"Okay, so it's not that. And from your scent, I assume I wasn't too lax. So, in that case, what should I have done? Nothing?"

"*That* for one," Dad mumbled, but when I gaped at him, confused, he waved at Mom.

She sighed. "It isn't that you should've done nothing, sweetie. There was a murder, probably by a wolf. Yes, we need to be on alert. But here are a few tips: first of all, getting the second scent marker—"

"Was too much?" I leaned forward. I was ready to fight this one. I may not know a lot, but this was important. "Because we need to find this wolf, and having two wolves, especially Tanner, who has an amazing nose and can move around with much greater freedom, seems really important to me."

Dad reached over to rub my back.

Mom's lips twitched. "Actually, I was going to say that that was your best call. You're right, having two noses, especially one of the best, on the trail, is great. Beyond that, Dad and I always ask for advice, especially if we're not on the ground when and where it happened."

"Ask?"

"Yes. We discuss it together," she raised her hands in a typical stop gesture. "And no, you don't have a partner ... yet, but that doesn't mean you can't discuss it with Aunt Allison, or Estrella, or Tanner. There are any number of wolves you can use as a sounding board or person to help you. Making big decisions on your own is hard and can be dangerous."

"What if the situation is time-sensitive?"

Mom sighed. "You were talking with Tanner. Use him, or whoever contacted you. You know the value of all our pack members."

I nodded slowly. "Got it. I'm not alone. I have a pack. I guess I should've thought of that. It's been a theme my whole life."

Dad gave me a half-hug. "College makes things harder. But yes, ask."

"Okay, so what should I have done?"

Tanner said, "Less." I turned to face him as he spoke. "We don't need a nightly patrol. Maybe two wolves twice a week. We don't know what's going on, and until we have a better idea, we shouldn't be overly cautious. Who is the dead person? Are they connected to anyone in the pack? Did the wolf come for that man? Is he targeting you or any of ours? If he is, everything feels off. If not you, why just off campus? If it's us, why the eastside of Madison? It's all cattywampus. For all we know, he's left town. It could've been a freak incident. A lone wolf who just happened to hit our territory. We can't be at high alert and efficient for too much time."

I was slowly nodding as he spoke. "Okay, that all makes sense." I turned to my parents. "Did you already tone down my orders?"

Dad smirked. "Sure did. But we won't always be here."

"I know. And ... well, thanks. I wish I could've done better, though." *I wish the boulder would leave my gut.* My arms and hands felt chilled and numb with the realization of my mistake. I felt awful for messing up so bad my first time out.

Mom stood. "Let's get food. It'll make you feel better."

She wasn't wrong. Thai food would warm my soul, though at the moment, little could make me feel better.

Chapter 25 – Xenagogue

Despite not having my premonition dream, I woke early on Saturday. At breakfast I texted Mom and asked about the rogue wolf.

Her reply came quickly. Like me, she tended to get up early. *No one in the group knew the man who he attacked. There hasn't been any sign of the dog in the area since the body was found. We'll stay alert, but there's a good chance this was a drive by.*

Part of me agreed this felt distant and unconnected to us, but another had a niggling doubt. Why come here to our territory if not to send a message?

I was so excited for my first day of my new job. I wasn't even really sure why. Giving a tour of a school I grew up knowing, talking to strangers who would ask basic questions, having to smile the whole time, and mostly walking backwards. None of this should sound fun ... but it did.

I'm going to have to tease Jade about this job. There would be no way she could have a job where you walk backwards while speaking to people about what they should be looking at. The mere idea amused me.

My tour started at ten and would last for about an hour and a half. We would start and end at Union South. It was a great place for the prospective students to hang out. It was quieter than Memorial Union, had great study areas, and wasn't as populated. I had my red school shirt on and was ready to give out information on the school, classes, programs, and history. In my bag, I had information cards with numbers for families to call when I couldn't provide answers. I knew a lot, but I wasn't omniscient.

There were fourteen people on my tour roster. Everyone had to sign up beforehand. In my work prep, I had name tags for everyone ... well, stickers and a pen, and a list of who had signed up. There was also a pole with a flag so if any of the people got turned around, they could easily find me.

While I waited for the tour participants to arrive, I double checked the names. A small half-chuckle, half-groan escaped me when, halfway down the list, I saw the name: Fern Meadow. *What are they doing?*

There wasn't anything stopping current students from taking tours, but why?

On a whim, I searched the area and finally spotted my friend standing off to the side. It was still about ten minutes before the tour started and none of the other families had checked in with me. "What are you doing?"

Fern gave me a sheepish grin. "I never went on one of these, and though I love the school, I thought it would be nice to learn more. I also thought you'd like some moral support on your first day on the job." Their face scrunched up and they started to speak faster. "If you really don't want me here, I can go."

"No, it's good. I'm ... it'll be nice to have a friendly face in the crowd. Just ... why didn't you tell me? We could've had breakfast together and walked over. Maybe stopped for coffee?"

A wide smile bloomed on Fern's face. "I didn't want to be teacher's favorite."

Amusement replaced some of my tension, and suddenly I was really glad Fern had shown up. "Is that possible? Don't all your teachers adore you?"

They winked and took a name tag to fill out.

The next few minutes got busy as the remaining thirteen people arrived, and check-ins happened quickly. I wasn't sure if I should take that number as a good or bad omen, or as just a number.

We were sitting just outside the union. It was a bit loud, and the wind was blowing away from me, towards the people I'd be leading on the tour. I almost missed that one of the prospective students, a gangly male in his early twenties who'd come alone, was a wolf.

My jaw tightened for a moment before I smiled. He didn't notice my tension. He also wouldn't be able to tell I was also a werewolf, not with the bear soap I used.

As I contemplated the wolf, I decided a bit more caution was to my advantage. *What he is the rogue who killed that person? What if he's looking for another victim? What if he's looking for me?*

All the people arrived, and it was time to start the tour. I waved my hand. "Hi, everyone, I'm Penelope, and I'll be leading your tour today." I made a mental note to tell my employers to change my work name to Penelope. Pebble was recognizable.

Fern's brow furrowed for a moment. I wasn't sure I'd ever told them my proper name. I thought I had when we met, but that had been a few weeks ago.

The man who was also a werewolf raised his hand.

"Yes?"

"Was there someone else who was originally supposed to lead this group? I thought I saw a different name on my paperwork?" He leaned forward and slowly breathed in.

I worked to keep a blank face. *If he is the killer, was that a test run?* A shiver ran down my back. *I will not give him any reason to think I'm anything but a tour guide.*

My family was well known in the werewolf communities. If he joined the tour and hoped to find 'Pebble Stone,' put a face to a name, I was doubly glad I'd given my proper name—not that my real name was that different. I'd used my nickname for so long that it was the only one most people knew.

I shrugged and smiled, trying to look vacant. I waved one hand. "To your left we have the engineering campus. If we walked up that way, we'd get to the stadium. On game days, this area is a sea of red and white. It's a wonder to see ... all puns intended." I guided the group to University Avenue, a huge street with city traffic dashing west. When we had a walk light, we headed into the heart of campus and towards one of the lakes.

The tour traced through campus, showing where some of the dorms were, where many of the major classroom buildings were located, Library Mall, and, of course, Bascom Hill.

One of the families, a mother with her daughter, stopped to ask some questions. "Is it true that the dorms have both boys *and* girls?" The poor teen looked scandalized at the idea.

I nodded. "Yes. All the dorms are co-ed. Some by floor, some by wing."

Her voice got softer. "I won't end up with a male roommate, will I?"

Trying to reassure her, I smiled softly. "No. That's not how it's done."

She nodded and her shoulders dropped. We continued to walk.

Fern came up and whispered, "Aw, bless her heart, poor thing's dim as a cave on a moonless night."

I clenched my jaw to keep from laughing out loud.

The werewolf snorted, eyeing me closely. There were enough people in the group that I let my gaze move away from him, trying to ignore him as best I could.

When we got to Bascom Hill, a popular place to take photos. While everyone gazed around and snapped photos, I quickly took out my phone and texted Tanner. *Giving my first tour. Dog in group.*

It took a few seconds for him to get back. *Where and when does tour end?*

Union South, maybe a half-hour.

He replied with a thumbs up emoji.

I quickly slid the phone back into my pocket.

Since State Street ended at Library Mall, part of the tour was showing off the state's capital and one of the more charming streets in town.

When we finally got back to Union South, I gave my wrap-up spiel.

"I suggest you all try out The Chocolate Shop, a local ice creamery with award winning flavors. You can stop by the Memorial Union, sit on the terrace, and enjoy the sunset over the lake. And, of course, you can spend time walking and shopping on State Street. Let me know if you have any questions and I hope you've enjoyed the tour. Thank you again for visiting us here at the University of Wisconsin."

I smiled as the group dispatched. I took out my phone and took a picture of the wolf. As he slid away into the crowd, I saw the shadow that was Tanner following him.

Chapter 26 – Study Break

Sunday morning, I had breakfast with Fern. Hollis liked to sleep in, but often Fern would meet me in the cafeteria. I brought them a travel mug with coffee so neither of us had to suffer. At nine, Trista was meeting me for a hike, but right now I wanted to wake and clear the cobwebs from the obnoxious dream.

"Are you and Hollis doing anything today?"

"Yeah, studying. I know you're taking the day off, but some of us need to work to learn."

I laughed. We finished our food and headed for the elevator. "I'll have you know I do study ... a lot. I just need to get away from campus once in a while. I sometimes feel overwhelmed being surrounded by so many people."

I don't know why I felt safe talking to Fern and telling them the truth, but I did. I couldn't tell them everything, but I had a feeling they understood emotions better than most. Almost like Bevin.

The elevator doors slid open, and we got in.

We hadn't made it past two floors when a sharp pain stabbed at my head. *No! Not here, not now. Not with Fern ... they're a good friend, and I'm willing to open up about some things, but not this. Not to mention, they're too perceptive!*

I pushed myself into the corner, hoping to stay on my feet. A bump on my rear let me know how successful I'd been along with a distant, 'Pebble!'

A black swan flew over a field of wolves fighting. It somehow held paper and pencil, taking notes. A loud bang and most of the wolves fell.

The swan dove down, at the last moment shifting to human form ... as hard as I tried, I couldn't recognize who it was. As it landed two wolves morphed to humans, also shadows, though I had an inkling of who it could be. The three stood proud and tall, all pointing in the same direction. 'Out!'

Most of the wolves vanished.

Then, from the depths of my soul I heard: *It isn't over ...*

My eyes shot open. Fern crouched above me, their soothing, woodsy scent relaxing me. "Pebble. Are you ... are you okay? I mean, that's a stupid question. Do you need medical help?"

I sat on the floor in the elevator. The doors were opening. I pointed. "Your floor. I'm fine." I put my hands on two of the elevator walls to push myself up. Gah, I hated that this happened in front of them.

They reached out to pull me to my feet. I accepted their help. "No," Fern said, "your floor. Let's talk."

Dread filled me as they let the doors close and then open. We crossed from the elevator to the student lounge. It was empty at this hour on a Sunday morning. We sat in two comfortable chairs facing each other.

Fern's face tightened. "Will you tell me what just happened?"

"It's complicated and I'm not sure you'll believe me or that you'll like what you hear."

They sighed, slumping a bit. "Is it worse than what I just *saw*?"

I shrugged. "Don't know, I've never been on that side."

"Pebble! How often does that happen?"

"Not that often, and you can see, I'm fine." My hands rose to the side, but Fern glared. "Okay, fine. But I really don't like having friends who are so clever. It's annoying." That got Fern to at least smile. "I have—" My hand waffled between us. "I don't know, visions? Maybe premonitions.

It happens from time to time. I see something then I move on. It's fine."

"That didn't look fine." One of their eyebrows went up. "And do these visions ever manifest?"

I looked at them desperately. "Can I plead the fifth in hopes to keep our friendship? I don't want to sound like someone you'd like to commit."

Fern's head tilted to the left. "Wait, is this why you're studying psychology?"

It wasn't, but I was willing to grasp onto anything. "Um, yeah. Learn about why I'm like me."

Their eyes narrowed. "So, that's a no. Does anyone else know about this? Hollis?"

"No! Well, yes, my family knows. But not Hollis. I just ... please."

Fern leaned back. "Okay, as long as people know, I'll keep your secret ... for now. But Pebble, that didn't look good."

My muscles began to relax. If Fern said they'd keep my secret, I believed them, not to mention, I could hear a lie.

Then their eyes narrowed. "Is that what that recurring dream is?"

I shrugged. "I don't really know. Usually when this happens, I get a spike of pain in my head first. In the dream, I'm asleep, so, no idea. Also, that's the first vision type thing that's ever repeated. It could be because I'm too block-headed to figure it out. The others have all come and gone."

"After what you saw came to be?" Fern persisted.

I just gazed at them blankly.

"Fine." Fern sounded frustrated that I wouldn't give them all the information they wanted. "How many others are we talking about?"

I realized the mistake I'd made in my wording.

"Fern, I need to meet my friend. How about we talk about this later?" *Or never.*

Their eyes narrowed. "Fine, but I'm not dropping this, Pebble. *I* have a feeling it's important."

"This path, it's like this park back home, you know in Tennessee. My home up in the mountains there, it was so pretty."

Trista and I hiked in the arboretum. We'd decided to take a few hours on Sunday to break away from school, homework, and anything stressful. The area was beautiful, and a few trees were starting to change.

We'd taken one of the harder paths and were navigating a rocky climb. "Wait. You're from Tennessee?" After my morning, I may have been mixing up what I remembered of her past. My mind was a muddle of premonitions, dreams, and having Fern learn more about me than was probably good. *At least I got away before revealing too much. Maybe I can continue to avoid that topic with them.*

"Yeah. Didn't I tell you that? My parents and I were on vacation in Florida when we were attacked."

I shook my head. "I could've sworn you said you were from Florida. I guess I'm mixing things up."

"Totally. I was only on vacation down there. That's why I headed back up to Tennessee to stay with relatives."

"Oh," I said intelligently. "Okay. That makes sense." We tackled a steep part of the trail before I continued. "Did you hike a lot when you lived in Tennessee?"

Trista spun, her face alight. "When I could. I love the outdoors. It's why my family would go on hiking and camping adventures. It's something we all agreed on, even if there was a lot we didn't."

She suddenly turned to face me, face tight. "Never mind about that. I don't want to speak ill of the dead. I have a lot of really good memories of my family. I don't want to remember the bad. Is that okay?"

I nodded and we continued our walk. Focusing on my connection, something I was pretty sure Trista forgot I could do, I could tell her emotions were a mess. Something about her family in general or her parents specifically made her unhappy. There was something dark there. I wanted to ask but worried I'd push her away. We had time.

"You didn't have any siblings, did you?" She'd never mentioned any, but I didn't want to assume.

Again her emotions spiked, but then she tamped them down. "No. Just me. But you have siblings, right?"

"Yeah. Jade and Owen. They're out in California and I really miss them." We got to the top of the trail and there was a scenic look-out that overlooked downtown Madison and the lakes. We found a place to sit and rest and enjoy the view.

At the mention of California, I thought she grunted, but that also could be the fact we finally had reached the end of our climb. *Stop letting Julez's words make you paranoid, Pebble. Trista is nice; just enjoy her company and the day.*

"There's a pack out there, right, in California? You could've joined them? But you want to be alpha."

I slumped. "It's more complicated. The plan had been for me to follow them out to California, but my parents asked me to take over the pack here. There are a couple of wolves who may have been strong enough to lead, but none of them wanted to. You need power as well as desire, and the heart to want to sort of be a parent to a lot of people."

"Pebble, you're eighteen. You're too young to be a parent."

I laughed. The sound echoed through the woods around us scaring birds, which caused a secondary ruckus. "I know. But I won't actually be taking over the pack for many years. My parents aren't that old yet. I have until after I graduate and then some. Probably until after I find a partner to help me. So, time, lots and lots of time."

Trista leaned back on her hands. "Then why am I in your head?"

"That was more training than the true start of me taking over." The amusement still rolled through me. The idea that I would be a pack leader this young was ... well, I knew they'd done it in California, but the pack had been small and young. It wasn't going to be my path. Bevin and José were amazing at what they did and they had each other. They were also crazy for taking it on while in college. *No, thank you!*

"So, I'm like training wheels?"

"That you are, my friend."

She laughed. The vanilla and citrus of her pleasure and amusement filled the air. Her joy swept through me, and I smiled.

I looked up at the cerulean sky with perfectly fluffy white clouds. "How is school going for you? You know, with you going for culinary sciences, we have high hopes and big plans for you in the pack."

This got Trista to snort. "Your dad already warned me. Your mom told me he's been recruiting for good cooks for years. I was surprised when I didn't have to do a food competition style test before they let me in."

"Oh! I may have to implement that in the future. Werewolf food wars!"

Her stomach growled. "Well, I obviously approve."

We both stood. "Let's go find a burger and fries, or cheese curds," I suggested.

She tilted her head. "Cheese curds? Others have pushed this on me, but I'm not sure."

"Breaded and fried cheese. What's not to love?"

"I come from the land of vegans and gluten free ... I don't know. It sounds awfully dangerous."

"Well, you're now in the land of corn and cheese. Come to the dark side, learn our ways!"

We walked for a few minutes, then a thought occurred to me. "Tennessee is the land of vegans and gluten free?"

There was a pause, and I felt Trista's turmoil. Then she laughed. "No, not the state, just my family. I can and will eat anything, especially after the change, but my mom was vegan, and Dad had celiac disease. Our meals were always an adventure, especially eating out."

Her story wasn't the exact truth ... I could hear, almost taste, the lies intertwined within her story, but there was also some truth there. I wasn't sure what she was hiding. "Trista. I'll remind you, I can hear lies. Why are you telling stories? We're just discussing fried cheese."

She blew out a breath, disrupting her bangs. "I don't know. I just ... I've always tried to hide things about my family. There are people in my family who are vegan and who don't eat gluten, it was all around me growing up. Associating it with my parents just seemed easier."

My shoulders relaxed. "Okay, that was truth. You know, you don't have to hide things from us. We all have crazy home lives, I get it, we all do. Telling half-truths or lies is just going to get the pack to not trust you and it won't go over well."

She smiled weakly. "Okay. Got it. Only the truth." Her emotions were still a tsunami, but her body language told me she'd heard my message. "I'm just not sure about cheese curds."

I growled. "As your future alpha, I insist."

She huffed out a laugh and nodded. "Fine, if you insist."

We were halfway down the path when my phone rang. I checked the display and saw it was Mom. I answered. "Hi, Mom, I'm with Trista. What's up?"

Werewolves had great hearing, and I didn't want her to say anything that she didn't want Trista to hear.

There was a pause and then she said, "Tanner told me to tell you the person you were worried about on your tour … you were correct, it *was* the same person he'd been looking for. He has taken care of it, and all protocols have been dropped."

Mom wants to keep this on the down low. I wonder why. Tanner had found the wolf from the tour. He *had* been the one to kill the person in the park, and Tanner had taken him out. Two dead people in as many weeks.

We didn't get many lone wolves in our territory, and most weren't violent. Hopefully this was an isolated incident.

"Did he get any other information?"

"No. The person attacked, refusing to talk." Mom sighed. "Look, I need to go, we can discuss this later. Love you, sweetie."

"Love you too, Mom."

I slipped my phone back into my pocket.

It didn't take long for Trista to ask, "So, what was that about?"

I'd taken those minutes to decide. Trista was pack. I could be honest, or I could lie. I didn't like to lie, thus Fern learning more about me this morning than I meant them to know.. "A lone wolf came into town. Normally not a big deal, but they killed someone. We had to deal with it."

Trista paused. Then she shook her head and continued. She looked pale and I could feel her emotions spiraling. Finally, she said, "Sorry, I just ... death is my least favorite part of being a wolf."

I gazed back up at the peaceful sky. "You're not the only one, my friend."

Chapter 27 – Music To My Ears

Trista dropped me off outside the dorms. Instead of heading up to my room, I walked over to Library Mall to get some alone time. Sitting out in the open area centered me. It was still early, the day was beautiful, and though I needed to study, this was becoming one of my favorite places to relax.

I sent a text to Mom telling her I was alone if she wanted to talk. Though Jade and I had decided we'd talk on Sundays, since we'd just spoken, we'd decided to wait until next week. Right here, right now, I had no responsibilities or anyone wanting my time. It was glorious.

There were students throwing a frisbee, others reading on benches, and locals and tourists walking around. Memorial Union was a hotbed of activity, buses driving in and out, people heading to the terrace, and others just sightseeing. It was a great balance of peace and chaos. After a few minutes, my phone rang. I checked the display. "Hiya, Mom."

"Hi, sweetie, are you really alone?"

A laugh burst out of me as I saw all the activity bustling in the area, but no one close. "As alone as I can be sitting in the middle of Library Mall."

"Okay, that's good. I doubt there are any ears that can listen in." I could hear her moving around the kitchen in the background. "Like I told you earlier, Tanner followed the dog from your tour. That person never checked his surroundings until he got to a parking garage and his car. Tanner confronted him and instead of answering questions, he just attacked."

A shiver ran down my spine. Tanner was huge and terrifying. Over six feet of pure muscle. He looked like the kind of person you were warned about, and he could hold his own in a fight. If I didn't know he was a big teddy bear to the ones he cared about, I'd probably run every time I saw him.

"The idiot dog saw Tanner and decided to grapple with him?"

Mom scoffed. "No, he had a gun."

A punch to the gut. "Gods above, is Tanner okay?"

"Yeah. Apparently the guy didn't even have time to click off the safety. He wasn't the brightest bulb in the package. The fight was short, but brutal. Tanner tucked the dog under a blanket in his own trunk and drove the car out of town. He did a quick search, but didn't find anything that gave any indication of what he was doing in our territory. He was from Oklahoma, of all places."

Mom sounded disgusted. I'd never heard of any wolves from that area. "Oklahoma? Is that even a thing?"

"Well, it's a state, sweetie. If you don't know that, there's this musical you can listen to."

"Gods, no! How many times did you force me to watch that when I was young?"

"Oh, Pebble, you loved it."

"Love is a very strong word, Mom." I laughed. "Okay, so one problem handled. And I didn't recognize the victim's name from the paper. I don't know who he was."

"Well, there goes my next question. We'll have to send out an email blast asking if anyone from the our group knew him. If not, it's a really odd coincidence."

Mom and I spoke for a few more minutes before I got off the phone and decided it was time to find Hollis and discuss dinner. I was starving.

I loved how close Chadbourne was to the library and Memorial Union, not to mention State Street. I felt like I was close to campus but also close to everything else. It didn't take long to make it back to the room.

Hollis was sitting at her desk studying. "Look at you, Ms. I Don't Have To Study."

I groaned. "Don't remind me. I'm utterly weak with hunger. Food, I need food." I flopped onto my bed. "Then my brain will work enough to get through my homework."

Hollis smiled wide. "Okay, let me text Fern and we can meet them down in the cafeteria."

I tucked my head in my pillow. My day had been long, the hike and sitting in the mall, and even with the few snacks, I was tired and hungry.

Hollis flopped down on top of me. "Oh, sure. First you tease me with being hungry, and now you're sleepy?"

I wiggled until she fell off me onto the floor, banging down with a laugh. "I never said sleepy. Let's go!" I leapt up, then reached out a hand to pull her to her feet.

"How are you this hyper for the swill they serve in the cafeteria?" Hollis shook her head.

"Eh, it's more the company. And it isn't *that* bad, just a bit bland."

Hollis shook her head. "We'll agree to disagree, my friend."

We reached the food line and had to wait. Once we got to the options, we separated. I selected lasagna, garlic bread, and corn on the cob. It didn't all go together, but the salad looked a bit wilted. I debated dessert, but I could come back.

As soon as I sat, I started eating. Despite filling it, my belly cramped with need. I wasn't sure why I was so hungry, unless searching Trista's feelings, skipping lunch, and taking a hike was enough. There had been two-meal days in my past, so lunch couldn't be the only reason. I'd text Bevin later and ask him. He would be the least likely to snarl at me ... probably.

Hollis and Fern sat down. Hollis said, "Look who I found!" Then she leaned over and kissed her partner.

I groaned. "Really. Every time?"

They both laughed and started to eat.

We chatted for a bit about homework and classes. Then Fern's eyes widened. "I almost forgot. I can get us tickets to see The Jagged Edges playing in Chicago in a couple of weeks. But I need to know by tonight if we want them."

My mouth hung open. "Really? The Jagged Edges? I love that band. How much? How will we get there? How many nights? I'm so excited! Yes, we have to go!"

Fern laughed. "I didn't know you liked them so much. There's this big show the week before Halloween. It's a Saturday concert. I'll text you the details. I take it you're interested?"

"Yes! I'm very interested."

Hollis's eyes twinkled. "I'm totally in."

Gazing back and forth between us, Fern shrugged. "Do you think you could procure a car? We could always take the bus, but not riding with strangers would be so much better."

"I'll find out. We can continue the discussion of transport tomorrow, but yes on tickets."

Fern smiled. "Sounds perfect!"

Chapter 28 – Of All The Bars …

In the back of my mind I could feel a cloud of sadness coming from Trista all week. I tried to text her a few times, but her responses were all vague. School was hard. She'd failed a test. And to top it all off, a friend was acting weird. Nothing more specific.

I made my rounds, but Julez and Piper's emotions were less intense. There were some spikes of happiness or frustration. Their exhaustion was a constant beat, like a slow bass drum in the back of my mind.

Moving the three to a separate head space so their feelings and day to day mood swings didn't interrupt my comings and goings wasn't too bad.

Though Trista and I had made some progress in the friend department, I knew I was mostly a stranger to her and didn't want to be too pushy. I let her know I was available if she needed someone to talk to, a shoulder to cry on, or just someone to sit with quietly. Then I planned on touching base with her every few days. Beyond that, I gave her space.

I called Bevin Thursday night. "Pebble, did you mean to call me and not Jade?"

"Yeah, do you have time?"

"Sure, is this private?" I could hear movement in the background and a door shut.

I sighed. "It isn't really private ... I don't think. I just ... can I ask you a few leader type questions?"

"Of course. You know that. Any time. But you have your parents, too."

I sat in Library Mall. The weather was getting colder, but there were still a lot of people milling about. "I know, I would just rather ask you."

"So what's your issue?" I could hear the smile in his voice.

"Most of the time, the people you have ... you know, they're background noise, nothing you really notice, right?"

"Pretty much."

"Okay, I have Trista, Piper, and Julez, and until this last week, it's been mostly radio silence."

"That's good, right?" His voice came to me, calm and soothing.

"Yes. Being in classes, that is definitely preferable." I leaned back to look at the darkening sky. "So, first question, and please don't tell me this is dumb."

There was a sigh on the other end of the phone. "Have I ever?"

"Well, no. I just ... okay. When you focus on one of the people, does that take energy? I was on a hike with Trista last Sunday. The adventure went longer than planned and we missed lunch. But afterwards I was way hungrier than I expected. But the thing is, I did experience her emotions while we talked. She was a whirlwind of ups and downs."

He laughed softly. "Depending on how long you're focusing on a person and how deeply, yeah. It's a power, it takes energy. Try to have bars on you at all times, just to be safe. Nothing like what your sister needs, but something. I know you have more control than most, but hunger is always dangerous."

Even though he couldn't see me, I held back rolling my eyes. I sensed he'd be able to feel it. "Yes, Mom."

His laugh got louder. "Okay, you know. Was there anything else?"

I paused for a moment. "I guess not. Trista's been loud this week, and I've tried to reach out to her, but she's been standoffish, but she really doesn't know me. I sometimes feel I'm in way over my head. Did Mom and Dad make a mistake?"

I regretted the question as soon as I asked.

"Pebble, we all make mistakes, we all have imposter syndrome. You will be an amazing leader. We all see it. Just breathe and imagine me giving you a big hug." I didn't want to cry, but his words were releasing a tension deep down I'd been building up for weeks. "Any time you feel overwhelmed, just call me or José. We had each other. And we had Jade ... and even Owen. I can't imagine doing it alone. We're all here if you need us."

"Thanks, Bev." My voice was small, but I was starting to feel stronger.

School finally hit a routine. For the next couple weeks, things seemed to smooth out.

The biggest disruption to classes, tours, and studying was Fern, Hollis, and I talking about the concert. My parents said I could take a pack car ... one of the SUVs.

When the Saturday of the concert finally rolled around, we planned to leave in the early afternoon. We could get to Chicago, just over a two-hour drive, have dinner, then get to the venue for the concert. It was at a bar, but underaged people were allowed in for the show with a special hand stamp.

Excitement bubbled in me. I'd been wanting to see this band since Jade and Bevin turned me on to their music. The two were head-over-heels jealous I was seeing them live. They almost got tickets to come out and join us, but five babies at home made them see reason.

The vehicle, a black Subaru Ascent, had two rows behind the driver's seat. First the bucket seats, then a bench seat. Mom pulled up in front of Chadbourne in the whale of an SUV. Maybe we could sleep in it, each of us taking a row of seats. Dad followed in a second car to drive her home. She popped the rear door, and we put in our overnight bags. We weren't planning on spending the night, but better safe than sorry.

I took the keys, gave both Mom and Dad hugs, endured their good wishes and warnings, and we headed off.

Fern sat next to me with Hollis sitting in the second row. Fern gazed at all the controls. "This car is ... wow, so many buttons to play with. Can I start pressing everything?"

I laughed. "Only if you can fix what you break. You know what they say ... you break it, you buy it."

Fern snatched their hand back.

Amused, I showed them the basic system so they knew how to adjust the temperature, what we listened to, and the GPS.

Soon we were on I90 heading west ... or south, to Chicago. Hollis leaned forward. "Have you two heard about the college Halloween party?"

There had been something in the email announcements, but I had ignored it. I wasn't sure what I wanted to do this year, but spending time with a ton of college coeds didn't sound like the top of my list.

Before I could say, 'no', Fern shook their head. "I missed that email or emails in the myriad of stuff that crosses my inbox. Do tell."

"Okay, this sounds amazing. If you sign up, which is free, it's an all-night event. It's school sponsored. You get a randomly selected costume. Step one is, in Library Mall at four-thirty, we meet. You have to find your partner, the person with a matching outfit. Step two, scavenger hunt. Step three, food."

I navigated around a semi-truck. "Like two people dressed as cats? And wait ... a random partner?" I already hated it.

"I think it's more thematic, like a Jack and Jill or Little Miss Muffet and a spider. You get a name tag to help you find who you're matched up with."

Next to me, Fern laughed. "That's fantastic. I mean, I would rather spend the evening with the two of you, but I'm guessing we can eventually find each other and celebrate."

"Exactly," Hollis said. "There's a scavenger hunt. They didn't give many details, but the partners each get a ticket. There's a party, and each ticket you find is worth an item at a food truck. The final location will be surrounded by food trucks. I'm sure we can all hang out then regardless of who we're foisted on. So, it's only the time we're searching that we'd be separated."

My stomach grumbled at the thought of a party with food trucks. "Food trucks?"

Hollis laughed. "I knew that would get your attention."

"Why do you know my loves in life? That isn't fair!" It really wasn't. Hollis was using my weakness against me.

Fern leaned back to look at me. "You really enjoy food, don't you?"

I grumbled low in my throat, too low to be heard over the noise of the road. "Yeah. Food is lovely. How can you not love it … it's brilliant!"

They shook their head. "I know you've gone on a few hikes, but I don't see you exercising nearly as much as you eat. I wish I could eat like you. Your metabolism must be top notch. You remind me of … never mind."

Winking, I smirked. "It's a family thing. We're all big eaters, and all seem to be able to get away with it." Though, their words made me think about Dad and his exercise programs. He hadn't given me one at the start of college so I could acclimate. He did threaten to give one to me, but miraculously there was nothing yet. I wondered how much longer he'd give me to get used to my new life.

"It's true," Hollis complained, tearing me from my sudden worries. "Though, since you're adopted, that makes no sense."

I laughed at our familiar discussion. "Maybe my family tree really does match up with the Stones' if you go back far enough. We never did check. Jade and I look enough alike."

"Really? You look like your adopted sister?" Fern seemed really interested.

"I do. It helped when I was younger to feel comfortable with the family. That and the fact that Owen, my brother, is a complete goof."

Hollis huffed. "Okay, this is fun and all, but Halloween? No changing the subject. Are we doing it?"

They both looked at me with big eyes and my resolve dissolved. So much for my avoidance of this farce. "Fine, I'll sign up. But I don't promise I'll enjoy it."

Both Hollis and Fern cheered.

We discussed families and then where we wanted to eat for the rest of the drive south. We ended up at a Chinese restaurant. We ordered four items and shared, family style. Then we went to the venue.

We arrived early, but that just meant we found parking. At the door, we got our hands stamped, ordered soda, mozzarella sticks, and nachos, and secured a table about halfway to the stage. We knew the crowd would get crazy when The Jagged Edges started.

They announced an opening band, The Rebel Phoenix. I'd never heard of them, but the sound was amazing. I leaned over to Fern. "Do you know this group?"

"No!" they yelled. "They're up and coming, but I really like them."

"So do I."

Hollis leaned across the small table. "Are we talking about how good this group is?"

"Yeah."

"I've looked them up." She waved her phone. "They're from Rockford. We can probably see other shows, maybe even in Madison."

My cheeks hurt as my smile got bigger. The buzz from everyone's enjoyment permeated the place.

When they finished, a couple of really cute guys came out to switch out the equipment. Then The Jagged Edges came out.

They opened with 'The Breaks,' their standard opener. We leapt up. The crowd rushed the stage, waving their hands, and creating a mosh pit. The air was electric.

"Gods above, the lead singer is handsome!" I yelled.

Someone behind me leaned down. "He's also gay."

I turned and my heart dropped when I saw Luna. *What is she doing here? Why is she here? Of all places?*

"And married, from what I understand. Doesn't mean I can't appreciate his beauty. Della is beautiful too. And I love Clyde's green hair."

Luna rolled her eyes ... again. Gods, she needed a new action. "You just think they're all pretty?"

"Is that wrong? They look good and make such amazing music."

Before Luna could answer, Dayna pushed her aside. "Ignore her. We're here for the music."

I decided that was great advice. Turning back to the stage, I beat my fist into the air and danced.

Chapter 29 – Let's Make a Deal

When The Jagged Edges finished their last set, my singing and laughing left my throat rough and scratchy. Fern, Hollis, and I headed out of the bar and started walking down the street towards the SUV.

The plan was to drive as far as we could tonight, probably all the way home. The drive was just over two hours, so we hoped we could make it back. If not, we'd either find a cheap hotel or sleep in the car. Probably the former if we became desperate.

We'd walked a block when I heard Dayna. "Hey, Pebble."

I turned. "Yeah?"

"I was wondering ... how did you three get down here?"

Hollis and Fern stopped when I did. One of my eyebrows rose. "Um, in a car. Isn't that the normal way?"

"We caught a bus. The plan was to catch a cab or order an uber back to my parents' place, then get a bus back to campus tomorrow." Her smile widened and I could smell a citrusy hope emanate from her.

"Okay, sounds like a great plan." I took a step backwards, bumping into Hollis.

Dayna sighed. "Would it be too much to ask that you take us with you?"

"What? You want to hitch a ride with us?"

Luna scoffed. "Are you daft?"

"No, I'm just trying to avoid a long ride with someone who doesn't like the majority of people in the car. It sounds odious." I hardened my face and stared at her until she shrugged one shoulder.

She smirked. "I'll sit in the back with Dayna and the quiet one. You won't even know I'm there."

I laughed. It was ridiculous. "You don't even know what we're driving. It could be a micro mini."

Dayna put up her hands. "Luna, please. For the most part, Pebble has been nothing but nice, even with you being ... you know ... you. And do you even know these other two?"

"I forgot you weren't there at the welcome to school game day after I lost and had a run-in with them. Don't you remember? This is the one that beat me." Her hand waved vaguely towards Hollis.

Dayna snorted. "So, you hate her for being better than you? Typical."

"What's that supposed to mean?" Luna snapped at Dayna.

"You know what it means. Aunt Joan beat you at Monopoly when you were like six and you never forgave her."

"I was six, Dayna. Who doesn't let a six-year-old win?"

I shook my head. "Is *that* what's wrong with you? Everyone let you win your whole life? And I thought you two said you met in the dorms ... same floor. But you're related?"

Dayna's hands flew out to her sides in a shrug. "I mean, I live in Chicago and Luna lives in Maine. We did meet in the dorms, in a way. There were a few times our families came together, but not many. My uncle married her mom and moved out east. He barely speaks to anyone in the family. Irreconcilable differences."

"You don't have to tell her this ... any of it. We're cousins, so what? And we don't need a ride. We can just take the bus tomorrow."

"Good," I said. And turned.

Fern put up their hands, relaxing me with their presence. "Pebble? We're better people than that."

I narrowed my eyes. "Are we?"

They stared pointedly at me.

"Fine," I snapped out. "If you want, you can join us."

Dayna walked up and put her arm around my shoulders. "Please tell me you didn't drive a Mini Cooper."

"Nah, we drove down in an SUV, you and Luna can take the back seat. Lots of space." I started walking, leading the group to the car. "You can even sit next to Hollis and give Luna her own row if you want."

"Excellent. Any chance we can stop at my house to pick up our bags?"

The drive from Chicago to Madison was pretty much one interstate, I90. Whereas Chicago traffic could be slow, once we got outside of the city proper, most of the cars dwindled away. The part of the interstate in Illinois had tolls, but the pack SUV had an iPass, so they didn't slow us down.

By the halfway point, everyone had fallen asleep, and a quiet had blanketed the car. I debated turning on some music, but I really didn't want to wake anyone up.

"Thanks for the ride."

I looked in the rearview mirror to make sure I picked out the right voice and my mind wasn't playing tricks with me. Luna gazed at me from the back seat. "Um. You're welcome. I didn't think you really wanted it."

She sighed. "I have a big paper due in my English class on Monday. Dayna knew I needed to get back earlier than the bus could get us to campus, that's why she pushed."

I continued to watch the road since I didn't need to watch her to hear her. She could whisper and I'd know what she said, not that she knew that. "Then why didn't you say something? You acted like it was no big deal."

In all honesty, I didn't expect her to answer. When the topic of conversation got personal, Luna usually pushed back. To my surprise, she stayed pleasant. Maybe it was because she was tired, who knew. "I don't like to be a burden. This feels like that's what I'm doing."

"But we're all going to the same place." Her argument seemed weak.

"No, you had to drive to Dayna's place to get our school bags. Then you have to drop us off at our dorms, then your dorms for Hollis and Fern. Then I assume you're driving to wherever this car goes. It'll be an extra hour of driving for you."

It would've never occurred to me her prickly attitude was for me. I was almost touched.

"It's no big deal. I'll sleep at home in a comfortable bed and wake up to real coffee and a homemade breakfast."

"Well, when you put it that way." Looking back, I saw her smile.

Luna smiles?

"Anyway," I continued, "I'm glad to help. And the concert was really great. I'm still buzzing from that. I've been wanting to see them live for a long time. My sister is going to be so jealous."

"Why didn't she come with? Is she younger?"

"No, older. She lives in California."

"Ah, then that makes sense."

We fell into an amiable silence for the rest of the ride.

Did this mean we were becoming friends?

Chapter 30 – Halloween

Sunday morning, I was tired. Every bone in my body protested getting up, but the smell of coffee, ham, and potatoes pulled me into the kitchen.

As I plodded in, Mom glided around, cooking. Nothing was quite done yet. "Hi, sweetie, how was the concert?"

A smile slowly spread across my face as I poured my morning ambrosia. I was too tired to speak pre-coffee. After half a cup, words made sense. "So much fun. Even the opening band was good."

"Well, eat up, shower, and get dressed. You need to get back to the dorms to study, unless you brought your books here."

"I did not."

She let me finish my first cup of coffee and poured a second before she asked more questions. "Have you made plans for next weekend?" She placed a plate of food in front of me.

"Yeah, Hollis convinced me to sign up for a school-sponsored Halloween thingy. Do you know anything about it?" I started in on the ham and potato hash.

"I don't. It isn't anything that affects faculty, so I tend to ignore it." She smiled at my look of disappointment. "But let me know afterwards. I'm glad you're doing things—it's why you're not living here, right?"

She wasn't wrong, but I still scrunched up my face at her and she laughed. "Oh, well. It shouldn't be horrible." I pulled out my phone and checked the school email account. "It says I need to dress up as—" I groaned. It *was* awful. "Gods above. I've been assigned Little Red Riding Hood. My partner will be the wolf. I have to go to Library Mall at four-thirty on Halloween and find him or her. Then the games will begin."

Mom couldn't hold back her loud laugh. "You were Little Red Riding Hood your first Halloween in Wisconsin, when you were five. I don't think that costume will fit you anymore. Jade was the wolf. Do you remember?"

Gods! "I hadn't, but now that you say that I do. Well, if Jade were the wolf again, this wouldn't be so bad. But this time it will be some stranger. I think they're trying to get us to meet new people."

"I think you'll have fun."

I groaned. "I guess it could be worse. I could be the wolf."

She got up to refill both our mugs. "I wanted to talk to you about Thanksgiving."

I watched as she added some milk and handed me my drink. "Oh. We have over a month to worry. Are we hosting the pack again this year?"

It was something of a tradition. We cooked with several pack members and had food for days. Everything ended up tasting amazing and afterwards we headed out for a run.

Sitting down, she shook her head. "No. We're thinking about doing something over the weekend with the pack, but on Thursday proper, the werebears invited us up to their sleuth for the meal."

"Wait, what? Why?" We'd never been invited to visit the werebears. They were incredibly private.

The high school gym teacher was a werebear. We only discovered them after Jade trained to find wereanimals with a touch, something only epsilon werewolves could do. The story I'd heard, during a dodgeball game, she walked in front of him, and he touched her arm to stop her and ask a question. That was it, the cat—or bear—was out of the bag. He probably regretted that question for years.

"I'm not entirely sure. Your old coach, Mr. Nelson, invited us. Dad and I think there's something he wants to discuss with us, but we don't know. It may also be to welcome you as the next alpha. But the idea of a big meal sounds pretty good to us." She watched me, waiting for my answer.

Slowly, I nodded. "Yeah, I've been wanting to see their territory for a long time. I'll be able to hold this over both Jade and Owen." I waggled my brows. "Which is only a bonus."

Monday night, I got a text from Piper asking if I would have dinner with her and Julez Tuesday night. It had been some time since just the three of us had hung out. When I was young and didn't like to hunt cute animals, Piper helped take care of me a lot. I thought it could be fun.

Knowing how busy the week would be, I made sure to get all my important homework done.

Piper picked me up at five-thirty from the dorms. Her smile was huge. "It's great to see you, Pebble. I feel like I never see you anymore."

I sighed as I sank into the seat of her Toyota Camry. "I know. I love college, and living in the dorms is a must with my schedule, but I feel so disconnected from the pack. We've had two runs, and those nights have been good for my soul ... and grounded me with everyone, but I feel like I *miss* all of you."

Piper laughed. "You've always had your finger on the pulse of everything happening in the pack. That started when you were five and Jade used you to get all the gossip."

"Yeah, that was amazing." A warm happiness filled me at the memory. "I was her sister spy because no one thought I listened in."

"You may be better than me at finding information"

I chuckled. "This from the forensics scientist? No. I don't think so. But I do tend to hear and see more than people give me credit for. And with the premonitions added in, I get a lot of weird information."

A seriousness overtook her. "Are you having many premonitions?"

"No. Maybe three or four. But there have been two that don't really make sense. One has been recurring since this summer. The really odd thing is, until these two visions or whatever, I'd never had anything recur before. It's frustrating. Sometimes I wish I had Jade here so I could talk to my wolf and get actual answers."

"Don't we all?" There was a wistfulness in her voice, and I wondered what she'd ask her wolf.

When I mentioned my premonitions, Piper's vanilla curiosity peaked, and her emotions swirled in my mind. The pack knew my visions were private, something Dad and I managed, but the two-pronged reading let me know how interested she was. Apparently, proximity amped up my ability to read emotions as well. No wonder Mom and Dad always snacked.

It didn't take long to get to Piper and Julez's place. As soon as I got in, I found Spruce in the living room and sat down to play with them. They were the best kiddo.

"Peb! Pay boxes?"

I smiled. "Yes. I'd love to play blocks with you. What should we build?"

"Kindom. I have two kings and two queens. They need house." Spruce breathed heavily as they got all the words out.

I assumed as soon as the kingdom was built, we'd become the monsters that attacked and tore it down. We'd played this game before.

"Are there any princes?" I asked.

"Yes. And princesses. All in pretty dresses."

"All of them?" I tickled them. They were so cute.

"All."

In the kitchen, Piper and Julez spoke quietly. I did hear Julez say, "No, I want Pebble to enjoy dinner. You just sit, I'm cooking."

I chuckled. Piper's mom was an amazing cook. That seemed to have skipped over her daughter.

A couple minutes later, Julez popped her head out. "Dinner's ready. Can you take Spruce to the bathroom to wash up?"

"Absolutely. We'll be there in a sec."

Spruce wiggled, but I got them clean. My hands were cleaned in the process. As we sat by the sink, they told me about their day. "And then I at Kimmy's and painted ... and snack. But I no like snack. Carrots today. But lunch was yum. Pasgetti and bread and then a walk."

The ongoing talk of their activities continued until I got them in their seat at the dining room table.

Julez made pork chops, hash brown potatoes with bacon and chives, and a salad. It all smelled wonderful.

Outside of Spruce's jabbering, we all ate quietly for the first few minutes. Then I leaned back, sipping my soda. "How have you two been? Work going okay?"

Julez ran her own cosmetology business. She'd always been good with the skills—hair, nails, skin and hair treatments, all of it. After she'd earned a business degree she had the confidence to start her own salon.

"Business is going really well. We have so many regular customers that I've had to hire two new staff. I'm debating opening a second location. It's slightly terrifying." Julez gave me a half-excited, half-worried smile. She had a citrusy vanilla scent, letting me know how pleased she was with all of this.

"That's really amazing. You deserve all the success you're building up, Julez."

Piper reached over to clasp Julez's forearm. "You really do, hon. I'm really proud of you."

Julez blushed. "Piper is doing great too. She keeps getting raises."

"They keep trying to promote me out of the lab, but I don't want to be a leader. I just want to do what I do."

I laughed. "Mom talks about that. They've asked her to be chair, or if she wants to apply to help in the dean's office. She's worked there for a long time. She keeps reminding them she just wants to teach math. The promotion doesn't really reward her if it takes her away from what she loves to do."

"Exactly!" Piper exclaimed with more passion that she usually showed other people. "Why don't people see that we go for the jobs we want? Not everyone wants to 'climb the ladder.'"

Julez gave Piper the kind of smile that filled the room with the love they shared. I cherished this type of connection.

She turned from Piper to me. "How about college?"

"It's good. Lots of work, but I like it."

"I miss college. I know it was all about running around and crazy assignments, but there was a freedom as well."

I knew what she meant. Despite having a few charges in my mini-pack, I really didn't have responsibility as an alpha yet. My only focus was passing and getting decent grades.

"I love coming over and catching up with you two. I miss having time here. I know we had weekly-ish dinners this summer, but was there any ulterior motive for all this? Worried I wasn't getting properly fed?"

Piper blushed, shrinking into herself a bit. Julez raised an eyebrow. "Well, if we're to be honest, maybe. We were hoping you'd take your favorite *nibling* out trick-or-treating on Saturday so we could have a date night. It's been a long time for us."

I blew out a breath. "I can't, I actually already have plans and—"

"Are they with her?" Julez snapped out. "With Trista?"

Anger exploded in me, but I held myself tight. "Does that matter? She's new in town, and as her pack it's our job to make her feel welcome."

"You don't understand, Pebble. There's something about her." Though she kept her voice level, I could feel her anger rising within me.

"Julez, it's my job as an alpha to help her acclimate to Madison. I can't just shrug off my responsibilities because you don't like her. It's her first holiday in a new city with a new pack. More than that, she lives on the other side of town, separated from us. She needs the touch of pack. You know that."

She grumbled, but relaxed. "It's not that I don't like her. There's something *off* about her. I wish you'd step back and take another look. Maybe have your wolf look at her."

"Trust me, I'm not doing anything blindly. You know me, Julez. I've never been blindly trusting of anything since, well, since my parents. Piper can confirm that. Moreover, I've been having premonitions, and nothing about her. I think you're off base here. I think you're being an overly protective mom, which is great, but she apologized. She's never misgendered Spruce, and she's trying."

Julez's face hardened. "She sure is." Louder she snarled. "I can't believe you're choosing her over Spruce."

"I can't believe you'd ask me to cancel my plans last minute when you have alternative options." I started ticking things off on my fingers. "I'm in college, you waited until now, not weeks ago, you have a full pack who would probably happily watch Spruce. If not Easton, Piper's parents, my parents—should I go on? In all honesty, I don't even know why you came to me at all."

Slumping, Julez shrugged. "We miss you, Pebble, and our last few interactions have been tense. We just wanted to get back to our normal friendship. But hearing you chose her..."

I wanted to scream, but instead I took a calming breath and modulated my tone. "I didn't. You just assumed. I signed up for a university event with assigned partners that we don't meet until the day of."

Julez sat back. "Oh."

Piper bit her lips, as if trying not to react in any way. Spruce was done eating and getting fussy. She got up and took them away, probably to get cleaned up and ready for bed.

"Yeah. So someone will be searching for me if I don't show. I have no way to back out now."

Julez slumped. "Okay, yeah, sorry I assumed. I still don't like Trista, but I get that you're legitimately busy."

It annoyed me that if I had plans with Trista it wasn't a valid reason to say no, but I was tired of the fight. I sighed and rubbed my face. "Have you tried Easton?"

Piper returned without Spruce. "He's next on our list."

"Why not first? He loves Spruce."

Julez shook her head. "Since we haven't told Spruce ... I don't know. We need to decide."

"For what it's worth, a bigger village is never a bad thing. I don't think Easton would try to push for more time with Spruce as his father than you're comfortable giving. He loves the kid, but knows you want to be exclusive parents."

Piper swung her gaze between us. "That's what I think. Before Spruce starts asking about their father, I think we should tell them. Spruce will be ours all the time, but Easton will help in any and every way he can. He loves his child."

Julez sighed. "I know, it's just a big decision. We'll call him and talk to him about this weekend."

The rest of the week passed slowly. There were quizzes and tests in every class but English, where I had a paper due. I had two tours to give on Wednesday and Saturday morning. I felt like I was running every second of each day. I found some time to speak with Trista on

Thursday. Our schedules had been all out of whack. She was doing much better with school and friends. She had a party to attend on Halloween and was super excited.

Beyond that conversation, I hadn't been getting many emotions from her, so I believed what she said, and was glad. I reminded her she could always call.

I wasn't sure how, but Hollis found a red dress for me to wear with long sleeves and a black belt. She also found a red-hooded, lined cape. They both came to just above my knees.

It wasn't unusual for Wisconsin to have a snowstorm on Halloween, so it was a pleasant surprise when the day had a high in the mid-forties. No one would freeze as we ran around searching for tickets.

Hollis had been assigned Bonnie of Bonnie and Clyde. Fern had Woodstock of Snoopy and Woodstock. I heard some people had food pairings like peanut butter and jelly and burger and fries. I kind of wished I had gotten fries.

Once I had the dress and cape on, I paired it with black tights and knee-high boots. I applied light makeup and used pins to make sure the hood stayed on.

Hollis took a picture then affixed the sticker on my chest with my character name and who my partner would be. I figured I'd send it to different family members later.

We met Fern in the lobby of Chadbourne and we walked over to Library Mall.

There were a lot of people milling around the area, a few hundred students in wild costumes. I wasn't sure how

I would find my person, except I knew I would be looking for someone who probably had animal ears.

It took a while, but the third person I found who was an animal, but not my partner—wolf of the wolf and three pigs— said he saw a wolf near the water feature. When I reached them, I tapped on the shoulders of a person I *thought* I recognized. With my gut clenching, I saw the tag that said, 'Wolf - seeking Little Red Riding Hood.'

Looking up, I said, "Hi, Luna, I guess we're partners ... again."

Chapter 31 – Find And Seek

Luna stood in front of me, sneering. *I guess our moment of peace in the car is over.* She wore the worst wolf outfit I could imagine. She had on a gray furry bodysuit. The tip of her nose shone with black paint, maybe nail polish, and she'd applied black whiskers. Even the ears were homemade. She had a headband with gray ears that mostly matched the body suit. There was a long tail and gloves with paws and claws.

Her upper lip twitched. "Why do we always get matched up?" She sounded exasperated.

I huffed out a laugh. "My bad luck, I'm guessing." She rolled her eyes. "That's a horrible wolf's outfit, you know." I bit the inside of my cheek to help keep my face blank. I wasn't sure why I was goading her, but her attitude annoyed me once again.

"Oh, and you've seen that many wolves in your life?"

"Enough to know they don't have cat ears and a cat's tail." One of my eyebrows rose despite my attempt to keep my stance neutral.

"And why would you have seen any wolves, city girl?" She crossed her arms over her chest and glared.

Part of me was worried, but most of me knew she wasn't from around the Midwest, and I could say anything I wanted. "I'm from Wisconsin, everyone knows these things." I stopped myself before I said, 'duh,' so that was something. "And if you really must know, my house backs up to woods. We have lots of animals back there. I've run and played enough to see just about everything."

She scoffed. "Let's just get this over with. I don't know why Dayna forced me to do this farce of an activity." She looked around at all the excited people. "I guess you're better than most of the people I could've been paired with."

The thought of subjecting a random coed to work with Luna for the night sent a shiver down my spine. I didn't know what Dayna had been thinking either. As much as we didn't get along, I hadn't planned on this being a fun night; at least Luna wouldn't be ruining someone's joy.

"Wow, that was almost a compliment. Did it hurt? Do you need pain meds?"

She turned and headed towards the organizers who were handing out a paper to each pair. "I was wrong. You are worse."

"Big bad wolf," I mumbled. "So very scary."

She looked at me over her shoulder. "I really am."

We got to one of the organizers and they smiled. "Here you go. There are five clues that will take you to five places around campus. Each correct clue location will give you two tickets, one each. The tickets are good for one food truck item.

Luna took the sheet, and we headed to a bench. She read through the clues and then gave them to me to read through. *Red light, green light. Visit me to learn to be civil.* The second one read: *A gatekeeper to many realms.* Next we had: *Most think of the deck and a view of the sea, but directional visage is for you and for me.* The fourth was: *We have more than books, you know.* It ended super easy. *You're in Bucky's house now!*

As locations popped into my head, I stood. "These weren't written to be hard."

Luna shook her head. "If we go in order, we'll be running back and forth across campus all night long, and that would be stupid. Look, several of the groups are heading off now. Why are people so ... peopley?"

I looked over the list again. "I take it you want to hit up the library and bookstore while we're here?" The locations of the second and fourth clues lined Library Mall.

She just looked at me.

I stood. "Right. Bookstore first? I see several groups heading towards the library."

"Fine." She somehow *implied* the eyeroll in her voice.

We walked in silence as we headed towards our target. The shop was buzzing with people shopping. We made a direct line for the information desk.

"Can I help you two? Nice costumes by the way ... are you a cat?"

Luna snarled and did a pretty good job at it. "I'm a wolf."

The guy nodded. "If you rotated the ears out a bit and maybe double up the tail so it was shorter and thicker you'd look more the part. And why the whiskers?"

She just glared at him.

I whispered, "Wisconsin ... we all know." Then I smiled at the man. "You're more than just books, right?"

His smile widened. "We sure are, and because you know that, here are two tickets."

Luna and I each took our ticket and headed out of the bookstore.

There weren't many people in Library Mall as we crossed to the library. There was a sign that reminded students that even on Halloween others were studying and to keep quiet.

At the help desk, Luna smiled. "Hi, you are the gatekeeper to many realms?"

She obviously was taking my strategy of giving the clue. The librarian took a moment, then nodded. "You want the other desk around the corner." Then she rotated in her seat, giving us her back.

Both my brows shot up and I mouthed, "Wow." If they didn't want students in the building, you'd think they'd make it easier to get us out.

There was an older lady at the other desk. She smiled at us. "You two look great. Now, don't eat her!" She laughed at her own joke.

Luna leaned in. "You know, it's crossed my mind, but not tonight."

The woman chuckled.

My jaw dropped open, and Luna snorted. "What? I'm staying in character. Don't look so scandalized, Pebble. You're not my type."

The woman handed us our tickets and we walked out.

"Not that I'm complaining, but what *is* your type?"

She just shook her head. "Next stop, Bascom Hill."

I sighed. "Only if you want to waste energy walking up the hill. None of the clues are for there."

"Of course one is." She waved the paper in my face. "Red light, green light? Civil? That's totally law."

"No." I spoke slowly. "That's engineering. Civil engineering, with the traffic lights."

Luna huffed. "You're wrong, and Bascom Hill is on the way to Union South."

"But it's a hill. One we could avoid." I shook my head. "Are you being oddly dense to avoid telling me your type? You're normally smarter than this."

She paused. "My type is ... complicated. I would tell you, but then I'd have to kill you." She slid her eyes over to look at me and sighed. "But, really, it is complicated. My family is picky. I'll find someone when I get back to Maine. So, now you know; can we go up the hill?"

"Fine, but when there's nothing there, you're buying me ice cream." We started towards the law building, which I knew was wrong. "So, is that why you're so arrogant? You're like royalty. Are you really from Europe? Some sort of princess living life as a commoner just to see what it's really like?"

She laughed. "Yep, you figured me out. What about you? What's your type?"

I sighed. "I don't really date."

Luna stared at me. "Why not?"

"I just ... it's not my thing. Maybe if I knew someone really well, felt comfortable around them, and built a friendship. But that hasn't happened."

"Oh, demi. Got it."

The way she said it was so casual, matter of fact, as if it were no big deal. I guess it wasn't, but it was new to me. Her blasé attitude—I wasn't sure if I loved it or hated it.

"You still with me?" We'd started up the hill as I'd lamented how simple everything was to her.

I shook my head. "What? Oh, yeah, sorry. I was just thinking."

Luna gazed at me again. "You know that term, right?"

That annoyed me. Who did she think she was? "Yes. I've even considered getting a flag for my room."

"Cool, just asking."

Am I really having this conversation with Luna? She's being so ... normal. A shiver played down my spine.

We got to the law building, but it was locked up tight. I smirked at her. "Can't wait for my ice cream. Can we go to Union South now?"

"Whatever." The snap to her voice was back, and I tried not to laugh.

After we were back on track, I bit my lip. "Have you known others? You know, like me?"

"Demiromantic? Yeah, a couple of my friends back home."

We walked for a few blocks in silence. It wasn't as tense as when we'd first partnered up, but I was a bit uncomfortable. I wasn't sure why I'd told her what I had. It almost felt for a moment like I was speaking with a friend or partner ... like partner in crime. But, no, it was just Luna.

We got to Union South, the third clue: *Most think of the deck and a view of the sea, but directional visage is for you and for me.* The University had two unions, one on the lake and this one, with a direction in its name. There were a bunch of other teams there, their grapefruit scented joy in the game filling the space. We'd lost time tromping up the hill, not that it was a race, but now we waited in line. When we got to the front of the line, I could feel Luna looking at me, but I was gazing off into space. She said, "Who needs a view of the sea when we can have this directional visage?"

The woman laughed. "Oh, I like that. I'm going to give each of you two tickets for making me laugh."

A small moan escaped me—an extra food item, yum!

Luna said, "Ice cream first, then engineering?"

"Yes, please."

We each got a small cone and headed out towards the engineering campus. There was a building with a huge bat over the door and lights on. We headed in and found someone sitting on a couch surrounded by a few other matched pairs. Once again, we had to wait.

When it got to be our turn, I walked up to him. "Are you red light or green light?"

He said, "Are you going to be civil?"

"I am," I confirmed. "But I'm not sure about my partner."

He laughed. "Fair enough." He handed us each a ticket. "For your troubles."

Outside the building, it was time to head towards Bucky's house, the stadium. It occurred to me, I was actually having fun. "One more stop ... and it'll have food trucks."

Luna narrowed her eyes. "That's why you came, isn't it? You're just after the food."

"Gods above, yes. Food trucks! Why else do any of this?"

She shrugged one shoulder. "I guess that's as good a reason as any."

It was only a few blocks to get to our final destination. Anyone who reached the final destination received a ticket and a hand stamp.

The person with the stamper yelled over the loud music, "This stops you from coming back for more tickets."

We both nodded.

Gazing over the trucks, my stomach grumbled. I leaned in to Luna. "This was surprisingly not awful. I'm going to go get food." *Lots and lots of food, but hopefully no one I know will realize that.* "What do you think will be your first stop?"

Her eyes narrowed. "Dayna said to meet her by the Bucky, so, that's where I'm heading. Don't you need to meet," she waved her hands, "your people?"

"Sure, but poutine, tacos, waffle cones, why wait?"

Eyes narrowed, she shook her head at me, then laughed. "You're going to make yourself sick."

"Maybe, but it'll be fun until I get to that point." She continued to gaze at me with a raised brow. "Well, enjoy whatever it is you get. See you Monday."

She nodded. "Yep."

There were almost two dozen trucks. I wanted to try them all. I had six tickets and a pocket full of cash. I figured without anyone monitoring me I could do some real damage. My goal was to see how much I could eat before Hollis and Fern found me.

Chapter 32 – You Again?

As the days got closer to Thanksgiving, the number of students in class shrank. Fern was returning back to Kentucky for a few days, and Hollis was spending time with her family.

On Wednesday, after stats, we all headed back to the dorms together. My English discussion class was canceled.

Hollis gave us each a hug. "Have a great few days and eat a lot. I expect you both to come back double your current size."

Fern laughed then hugged me. "I can't believe it's only been a few months." They looked at their watch. "Okay, I have to catch the bus in an hour. I'm going to head down and grab my bag and head over to Memorial Union. I'm going to miss you both. I know this is a prelude to winter break, but I really like it here better than there. I feel so much more myself."

Hollis gave them one more hug. "I'm glad. You deserve to be you."

After Fern left, I sat on my bed. "I can't believe my family isn't cooking and I'm going up north to celebrate. At least I'll be back for the weekend. Maybe we can see a movie together?"

"Yes, please, don't leave me with my family. I love them, but they're bound to yell at me about dating a trans nonbinary person. My dad will say something horrible, I know it."

I scrunched up my nose. "Let me know. I can come back here, too. Maybe not before Saturday night, but I can come back then."

"Good."

We hugged again, and I headed down after Mom texted me.

I put my bag into the trunk and slid into the passenger seat. "Hi, Mom! Happy time off."

"Hi, sweetie. I really need these days. A small respite, and then the final push to the end."

I leaned back into my seat. "I am so looking forward to that." There was an ironic edge to my voice.

Mom laughed. "Have you heard about the Colorado winter program?"

"Professor McCrea said he'd send out emails after Thanksgiving."

Mom navigated through the students and cars causing heavy congestion around campus. "That's exciting. I hope you're selected. Travel and study are such great opportunities."

"Thanks, Mom."

It didn't take much time to get home, and we talked about what homework I did need to finish up over break and what plans I had with Hollis.

After I settled in, Mom and I baked two apple pies and one pumpkin pie to bring the next day. We planned on leaving at eleven. The drive to Viroqua would take just over two hours and Coach Nelson requested we get there between one and two.

After dinner, I went to my room to relax. Being alone in my room was so novel. My phone rang and the display flashed 'Trista.'

"Hiya, Trista, how are you? Happy Thanksgiving."

"You too." She sounded relaxed.

I shifted so I was lying down. "Do you have plans for tomorrow?"

She snorted. "No. I was hoping for a pack dinner, but since there isn't one, I don't know what to do."

I closed my eyes and tried not to feel guilty. It wasn't a pack rule that we celebrate Thanksgiving together, and our pack didn't *every* year, they just did most years.

The werebears were a secretive and elusive bunch. When they invited us up, they said they had something they wanted to discuss. Dad asked if we could bring any of the pack, and Coach Nelson requested that this time we only bring immediate family. Apparently, he wanted to see how the wolves and bears socialized before adding more.

With a sigh, I tried to sound supportive. "I get it. And we'll probably do something next year ... which doesn't help you now. There are a lot of restaurants that do Thanksgiving. You could try one of them. Or if you want, I'll contact a few pack members I know are always up for more company."

"I don't love the idea of a restaurant alone, especially if there are families eating around me, but yeah, if you could call other pack. Hannah and Chloe have been really nice, as have the submissive wolves." Her voice had perked up a bit.

A plan started to form. Though she was in my mini-pack, I wasn't her 'mom' or 'keeper,' that wasn't what it meant to be pack. That said, I wanted to make her transition to living in Madison as streamlined and positive as possible. "Okay, let me call you back."

It didn't take long to confirm Chloe and her dads, two of our submissive wolves, would happily have her join them. One more call to give Trista the time and address, and my day was ending on a great note.

"Thanks, Pebble. You're really nice. I ..." There was a long pause. "Never mind. It's just that you're nice."

"Well, everyone should be nice to you."

I could feel her pleasure in my words. There was something else, but I couldn't quite decipher it. Translating other people's emotions was weird when they were coming through the filter of distance and your head. I could talk to Mom and Dad, but I really wanted to sit down and talk with Bevin and José. I wondered if I could sneak off to California in early January for a few days before the second semester started.

Over the summer, I planned to travel to meet all the different pack alphas, just like all new alphas did, but for now I was leaning on the ones I knew.

There was the sound of movement over the line. "Well, I should go. I hope to see you soon, Pebble. Thanks again for being so nice. You know, I didn't expect that."

It took me a second to wrap my head around that. "Really? Why not?"

"Um. I don't know. But I'm getting a call on the other line ... I think it's Chloe. I'll talk to you soon. Gotta go. Bye."

She hung up before I could say bye.

I wondered if she was just one of those people who didn't do well with compliments or other people being nice to her. I needed to spend more time with her and really get to know her.

Thursday morning, I had one of my premonitions again. I was tired of the two. I really wished they'd manifest so I knew what was going on.

The bear's roar was deafening. Maybe that was why I couldn't hear anything else. It ran towards me, but I held my ground. The amusement poured off it as it passed. Was there something familiar in the way the bear felt? In its eyes? Did I know those eyes? It's aura? *Why am I thinking about auras?*

Did I know this bear? Around me were wolves.

I looked up quickly. The bird, it wasn't a swan. I was sure of it. Was it a ...

"Pebble, wake up. We need to get ready to go." Mom shook me. "You need to do Dad's routine, shower, then dress. Then there's breakfast."

With a groan, I rolled over and snarled, "I'm up!"

The drive to Viroqua was nice. We were just outside of Madison when Dad rotated in his seat. "Applesauce, we need to talk."

Dread slammed into me. "What? Did something happen? Did I do something wrong?"

His face hardened. "Yes, yes you did."

The citrusy scent of amusement came from Mom, so I took a breath and tried to release some of my tension. "Okay, what did I do?"

"Well," a small smile spread on Dad's face, "it's more about what you didn't do."

My eyes narrowed. "What I didn't do?"

"You've stopped your morning exercise routines." He held up his hands. "I know, we discussed you taking off a couple of weeks, but it's November ... the *end* of November. Don't you think with your first class starting at almost ten you should be doing something? And I did mention I'd have something for you, but with your first duty as alpha ..."

I slumped. "Yeah, probably."

"Good, I'm glad we have that settled." He handed back a notebook with a grin. "I didn't want to wait until Christmas to give this to you."

I grumbled as I took the book. Paging through it, I saw he'd set up several months of cardio and weight training. Over winter break, he'd included some full pack training, with notes that he hadn't set them up yet, but he would after Christmas. There were alternative options if pack members weren't available.

Then he tilted his head. "Have you figured out any of your premonitions? You have two recurring ones, and the one about the last battle in California."

I sighed. "No, and it's really annoying. And you only *think* that one is about California; we don't know. If something doesn't come to fruition soon, I may scream."

Mom nodded. "You've never had it like this. And you said that last one your new friend Fern was there when you went down?"

"Yes."

Dad shook his head. "You told them about your visions."

"Again, yes."

"Why didn't you lie?" He sounded truly perplexed.

My mouth opened and shut a few times. "Because people smell lies. I just ... I don't lie. It's not something I do, not really."

Mom laughed. "Is this Fern a werewolf?"

"No, you know they're not."

"So, sweetie, how would they smell a lie?"

I gaped at her and then at Dad who chuckled. "I mean ... but. I just. You want me to lie?"

Dad shrugged. "I want you to be safe. I know you've mostly been with our own kind, but sometimes it's better to just ... not tell the truth. Especially around norms."

The idea of lying to my friends, especially Fern or Hollis, made me feel dirty. I didn't know what it was about Fern, but they felt safe. And Hollis, she'd had my back my whole life. "I'll think about it. But Fern and Hollis—I trust them. I wish you knew them better. I think you'd see what I see."

Mom's eyes darted to me for a moment. "You really trust them."

"I do."

"Okay, we'll find a way to learn more about them. Some norms, like Piper's mom and Milo out in California, end up being worthy of knowing more." Dad's face hardened, but he didn't contradict Mom.

After that, we focused on getting to Viroqua. The drive was uneventful. The day was cool, but clear. I had an English book I could read in the car. That really helped the time fly by.

We were told that the meal was happening at Coach Nelson's house.

Dad turned to me. "So, now that you've graduated, will you start calling your old coach Stanley?"

I shivered. "Gods, no. I can't ... just no."

He laughed. "You call his wife Suzie."

"Well, that's how she was introduced. When I tried to call her Mrs. Nelson, she told me that was her mother-in-law, and she'd nip off my wolf's tail if I did it again. I was seven at the time. I wasn't going to chance it."

Both my parents chuckled low.

Mom navigated into a residential street with a lot of cars. "Well, it looks like we'll be meeting a lot of bears. Are you ready?"

"It helps that they have the soap and none of us will be triggered by scent."

Dad nodded. "That's true. But I don't know that they use the soap for intimate gatherings like this."

"Well, I did. I'm just used to doing that."

"That's a good habit, Applesauce. I still want you focused on school and not potential battles."

Mom parked and we all got out of the car. Since we'd made three pies and there were three of us, the division of labor was simple enough. Mom rang the doorbell, and Suzie opened the door. "You made it! And you brought pies, excellent. There are never too many pies in this crowd."

She led us to a large room filled with food. "Laci, Levi, show our guest where to put the desserts they made." Suzie turned to us. "They're my brother Tom's twins. They'll be graduating high school next year."

We watched the two teens run in. Instead of guiding us, they took the pies and ran off without a word. Dad cleared his throat. "How many of the sleuth will be here today?"

"Not many. We're welcoming one of our lost souls back for a meal with his family. We decided since he wanted a small celebration, we'd invite you as well. Also, his daughter is attending college in Madison. We thought we'd get all the introductions out of the way."

I leaned in. "There's a werebear at the university? And they aren't part of your sleuth?"

"We used to be, but Dad left when Uncle Stew moved to Maine and was kicked out. You know, what's good for the goose is good for the ... other goose?"

I turned around and gaped. Dayna stood in the doorway to the kitchen.

Chapter 33 – Secrets

Dayna and I sat in a swing set Coach Nelson and Suzie had in their backyard. No one else had followed us, preferring the warmth of inside.

"Why do they have this? Is it for the sleuth kids?"

Dayna looked at the swing set that was attached to a full play structure. "Yeah, I mean, bear cubs like to play and climb, but you do know Stanley and Suzie have a daughter, right? She's either about to start high school or *in* high school."

My eyes narrowed. "Does Coach Nelson drive the two hours to work every day?"

"No. He has an apartment in Madison. He drives down each week. He didn't want his real work life and bear life to combine."

I nodded. "So, you're a bear. And your cousins with Luna ... because she's uncle Stew's daughter ... an uncle who was thrown out of the sleuth." I turned to her, hoping she'd fill in the gaps.

"And you're going to be the next werewolf alpha. You're a wolf, and don't smell like one ... but you're friends with the bears, so I guess that makes sense—we get our shower products at the same place."

A small growl bubbled up from my gut. "Are you going to make me specifically ask the questions?"

"Probably."

"Okay, why isn't Luna here if she's your cousin?"

Dayna nodded. "She doesn't know about the werebears. My uncle decided if she didn't shift into a bear he wasn't going to tell her." I just stared at her. She had to know I could hear her lie. "Okay, fine, he was told he couldn't. So, when Luna didn't become a bear, thus ending the werebear line with her dad, the family secret ended with him ... at least in that part of the family."

My head pounded. "So, you two live together in the dorms ... at least are on the same floor."

"No, we are in the same room, you were right the first time."

"Gods, you two. So many half-truths."

She shrugged. "To be fair, it was mostly Luna covering up our relationship. I'm not really sure, but I think she felt if a group of three had cousins who lived together, you may feel like a third wheel."

A laugh bubbled out of me. "She was trying to make me feel more welcome?" Dayna nodded with a wide smile. "You know, I can't even imagine that."

"I told you, she grows on you. At heart, she's a good person."

In no world could I fathom it. Not really. The times Luna had been decent were few and far between. When other people were around, she'd always reverted back to her snappish self. "I'll take your word for it." We sat for a few moments. "I do have to ask that you keep my secret." I held up my hand. "I know you said she doesn't know about you and the bears, and part of me believes you ... part doesn't. I could hear a part lie in what you said." My eyebrow rose as she started to protest. "Anyway, living together, it would be so easy to let something slip."

Her face shifted into one of disbelief. "Does Hollis or Fern know about you? Didn't you say you knew Fern for like, all of your life?"

"Hollis. I just met Fern this school year. And they're friends, not family."

Dayna grunted. "I'm not sure if that's really much of a difference. But, to alleviate your fears, I know how to keep a secret, and I understand your need for secrecy. Luna will not learn you are a werewolf, at least, not from me. I assume I can expect the same respect."

"Thank you, and of course." I could hear her truth. I narrowed my eyes. "Werebear. I can't believe you're a werebear who supports the Bears."

She snorted. "It's great, no? I feel like the whole sleuth should, but they don't agree."

My heart started pounding. "Have you ever run with wolves before? Do you know of other ... animals?"

Dayna turned to me, eyes narrowed. "You mean besides wolves and bears? I'm pretty sheltered, even though I'm from Chicago. Why? Are there others?"

"You never heard the story of my sister, the panther?"

Her eyes widened. "Oh, my gods. That story was real? The boop on Stanley's nose? It's really real? Werepanther? That's three wereanimals. We should find out if there are more."

Something in her body language told me she may have known more, but the whole shifter world was so secretive. It didn't surprise me she wasn't saying anything else.

It occurred to me that this could be what one of my premonitions was hinting at—Dayna running with the pack. "Would you want to run with our pack during the next full moon? Or any time? My pack has a large wooded area that would be a safe place for you while you're in Madison."

Her face lit up. "That would be great ... and running with wolves? How fun!"

Laci popped her head out the door. "Dayna ... um, Pebble, it's time to eat. You're supposed to come in now."

Dayna and I stood and shared a smile. I thought this was the start of a great friendship.

Chapter 34 – Decision Made, Trip Taken

Saturday night, Hollis and I headed out to see the latest action movie. We bought popcorn, candy, and huge sodas. The theater was filled with people who were visiting family but didn't want to socialize ... at least, that was my theory. During the opening credits, Hollis and I made up stories about the different individuals, laughing at how crazy our stories got.

One group came with two older people and three teens, who all looked angry at the world. Hollis leaned in. "I bet the parents are on a date, thrilled to finally be away from all that attitude. The one set of grandparents drew the short straws and will go home, happy to not see their sweet grandbabies for another season."

I snorted and pointed to a cluster with a young boy. "Gods, do you think that kid will last without crying? I've heard this isn't a movie for young'uns."

Hollis slumped. "Why do parents do that?"

I shook my head and pointed to a trio with two women and a man. "Third wheel, like when I crash a date with you, or a throuple?"

"Oh, definitely a throuple. But the thing is, the women, they really just want to be an amazing lesbian couple. Give it two years and they'll dump the guy." She rested her head on my arm. "And you're always welcome to the events I invite you to. When I don't want you there, I always let you know."

I chuckled, but then the movie started, ending our game.

Afterwards, Mom dropped us at the dorm. Hollis smiled. "So, how was the family friend's feast?"

I sighed. "Good. A lot of new people, more food than a herd of elephants could eat, and a hike in the woods afterwards." Well, a run, but it was easier to explain that way.

"You moved after Thanksgiving dinner? You obviously didn't eat enough," she said with a laugh.

"I tried to eat enough to double my size, just like Fern demanded. It just didn't work." I fell down on my bed. "How about you?"

"Same as always." She sighed. "My parents made a fine meal, but Dad doesn't approve of Fern. Mom was quiet and wouldn't say anything one way or another. I think they're talking less and less when I'm not there. I don't know why, it's just a feeling. A tension I felt in the air. When we weren't eating, I pretty much stayed in my room."

"So, high school all over again."

"Yeah. I'm so glad I was in Europe last summer. I have no idea what I'll do to survive next summer, much less winter break. I have to figure something out." She flopped back. "Maybe I can get a job as a camp counselor somewhere. Anything but stay there for three months. It was so oppressive."

"Well, you have time."

"True, however, winter break is just around the corner, too. Maybe I can visit Fern at their home in Kentucky. Though it doesn't sound much better there. I know, if you get to go to Colorado, I'll hide in your suitcase."

I chuckled. "I guess it's time to get your old job back at the ice cream shop ... I loved that one." She threw a pillow at my smirking face. "What? Then you wouldn't just be at home all break. And, bonus, you know I'd come and visit."

She chuckled. "Yeah, I guess." Her head dropped back, and she gazed at the ceiling. "Sorry I'm being such a downer."

"It's no problem. You know I'm always here for you."

"I do."

After a few seconds of silence I leapt up. "Let's head down State Street, find something sweet to eat. No more moping around here."

Hollis's smile returned. "Now that's what I'm talking about."

By noon on Sunday, Fern had returned, and everything was starting to feel like normal. I wasn't sure when college, dorms, and classes had become my normal, but it was nice having my friends around again.

Hollis sat on her bed, Fern next to her, when I decided to check my email. "Oh, my gods! I got it. I'm in."

Fern narrowed their eyes. "You do know you have to use all your words, right? We can't read your mind."

"For real?" Hollis squealed. "When do you leave? Does it give all the names of the people going? Will I see you at all over winter break?"

Fern rubbed the ear closest to Hollis. "Okay, I guess only one of us can't read your mind. *I* would still like to know what you're talking about."

Giddiness bubbled within me, and I couldn't shrink my smile. "I'm one of the students my bio professor selected to go to Colorado to help him study pronghorns. Hold on."

I went back to the email to read. "It says we leave December twenty-sixth at eight in the morning from Memorial Union and should be back on the thirty-first."

Hollis leaned forward, putting her elbows on her knees. "So, there's a chance we can spend New Year's Eve together?"

I relaxed back. "That's the plan."

Fern smiled. "That sounds so exciting. Colorado? I mean, it's a school thing, but it's also working with animals. I must admit, I'm a bit jealous."

They wanted to be a vet. This type of adventure was right up their alley. "I bet you'd have fun if you'd been in class and could've signed up. Maybe next time."

"Maybe."

The three of us sat up talking well into the night, not thinking about classes starting early Monday morning. When we did get to bed, I set my alarm for an obnoxiously early time. Dad had given me a new torture notebook ... training was back in my life and there was no avoiding it.

The next two weeks were a tornado of classes, final projects, and final reviews ... with a topping of sore muscles from exercise. There was a full moon the Monday of finals. Trista had decided to go home to visit her relatives back in Tennessee, so I only had Piper and Julez in my mini pack, though I made sure to mentally keep track of Trista since she was on her own.

I sat in the kitchen as Julez cooked. Piper's dad, Greg, helped. They were making homemade pizzas for dinner. Julez slid a pressed out pizza round to me and I sauced it, sliding it back to Greg to get the rest of the ingredients added. "I think if Mom decides on an individual run, I'm heading south. We usually don't go that way."

Greg gave me a hard stare. "Don't the wild turkeys live down that way?"

"I'm tired of being afraid of all the fowl. So many birds, so much fear."

Julez passed me another pizza. "I'm game ... you know, to go after the game." She snorted. "Maybe we can have a second Thanksgiving dinner."

A smile slowly lifted the sides of Greg's mouth. "You're just full of bad jokes. I like that."

"I know, I can't help myself." Julez giggled and shimmied her shoulders.

Greg shook his head. "You're making pizza, not pizazz."

"That's it, I'm out. Tell me when dinner is done." I stood and headed out. The two of them were too much.

"She just called foul on us," Greg stage whispered, and they laughed as they continued to assemble the meal.

I headed down to the basement to play with Spruce until we were called up to eat.

After we all were stuffed with pizza, we headed out to run. The shift was quick, and my wolf howled with her joy of being in control of our shape, not that I wasn't aware and able to give commands as well.

Before we ran, I saw Dayna walk through the back door, a huge grin on her face. Excited at the addition, I trotted up and bumped her legs. She'd watched me approach and was braced, so she barely flinched despite my rough hello. Reaching down, she scratched my head. "Hiya, Pebble, thanks for the invite."

Chloe walked behind her and pointed to one of the privacy walls. Dayna nodded and turned in that direction. "Thanks, I think I know what to do from here."

The wolves watched as Dayna crossed the backyard and slipped behind the wall. She'd worn the bear products and smelled like a norm, but the fact I hadn't knocked her down let them know to expect something else. Despite that, I doubted anyone but me, Mom, and Dad knew what was about to happen.

After a few minutes, a huge brown bear emerged and roared. Her eyes sparkled and Dayna looked as amused as my premonitions promised. On instinct, I glanced up, but no swan ... or other bird flew above. I could feel a tension from the pack, but Dayna's amusement quickly relaxed everyone.

At a signal from Mom, we ran.

After an hour, we split apart. I ran south, and sure enough, found the wild turkeys. I heard a honk and saw a V-formation of geese above. *There are mean birds everywhere.*

Julez and Piper had followed me, and we took down one of the turkeys. An earth-shaking roar scared the others away and let me know Dayna had joined us as well. I turned and threw myself at her with a snarl, though my scent had to give away my joy.

She rolled, amusement clear with her snuffling sound.

Though Piper and Julez seemed worried, a nutty scent wafting from both of them, Dayna smelled of vanilla and citrus, delight and excitement. She knew I wanted to play.

She got to her feet and swatted at me. I ducked and tried to push her into a roll again, but my body weight wouldn't move her if she was ready. It was like throwing myself at a furry wall.

After a few more rounds, I sat, my tongue lolling out in amusement. Dayna's eyes sparkled back at me. We both turned to see wide-eyed wolves watching us. I darted forward to take a bite of the turkey. When I backed away, Piper and Julez each ate some. Finally, Dayna finished it off.

Once we'd eaten our fill, we headed for a river. It may have been cold, but I liked to splash after a hunt.

When we finally returned to the pack den, it felt late, well past midnight. I knew we'd spent too much time frolicking, but how often does one get to play with a bear?

I had a final the next morning at ten, so I curled up under the treehouse ... I didn't want to chance Dayna following me up into the structure—it wasn't rated for bear. The others curled around me, and we slept.

It was surprising how quickly December twenty-sixth came. Dad drove me to Memorial Union, despite the early hour. He had work and Mom didn't. We found the van with a sign that read: 'Professor McCrea's research team'.

After giving Dad a big hug, I grabbed my bags and found Professor McCrea. He stood by the open back, and I stuffed my bag in. "Ah, Pebble, you're here, excellent. I have matched everyone up by how I think they'll best work. I think this trip will be great."

"How many students did you select?"

"Four. Two from your class and two from my afternoon class. Though several people applied, your group's research impressed me the most."

His compliment warmed me ... and I was thrilled my plan had worked out so well. "Thanks, Professor."

"No, thank you. Now hop in the van. You're the first here, but once we get everyone packed in, we're off."

"Sounds good."

I got into the back, sitting in the second row. Though I probably could sit in the front passenger seat, I was used to sitting further back. I pulled out my phone and found a book to read. *Wyldling Snare* by A.R. Grimes. I had downloaded it and *Nomad* by Lawrence Henry. I was excited about both.

A male student was next. When he got in the van, he introduced himself as Nick.

Next was another male. Before he could say anything, Nick smiled wide. "Dalton! I didn't know you'd been selected. This trip just got a lot more fun."

"I agree. I brought my cards. If you have money to lose, I'll make sure to liberate it from you."

Nick just laughed.

Dalton turned to me, reaching out his hand. "I'm Dalton, nice to meet you."

"Pebble, same."

Then we all focused on our phones.

It took a few more minutes, but finally the last student pushed their way into the van. I stiffened as I saw Luna. Of course it was her. It was always Luna.

She saw me and her face contorted. "Why is it always you?"

"I was thinking the same thing."

She scoffed and plopped down, ignoring the others.

Professor McCrea got in. "Well, we're all here. I'm going to see how far into Nebraska we can get today. It's roughly a fourteen hour drive to Spinney Mountain State Park. If we can make it ten or eleven hours today, that will be so much less travel time tomorrow. Maybe we can even get some work done."

I covered my mouth before I chuckled. Luna glared at me.

The professor continued. "I, for one, am already sick of this van. I will see if we can get to camping sooner than later. Life under the moon and stars in winter! What can be better."

We all got situated, the boys in the back row, a bench seat, and Luna and I in the center, two individual bucket seats.

Once we were out of Madison, Professor McCrea grabbed his bag, that had been sitting on the passenger seat and tossed it to the floor by my feet. "Okay, we have a long drive ahead of us. I have some binders in there that will give you a rundown of what we're doing. There will be two basic goals for the trip, tag 'em and bag 'em, so to speak."

There was a pause while he navigated around some thick traffic. It was Monday morning and the day after Christmas, but apparently people wanted to get home ... or maybe to Chicago.

"Okay, back to the details. Nick, you have been working as a phlebotomist for the last few months."

"Sure have, sir," Nick said from behind me. Though he hadn't technically been asked.

"You and Dalton will work to get blood samples from the pronghorns. I want a variety of as many samples as you can procure. Male and female, maybe some youth if possible." He shifted lanes to pass a semi- truck. "Meanwhile, Luna and Pebble, you'll be tagging the animals we've worked on. You'll also be documenting any characteristics you can of the tagged beasts. I have a chart we can use for each pronghorn we bring down. We'll need to get everything uploaded to my database."

There was silence for a few minutes as he drove. Then I asked, "So, we're all working on the same one, we just each have a different goal?"

"Exactly," he confirmed. "Now, Pebble, if you could pass out the binders, they're labeled with your names. It's mostly the same information, but some of it is person specific. I have assigned each of you exactly what I want you to be doing while we're working. We have at least seven hours on the road, with some time for gas and food breaks. We can discuss questions when I'm not driving."

I handed out the binders, then put away my phone. The information about pronghorns was interesting and my specific role in our research had me excited. I skimmed through the first part to get an idea of what it was about, then reread it more slowly.

Though I thought Luna would be annoyed about having to read so much background information, the overpowering scent in the van was a woodsy determination as we all made our way through the literature.

Everything was going well until we got to the hotel, and Professor McCrea secured two rooms, one for the males, one for the females. It was at that point I realized I would be spending all my time for the next five days with Luna Zweck.

Chapter 35 – Cobra Chicken

"**I**'m taking this bed." Luna dropped her bag on the bed closest to the door. She moved to the window and cracked it open. It was close to freezing and she didn't ask if I cared ... I didn't, but it was still rude.

I took a deep breath. There was no way I was going to spend the better part of a week fighting with her. If she wanted to see how far she could push me, fine. I would do as any parent learned early with toddlers and I would choose my battles.

"As you wish." I turned my back and smiled. If nothing else, I was amused at the movie quote.

She brushed past me and shut the bathroom door. I sighed and lay down on the bed. On my phone, I found my Dad's contact. *Made it to Nebraska. We should get to Colorado tomorrow. At a hotel, leaving tomorrow early.*

He replied with a thumbs up.

I sat and picked up my bag. When I had packed, I had selected two sets of pajamas. Mom had teased me that I should bring the goose pajamas everyone in the family had, but I decided to go with basic sweatpants and a t-shirt. Despite that, I found the patterned ones on the top of my duffle. *Dad strikes again! No one can trust that man.*

As I waited for Luna to finish, I selected clothes for Tuesday, including something to exercise in, and the shower bag. I'd put everything in the bathroom for the morning.

Professor McCrea said we'd be leaving at eight, after we all ate. Breakfast came with the reservation. I set my alarm for five so I could use the exercise room before the others probably woke. Shortly after that, Luna was finally done. She came out wearing shorts and a tank top.

If she weren't so ... bristly, I could see being her friend. It occurred to me she was even pretty. She'd make someone happy one day, if she treated them like she did Dayna.

Once I was done in the bathroom, I emerged to find the room dark, though a bit of light shone in from the parking lot. *Of course. This is all about her.*

"What is on your pajamas?" *Does she sound offended?*

Halfway to my bed I paused, gazing at what I'd thought was the sleeping form of Luna. "It's a really long story. It's late, you can ask me later."

"Oh, I will. Trust me. Those are ..." She laughed instead of continuing.

I crawled into my bed but couldn't fall asleep right away. I turned and tried to get comfortable, but all the inactivity of the car ride left me restless. I debated leaving the room and walking around, but it was late, and I didn't know the area. Instead, I just shifted and turned until I finally fell asleep.

Professor McCrea had driven until ten at night on Monday. We'd made eleven of the sixteen hours on the first day. That left five for the second.

We all ate big breakfasts, as per his rules. I was one of the first into the dining area and was on my second plate by the time the others started showing up.

"That's it Pebble?" Nick teased. "We're supposed to eat enough to make it all the way to Spinney Mountain State Park. Eat up. We're not stopping for you, girly."

A snarl started to reverberate from my gut, but I bit it back. "You don't have to worry about me, Nick, this is just my appetizer." I debated challenging which of us could eat more, but I wasn't stooping to his level.

"Look at you, practically skin and bones. I bet you're afraid of eating."

I wanted to slap his smirk off his face. "Not that it's any of your business, but if you're *that* worried, make me a plate of food. I already exercised this morning and don't feel I need the extra steps."

He gaped at me. "You exercised and that's all you've eaten? Fine, but I bet you won't eat it all."

Amusement bubbled within me that I'd found a way to make him do my bidding. Smirking, I leaned back, entertained at how easy norms were.

Luna dropped her bag at the seat next to mine. "Nice work. Getting the boys to work for you already. I didn't think you had it in you."

Her compliment made me feel dirty.

It didn't take long for everyone to eat and get into the car. Nick and Dalton continued talking about me and my breakfast for the first hour of our drive. "But did you see that? I gave her more than my plate and she ate it all."

"It was epic! You thought she was a wilting flower, and you were so wrong, bro!" Dalton laughed.

I tried to ignore them, but my eating became the entertainment they needed on the long drive.

Luna leaned over. "Idiots. I keep trying to tell you. We're surrounded by idiots."

"They're on this project with us. They can't be that dumb."

She shrugged. "Their skill set is being utilized because Nick can use a needle and Dalton can entertain Nick. I don't think that proves anything."

I wasn't sure I wanted to get into a full discussion with her putting down the others in the car, but we were speaking quietly. "But you think everyone is beneath you, present company included."

Her eyes traveled up and down my body. "I watched you in the classes we shared. You aren't a halfwit like most of the people in class."

Was that a compliment?

It took everything in me not to gape at her. "I'm shocked I passed the Luna screening."

Her eyes narrowed. "Barely. You're missing a few criteria, but you're mostly tolerable."

And she was back. I leaned back and pulled out my phone, ready to just sit and read for the rest of the ride.

By the time we got to the park and checked into our rooms, it was just before three. Professor McCrea took us out to where the wild pronghorns grazed. We could see them off in the distance.

"Okay, we each have a tranquilizer gun. I want to tag as many as we can. The serum will keep the animals down for one to two hours. I do have a counter that will help them revive quicker. We'll do all of this tomorrow. Are there any questions?"

Dalton nodded. "Can we practice shooting the dart gun? I have some experience, but I don't know about the girls."

Luna scoffed. "Sexist much? I live on a farm. I'm probably a better shot than you."

Professor McCrea sighed. "Enough. That was a question on your application. Only Pebble doesn't have experience, but she has a strong understanding of pronghorns and a background working with animals. We should be fine."

Once everyone nodded, he spun on his heel. "You have the evening to explore the woods or relax. Tomorrow we work.

I headed over to a rock and sat, pulling out my phone. Earlier in December, I'd texted Heather, our former packmate now part of the Colorado crew, to tell her I would be in the area. She said she would drive out and have dinner with me, I just had to let her know when I landed, so to speak. She knew my basic itinerary, but I wanted to let her know I'd be free tonight. Professor McCrea already okayed the outing.

Once I sent that text, I wandered into the woods. I really needed some time away from people and to connect with nature. There had been the run the previous Monday, but with finals, Christmas, and the drive, it was too little and too long ago.

After about twenty minutes, my soul began to sing. The smell of the trees and crisp air centered me, and my body relaxed. I turned to take in all of the nature around me, and spotted Luna, following me. "What are you doing?"

"I was curious as to what you were doing, city girl." Her voice was more curious than sharp.

I closed my eyes and took a slow, deep, breath. The wind wasn't in my favor, but I couldn't smell anyone else from our group. When I sorted all the unusual smells from the woods, I could pick up Luna, but only when I focused. One more deep breath, and I realized there was something else odd. *Is that wolf?*

I opened my eyes and searched, trying to see if I could see the wolf. "Luna, we should head back."

"Why? You walked all the way out here and now you want to leave? Are you scared? You really are from the city."

"It's not that, it's just—"

The tawny wolf leapt from a copse of trees, right towards Luna. I shot forward, tackling the beast. The scent wasn't fully animal—this creature was a were.

It ... he, snarled at me, snapping at my arm. I wrapped my legs around its body, my arm around its neck. "Luna, get out of here, run!"

"Are you sure? Do you need help?"

I saw glowing eyes in the leaves and bushes behind her. "Luna! There's another one behind you. Go! Now!"

Her eyes widened, then she squatted down. A gray cloud surrounded her, and I wanted to swear. "A shifter? You're a swan?"

Then a goose flew into the air, honking in disgust.

Chapter 36 – Battle To Truth

The second wolf, a small gray beast with black paws and a white belly, darted to where Luna had been. When she flew off, he howled, then changed directions to help his friend with me.

I wrapped my arm around the snapping snout of the one I held down with my body using a wrestler's hold and yanked his neck to the side. The snap reverberated through the woods.

I rotated so the second wolf's teeth embedded into the belly of his companion, not mine. Moving fast, I crab-walked back to get away from the two. Once the second wolf realized I was getting away, he leapt at me. I kicked up, smashing my foot into his underside, sending him over my head. I heard him slam into a tree.

With a grunt, I spun around and pushed to my feet. The wolf was already on his paws. His legs were wide and head low. He snarled.

Growling, I released my mantle, the full power of alpha. I wasn't sure why he'd attacked us. I knew I didn't smell of wolf, but now he was going to get the full impact of my strength.

His eyes widened and he dropped.

I walked over and knelt. "I don't know what your plan was, but *shift.*" I put power behind my word.

As his body began to contort, I pulled out my phone to call Heather.

"Hiya, Pebble. I'm heading up with one of my pack friends."

"I was just attacked by what I *hope* are two lone puppies, because I took care of one, and the other is shifting." My words were choppy, and I was breathing hard. "Please say you're close."

"Yeah, we should be there in about ten minutes. Send your coordinates."

I hung up and texted my location. I had a tank top under my sweatshirt, so I stripped it off, and when the man was done shifting, I tied his hands behind him. He just glared at me. "Who are you?"

"Why attack me if you don't know who I am?"

"I'm hungry, you's easier than the animals," he spat.

"Apparently, I'm not."

Behind him, a goose dropped down in a space between some trees. In the confusion of the fight, I'd completely forgotten about Luna. *Gods above. Too many secrets!*

The gray cloud surrounded the bird, and Luna appeared again, squatting. *And still dressed? I need to talk to Jade.*

She walked over. "You and your friend were pretty dumb attacking *my* friend, weren't you? Two werewolves taken out by a city girl. Idiots, I tell you."

The ease with which she said the word told me Luna knew a whole lot more than Dayna led me to believe. We needed to have a long conversation. *And did Luna just call me her friend?*

The man made a face but didn't say anything. I pulled Luna away from the man, far enough that he couldn't hear us, even with werewolf hearing. If he tried to run, I was pretty sure I could outrun him.

"So, you know about werewolves?"

"You know about shifter ... swans?" She snorted out a laugh. "Figures. They're such goody two-shoes."

"How do *you* know about shifter swans? Just because you're a deadly cobra chicken doesn't mean you know all the shifter birds."

"Cobra chicken? That's hilarious. But you're right, I don't know about all of them. This is the first I've heard about swans. They just sound frou-frou."

I shook my head. "Okay, important stuff. How many wereanimals do you know about? You weren't at all shocked about the wolves."

Her brow went up. "Right back atcha, girly. If you smelled were, Dayna would've told me during the first week of class."

"I knew it! She said you didn't know about her, but I knew she wasn't telling me the truth."

Luna's mouth hung open. "You know about the bears? Why didn't Dayna tell me about you? I'm going to have to talk to my cuz."

I held up my hand. "Okay, start over, take three, or is this four? Does the rest of the sleuth know about you knowing about them?"

"No." Luna scowled. We both still watched the nameless lone wolf, but I could see her face contort in anger. "I'm not supposed to know about my dad because it's a group secret. As if I wouldn't notice him lumbering off into the woods as a huge furry bear."

"Got it. And your mom's family are the shifter geese?"

"Look at you, putting two and two together."

"And shifter birds can shift with their clothes on?" This was the piece that was going to make me the most jealous. I mean, I knew the answer. I saw her go from human to bird and back, all with her clothes on.

Luna laughed. It was a hearty sound that echoed throughout the woods, scaring birds all around us. "I love watching you weres shift. It's such a show. I'm assuming you're a were … what, werewolf? You forced that jerk on his butt by just looking at him."

"Yeah, I'm a wolf, and I'm a bit more powerful than him. He's pretty low power."

"And how do *you* know about shifter birds? They are pretty secretive."

"It's a long story … like a really long story, but my sister is a shifter swan."

Luna looked at me, eyes twinkling. "And she strips when she shifts?"

"Well, not anymore she won't."

With a chuckle, Luna put an arm over my shoulders. She said something, but I didn't hear it. My head pounded, my vision blurred, and all I heard was the phantom voice screaming, "Find me!"

Chapter 37 – Family Affair

There was something sharp poking into my back. The pillows my head lay on were stiffer than normal, and my head pounded. *Why do I have a headache?*

"Pebble, are you up? Your breathing changed." Luna's voice was full of concern.

My body stiffened at hearing her voice. Then a groan bubbled up from my gut. "Why is this bed so uncomfortable? And why are you in bed with me?" The word 'mate' floated through my head, but I figured that was part of a nightmare I couldn't remember.

"I put my arm around you, and you collapsed. Then the idiot man tried to run, but two women appeared, saw you, then ran after the man. I decided you shouldn't be lying on the ground alone, and here we are."

I finally opened my eyes and stared up into Luna's stormy blue eyes. *Is there concern in her eyes? How bad do I look?* "I can sit up."

She sighed. "Just rest. I don't want you randomly falling again."

I shook my head, which I now realized was in her lap. "I'll be fine ... I, it's a long story. It won't happen again ... and the rock that's poking into my back hurts."

"Fine, but don't topple over."

I huffed out a laugh. "No promises." Once I was sitting, I pulled my knees in. "So, Heather and her friend went after the other one?"

"Yeah. And the wolf who you took out has shifted to a man as well. This is way more adventure than I expected when I signed up."

I nodded.

"Okay, can you tell me why you collapsed? Is this something that will happen again during the trip?"

"No. It's ... um ... okay, there's been a puzzle I've been trying to figure out for a few months. It may have solved itself."

Her eyes narrowed and her voice went back to the mocking tone I knew and didn't love. "Let me get this straight. You've been working on a puzzle. I put my arm on you. You solve your mystery and pass out?"

I gazed up through the branches and leaves to the sky. "When you say it that way, you make me sound a lot less sane than I am."

"Are you sure? What kind of puzzle?"

"I don't know if you learning more of my secrets will be a good thing, Luna. You already think I'm weird. Knowing more isn't really the best idea."

Where are Heather and her friend? Save me from this.

"Oh? Who am I going to tell?"

"Dayna? Who will then tell her family or the sleuth." My head continued to pound. Headaches were rare to unheard of in wereanimals, so I was pretty sure it was psychosomatic.

Luna rolled her eyes. It hadn't happened since we left Madison, and I'd hoped we were past that. "I don't tell my cousin everything."

I rubbed my temple. "You're not going to like what I tell you. If I don't tell you, maybe it'll just be better ... you know, go away."

"Wait, is my touching you part of the reason you passed out?"

I rested my head on my arms and thought. I was trying to puzzle together the pieces of the dream. The honking cars were a goose honk? Luna was the phantom? She was who I was supposed to find? That was what this was all about?

Deep inside me, my wolf howled as if thrilled I finally got my head screwed on.

Lifting my head, I gazed at Luna. "Yes, I believe it was your touch that was the catalyst for all of this." I squeezed my eyes shut. "I need to back up. You're probably not going to believe me, but I have premonitions ... um, visions.

"I know what premonitions are, city girl."

"Right. Well, usually they are one and done, but there's been one that's been happening over and over for a while. It involves a phantom reaching for me, urgently telling me to find them. With a honking sound outside the window."

One of Luna's eyebrows rose. "Okay, so what does this have to do with me?"

I took a deep breath. "When you touched me, aspects of the vision flashed through my head, as well as the word 'mate.'"

Luna sat up straighter. "What are you talking about? I'm not a werewolf and I'm not marrying you. I know lesbians do the whole moving truck on the second date, but just no."

A laugh burst out of me. "First of all, we haven't even had a first date. Second, I do believe I told you you wouldn't like what I had to say. And third, marriage? Gods above, you already told me I'm not your type. I assume your type includes someone you like."

Before she could answer, Heather returned alone. "Tammy is taking care of the wolf. She'll meet us at the restaurant. It isn't far, if you're willing to walk." She came over and wrapped me in a hug. "Gods, Pebble, I've missed you. Now, I'm used to Jade doing too much with her abilities and passing out, but not you. You need food. But first, look at how big you are—in college, all grown up. And you're going to be the next—" She shot her focus to Luna.

"It's okay, she saw everything and pieced it together."

"Okay, got it. I'm proud of you and excited that you'll be the next alpha."

Luna gasped. "Alpha? You're taking over your pack?"

Oops.

Heather laughed. "If you knew Pebble, you wouldn't be surprised."

I held up my hands. "How about we just get something to eat. I came out here to relax, and that was a fail. Tomorrow we work, and Thursday we head back to Wisconsin. This is my only time to catch up with you."

Luna stood. "I guess that's my cue to leave."

Before I could say anything Heather spoke up. "Join us. There's nothing back where you're staying."

Luna's eyes narrowed as she looked at me. I shrugged. "Up to you, but we're going to be talking about a lifetime of memories."

"Whatever, as long as it isn't norm crap, I'm in."

Heather smiled wide. "I love that. More friends, awesome."

Despite her cheer, my gut tightened with the idea of how much Luna was about to learn about me.

Chapter 38 – Your Destiny Isn't Mine

During the meal, Heather told us about the man she captured and what she'd learned from her interrogation. His attack on me and Luna really had been completely random. He and his partner were out of control and had turned rogue: wolves that had gotten the taste of human. They needed to be put down.

In questioning them, Heather hadn't figured out where they'd come from, but he was being taken to her alpha for further interrogation. I could probably have done it, but that wasn't my role or position while in

Colorado. It was chancy with my professor around and undiplomatic.

After that, the meal centered me in a way the walk in the woods hadn't ... even with Luna there. Heather and I told stories of her brother, Bevin, the California pack in general, and what it was like growing up as pack kids in Wisconsin. During most of the meal, Luna and Tammy, Heather's pack mate, laughed and enjoyed our stories.

On Monday, we collected information about three pronghorns. While Nick and Dalton worked on labs, Luna and I got GPS collars around the animal's necks.

They were beautiful. Once we had the information we needed, professor McCrea administered an antidote and we moved away, watching over them until they woke and ran off. We didn't want the majestic creatures attacked by any predators.

Once the pronghorns were sedated, the actual study didn't take much time. The whole process took the day. When we finished, the professor ordered pizza, happy with our success, and we played cards late into the night.

By the time we all headed to bed, I just crashed. Rooming with Luna hadn't been an issue for three nights. We kept getting in too late for anything but using the room to sleep.

On Tuesday, we got up early to start the drive back home. In the van, Nick immediately fell asleep. An hour into the drive, we drove up to an all-you-can-eat buffet next to a gas station.

"Okay, crew. Fill up here. This is the only meal out before we hopefully make it to Iowa."

Back in the van, I turned on my phone and started to read. At first I couldn't concentrate on the words. My mind kept drifting back to Luna helping me in the woods, making sure my head wasn't on the ground, and calling me her friend to that rogue wolf. Her laughter at dinner lightened the mood and as much as I feared her learning about my past, it wasn't awful.

At least she never got the story about the geese. Thinking about my pajamas, my face heated, and I decided it was time to focus on reading.

The drive back seemed longer, but everyone was quiet as we passed through the states and finally made it to a hotel just after ten.

In the room, I hoped for a repeat of every other night—silence until both me and Luna were in bed.

"You can shower first." I was surprised. This was the first time she'd changed the order. I got my outfits for the drive and exercise and headed into the bathroom. Afterwards, I sat on my bed, and waited until I heard the shower start.

I found my phone and called Jade. I hadn't talked to her since Christmas.

"Pebble! Aren't you on your school adventure?"

"I am, I just wanted to call and tell you something I learned. I don't have much time, so this will be quick." I'd been thinking about how to tell her this for days. Technology was tricky, so I had to be careful.

"Okay, talk."

"I want you to test something out for me. Leap from the platform but leave your clothes on."

There was a pause before she grunted. "Did you see something?"

"I did, but not in the way you're thinking. Just ... do this for me and tell me how it goes."

"Okay, I assume the jump is optional."

I laughed. My body relaxed speaking with family ... someone who understood me so well. "Yes."

Her voice got muffled. "Owen! Come talk to your sister for a minute." There was a shuffling sound, then Owen's voice. "Pebble, it's been days. How is your school thing?"

We talked for a few minutes as I filled him in.

"Oh, my gods! Jade, what are you?" His voice interrupted my story. I waited, knowing his reaction would tell me everything I needed to know. "Whoa, this changes everything."

"So, it worked?" A giddy excitement tingled through my body.

"This came from you? This is totally not fair! It also means I have to adjust a ton of training manuals." He sounded glum, but I knew this made things better for his job. "But, gods above, why didn't those ... for the love of ... we should've known this."

Owen kept mumbling until Jade took the phone back. Her voice was light. "That was fantastic."

I heard the shower turn off. "I need to go, I'm in a hotel room and the shower turned off. I'll call when I'm back in Wisconsin. Love you lots."

They both said, "Love you, too." And I ended the call.

A couple minutes later, Luna sashayed out of the bathroom. She never did anything plainly. "Oh, you're still up. Good. Can we talk?"

I slumped. "I guess. I figured you wouldn't want to."

"Look, Pebble. That stuff from the woods ... mates, you don't believe it, do you?"

I rubbed my face, really not wanting to get into this, but knowing it had to happen. "Mates in the werewolf world is pretty rare. I know maybe two other matched pairs. In both cases they are very much in love and happy with the situation."

"Like, from the moment they met?" She sneered at me.

"No, well yes. I don't know much about my aunt and uncle, but there is an alpha pair in California. They were always friends, but the 'more' took longer. I don't know their full story, I was young during all of that, I just know they are the most amazing couple I know."

"So, they're your friends?"

I nodded. "Yeah. They grew up in the Wisconsin pack and headed out west to create a new pack. My sister and brother joined them."

"Oh, wait, that's what Heather talked about. Her brother is that alpha?"

"Yeah."

Luna paused for a few seconds to think. "Well, I don't believe we're really mated, whatever that beast in you said."

I shrugged. "Look, considering you've made it plainly clear you don't like me, I'm fine with that. The idea that I *have* a mate and that she doesn't like me seems pretty awful to me. I just want to find someone who can help me run the pack in five to ten years. Someone strong and smart, who challenges me but also respects me, and that we both enjoy spending time together."

Telling Luna my wants should've been awkward, but it felt good to delineate for myself exactly what I wanted. That it was her no longer mattered.

"You said on Halloween you were demiromantic. How many people have you dated?"

My head hit the headboard behind me.

Luna sighed. "Have you done anything with someone else? Kissed?"

"Does spin the bottle in eighth grade count?"

I pulled my legs up to sit cross-legged on the bed.

"Only if you were interested in someone and you got to kiss them."

"Well, I figured out Hollis and I were only ever going to be friends, so kind of."

Luna's head rocked left and right. "Okay, well that's something. You kissed her and it showed you what you needed to know. Maybe that's how your wolf let you know the relationship was a 'no.'"

"Maybe. My wolf is more perceptive than I like sometimes. It helps when it saves lives."

Her eyes widened. "That's happened?"

"Yes, but we're not telling stories now."

"Okay, fine." But she gave me a look like she would find a way to learn more about me. I wasn't sure if that made me wary or scared. "But let's kiss. You'll see there's nothing there and we'll move on."

"Are you hitting on me, Luna?"

She scoffed. "The opposite. I'm proving a point. Now move over."

I did as she demanded, amused by her conviction. She lifted her hands to wrap around my shoulders, the warmth seeping into me. I tried to ignore the sense of connection I felt at her touch. This was Luna—it was all wrong.

Then she leaned over and gently pressed her lips to mine. My body tingled with the touch and within my mind, my wolf sang.

She slowly pushed back. Staring down at the bed, her voice softer, she whispered, "See, nothing."

I wondered if she really felt nothing. Gazing at her, I refused to agree with her assessment of the kiss. If this is what Hollis always felt, I understood her conviction that I date more, I just didn't think I would feel that with other people.

But why is the feeling attached to Luna?

Chapter 39 – Happy New Year's

I spent New Year's Eve with Hollis. We went to a citywide party and danced the night away. After the 'ball dropped' we each went home with promises to hang out later in the week. Now that the dorms were closed for a few weeks, it was weird not seeing her every day, but having my bed back was amazing.

On the first, I woke up late and trudged to the kitchen. After the trip, dealing with Luna, and staying up late with Hollis, I just needed a day of rest with my family.

Mom was in the kitchen cooking fried potatoes and eggs and making a lot of coffee. A groan sighed out of me as I poured a large mug and sat at the counter to watch her cook.

"Morning, sweetie, how was your trip?"

"Good, we got information on three pronghorns."

She smiled. "I bet everyone involved will be happy. Will there be follow-up work? Another trip?"

"Maybe. Professor McCrea said there was work we could do for independent credit. He plans on heading out again this summer, so that's a possibility. I don't know. I loved it, but biology isn't my focus."

"It could be. You're still a freshman, you can adjust what you study or have a double major. You know there's no urgency in your time at university. You're in no rush ... enjoy your years in college."

Warmth infused me with her words. My time to take over the pack was a long way off. I had years. Why not take every advantage presented? "You're right. I'll send the professor an email in the next few days or talk to him when the semester starts. There's no rush."

"True. He probably won't be looking at his email today anyway."

Dad shuffled out. "Heya, Applesauce. I want to catch up and move, want to take a run? It's oddly warm today."

It had been awhile. "Yeah, that sounds great."

We ate breakfast, talking about the study and the trip. Then Dad and I got ourselves dressed for our run. Our jog to the running path was slow, letting us warm up. We didn't talk much as our bodies adjusted to the cool temperature.

When we got to the path, we set our watches and started to really move. Once the run was going, Dad asked, "What's on your mind? You seem pensive."

Dad could always read me better than anyone else.

"There's this person from school, she's been a bane to my ... I don't know, my everything."

"Is this that Luna girl you spoke about in the beginning? The one in a couple of your groups?"

"Yeah, that's her." I went on to explain everything about her.

"A shifter goose? Is this why you've been attacked by a goose all semester?"

My jaw dropped. "Gods above, why didn't I put two and two together? I never even thought about that. Do you think all those attacks were her?"

"You say your wolf thinks she's your mate?"

"It's awful, right?"

"And she refuses." As we approached the turn around, we slowed our pace. Years ago cameras were put up to find what authorities thought was a dangerous out of control wolf. In reality, it had been scared teens who'd gotten a picture of Jade. None of us were sure if the camera feed was still being monitored, so everyone in the pack made sure to run human slow at this point of the path.

"Is that bad? She obviously doesn't like me."

"But you two seem connected. Give it time. I don't know that your wolf has ever been wrong."

I grunted. His words didn't warm me at all.

On the way back, we talked about shifter birds and their ability to shift dressed, and what that would mean to both Jade and the government.

When we got home, Mom paced the kitchen. "Good, you're both home," she said in a clipped voice

Dad moved up to her quickly, wrapping his arms around her. "What's wrong? Is everyone okay?"

She shook her head. "No. The Tennessee alphas, Iris and Kendall, they were attacked last night. River, they were killed."

The world dropped out beneath me.

"What happened?" Dad sounded calm, but I could smell the nutty scent of his worry.

"They went out for New Year's, just the two of them, on a date. They were attacked by a group of wolves. There were indications of at least five animal attackers. One of their pack could smell the different wolves."

"That's awful." Chills ran down my spine.

Mom nodded. She almost looked manic. "There were also gunshot wounds. It was like they shot them to incapacitate, then attacked, to kill and possibly eat. It was awful ... terrifying."

I licked my lips. "What will happen now?"

"That's just it, the pack doesn't have any alpha level wolves. They don't have anyone to lead them." She looked at Dad. "We have to go. Our pack is in the best position to send help fast. Not only can you take time off or work remotely, I can take a semester off. I already called the chair. I told them it's a family matter ... an emergency."

Terror washed through me. "What about our pack?"

Concern filled Dad's eyes as Mom slid my hands into hers. "Pebble, sweetie, you need to step up. We can't lead two packs, and we can't be alphas of this pack from Tennessee, not for months at a time. You've been training for this. You're ready."

Thank you for reading Xenagogue!
Please leave a review <u>online</u>.

Check out my <u>website</u> to find all the links to my socials
and find information on my next series!

Coming Soon:

- A new dystopian fantasy series: Chameleon

    - Ivy is alone in the world, trying to survive without people questioning her magic. Petra lives with her dad, though after her mom was caught lying by the government, his reprogramming meant he'd never be the same. After meeting at work, can the two trust each other enough to share their biggest secrets? Are they strong enough to fight for better lives for themselves?

About the Author

Huckleberry Rahr is a mathematics instructor at the University of Wisconsin-Whitewater.  She spent many years teaching math around the Midwest and in Papua New Guinea with the Peace Corps. Her parents instilled a love of reading from a young age.

She grew up with lesbian moms who had a huge collection of women authors with heroines as the protagonist. Her favorite genre was fantasy and science fiction, that is, until she discovered urban fantasy. What her mom's library lacked were books with characters that looked like her family: diversity in background, gender identity, and sexuality. She decided if she couldn't find that series, then she would write it.